Talking
to
Dragons

READ ALL OF THE
ENCHANTED FOREST CHRONICLES
BY PATRICIA C. WREDE

Dealing with Dragons
Searching for Dragons
Calling on Dragons
Talking to Dragons

and

Book of Enchantments
featuring tales from the
Enchanted Forest

Talking to Dragons

THE ENCHANTED FOREST CHRONICLES

Book Four

PATRICIA C. WREDE

HOUGHTON MIFFLIN HARCOURT

BOSTON ✸ NEW YORK

For information about permission to reproduce selections from this book,
write to Permissions, Houghton Mifflin Harcourt Publishing Company,
215 Park Avenue South, New York, New York 10003.

www.hmhco.com

The text of this book is set in Palatino LT Std.

The Library of Congress has cataloged the hardcover edition as follows:
Wrede, Patricia C., 1953–
Talking to dragons/Patricia C. Wrede.
p. cm. — (The Enchanted Forest chronicles; bk. 4)
Sequel to: Calling on dragons.
Summary: Queen Cimorene sends her sixteen-year-old son, Daystar, into
the Enchanted Forest with the only weapon that can combat an evil wiz-
ard's magic in an effort to restore the balance of power in the kingdom.
[1. Fairy tales. 2. Magic — Fiction. 3. Wizards — Fiction. 4. Kings, queens,
rulers, etc. — Fiction.]
I. Title. II. Series: Wrede, Patricia C., 1953–
Enchanted Forest chronicles; bk. 4.
PZ8.W92Tal 1993
[Fic] — dc20 92-40719

ISBN: 978-0-15-284247-0 hardcover
ISBN: 978-0-544-54148-1 paperback

Manufactured in the United States of America
DOC 10 9 8 7 6 5 4 3 2 1
4500539709

For NATE *(who started it)*,
and for the rest of the Scribblies:
STEVE, PAM, KARA,
WILL, *and* EMMA

Contents

Introduction

Talking to Dragons is different from the other books of the Enchanted Forest Chronicles. I wrote it first, when I was still very much a new writer—it was my third novel ever. It was my first try at first-person narration, and the first time I wrote a book without having any idea what it would be about when I started. (I didn't have a clue what was going on until nearly halfway through the manuscript.) Also, it was not what I was intending to write at the time.

The book came about almost by accident. I had just turned in my second novel, and my publisher and I were arguing about titles (they didn't like the ones I suggested, and I didn't like the ones they suggested). I was at a local party, complaining to a friend that I had plenty of good titles that didn't have books to go with them, and, apparently, a perfectly good book with no acceptable title, and wouldn't it be a fine thing if some of them would match. My friend got tired of listening to complaints, and in order to distract me asked for some of the good titles. I rattled off four or five, among which was "Talking to Dragons."

"'Talking to Dragons' sounds like a great book," my friend said. "You should write that one."

"I don't have a story to go with it; it's just a title," I grouched. "That's my whole problem!"

The conversation and the party moved on, but I kept

thinking about that comment. It floated up again while I was driving home. "'Talking to Dragons,'" I thought. "That *does* sound like a good story. *Mother taught me to be polite to dragons* . . . Hey, that should be the first line!"

I drove the rest of the way home repeating the opening under my breath so I wouldn't forget it, and the minute I hit the house, I grabbed a pen and paper to write it down. Only when I started writing, it didn't stop with 'Mother taught me to be polite to dragons'—it kept going for several more sentences.

"Cool," I thought. "When I figure out what is going on, I have a whole first paragraph." And I went to bed.

The next morning, I woke up knowing what the second paragraph was. So I hunted up the paper I'd written the night before, to add to it. When I finally looked up, I'd written two and a half pages and it was the middle of the morning. I really wanted to know what was going to happen next . . . and the only way to find out was to keep writing.

So I did. I didn't have any more idea what was going on than my protagonist did, which was frightening. Until somewhere between half and two-thirds of the way through the book, I didn't know if I was going to have a story or just a lot of random incidents. I felt like a highwire walker working without a net.

Because it was the first book I wrote in the series, *Talking to Dragons* is the place where I made up a lot of the things that people have asked about in *Dealing with Dragons*. All of them occurred because of the necessities of storytelling—for instance, the fact that a female dragon is King of the Dragons came about because my characters had just met their very first actual dragon and I wanted to show that dragons weren't just humans dressed in lizard suits. I wanted a fast way to demonstrate to readers that dragons don't see things the way we do—that they *think* differently. So I made King of the Dragons a non-gender-specific job title . . . as far as the dragons were concerned.

When I finally finished the book, I sent it off to my agent, who promptly informed me that she was going to send it to some children's book publishers. I panicked. I hadn't set out to write a children's book, and I wasn't at all sure children would understand or like it. So I called up two of my writer friends who had children of the right age and begged them to give the manuscript to the kids as involuntary test readers. They humored me, and when Annie and Paul liked the story, it made me feel much calmer about my agent's recommendation.

Then came a snag: the editor liked the book, but said the pace was too slow. So I sat down with my three-hundred-page manuscript determined to cut thirty pages, hoping that would "pick up the pace," whatever that meant. Unfortunately, every time I tried to cut a scene, I had to add one somewhere else to cover the important information that had dropped out.

Finally, I figured out that if I cut three lines per manuscript page, I'd get my thirty pages. I spent the next three weeks hunting for unnecessary sentences, three- and four-word phrases that could be changed to one- or two-word phrases, and dialog that could be rearranged and tightened enough to get rid of three lines on every page. They were some of the more difficult and painful weeks of my writing life, but the book was vastly improved as a result, and I learned an enormous amount about revising in the process.

The original version of *Talking to Dragons* came out in 1985 as a mass market paperback, which attracted the attention of Jane Yolen. That eventually led to the development of the other books in this series, all of which are technically prequels. When we worked our way back to this one, it needed surprisingly little attention—some of the background had changed slightly in the course of writing the first three books, but it didn't affect the main story line.

The four Enchanted Forest books are undoubtedly the most popular and longest-lived of the books I've written, and I am very grateful to all the readers who made that happen.

Talking
to
Dragons

In Which Daystar Leaves
Home and Encounters a Lizard

Mother taught me to be polite to dragons. Particularly polite, I mean; she taught me to be ordinary polite to everyone. Well, it makes sense. With all the enchanted princesses and disguised wizards and transformed kings and so on wandering around, you never know *whom* you might be talking to. But dragons are a special case.

Not that I ever actually talked to one until after I left home. Even at the edge of the Enchanted Forest, dragons aren't exactly common. The principle is what matters, though: *Always* be polite to a dragon. It's harder than it sounds. Dragon etiquette is incredibly complicated, and if you make a mistake, the dragon eats you. Fortunately, I was well trained.

Dragon etiquette wasn't the only thing Mother taught me. Reading and writing are unusual skills for a poor boy, but I learned them. Music, too, and fighting. Don't ask me where Mother learned to use a sword.

Until I was thirteen, I didn't know we had one in the house. I even learned a little magic. Mother wasn't exactly pleased; but growing up on the edge of the Enchanted Forest, I had to know some things.

Mother is tall—about two inches taller than I am— and slender, and very impressive when she wants to be. Her hair is black, like mine, but much longer. Most of the time she wears it in two braids wound around and around her head, but when she really wants to impress someone she lets it hang straight to her feet. A lot of the disguised princes who stopped at our cottage on their way into the Enchanted Forest thought Mother was a sorceress. You can't really blame them. Who else would live at the edge of a place like that?

Sometimes I thought they were right. Mother always knew what directions to give them, even if they didn't tell her what they were looking for. I never saw her do any real magic, though, until the day the wizard came.

I knew right away that he was a wizard. Not because of his brown beard or his blue-and-brown silk robes—although no one but a wizard can walk around in blue-and-brown silk robes for very long without getting really dusty. It wasn't even his staff. I knew he was a wizard because he had the same *feel* of magic that the unicorns and griffins have when you catch a glimpse of them, farther on in the forest.

I was surprised to see him because we didn't get too many wizards. Well, actually, we'd never gotten any. Mother said that most of them preferred to go into the forest through the Gates of Mist and Pearl at the top of the Crystal Falls, or through the Caves of Fire and Night if they could manage it. The few that went into the forest in other ways never stopped at our cottage.

This wizard was unusual. He turned off the road and walked right past me without saying anything, straight up to our cottage. Then he banged on the door with the head of his staff. The door splintered and fell apart.

I decided that I didn't like him.

Mother was cooking rabbit stew in the big black pot over the chimney fire. She didn't even look up when the door fell in. The wizard stood there for a minute, and I sneaked a little closer so I could see better. He was frowning, and I got the impression he wasn't used to being ignored. Mother kept stirring the stew.

"Well, Cimorene, I have found you," the wizard said at last.

"It took you long enough," Mother said without turning. "You're getting slow."

"You know why I am here."

Mother shrugged. "You're sixteen years too late. I told you, you're getting slow."

"Ha! I can take the sword now, and the boy as well. There is nothing you can do to stop me this time," the wizard said. I could tell he was trying to sound menacing, but he didn't do a very good job.

Mother finally turned around. I took one look at her face and backed up a couple of steps. She looked at the wizard for a minute and started to smile. "Nothing, Antorell? Are you sure?"

The wizard laughed and raised his staff. I backed up

some more. I mean, I wanted to see what was going on, but I'm not *stupid*. He paused a moment—for effect, I think—and Mother pointed at him.

"Argelfraster," she said, and he started to melt.

"No! Not *again!*" he screamed. He shrank pretty quickly—all but his head, which was shouting nearly the whole time. "I'll get you, Cimorene! I'll be back! You can't stop me! I'll—"

Then his head collapsed and there was nothing left but a little puddle of brown goo and his staff.

I stared at the puddle. All I could think was, *I never knew Mother could do that.* Mother let me stand there for a while before she told me to clean it up.

"Don't touch the staff," she said. "And don't forget to wash your hands before you come to dinner."

I went to get a bucket. When I came back, the staff was gone and Mother was stirring the stew as if nothing had happened. She didn't mention the wizard again until the next morning.

I was out by the remains of our door, trying to fix it. I didn't think my chances were very good. I picked up the hammer, and as I looked around for nails I saw Mother walk out of the Enchanted Forest. I was so surprised I dropped the hammer and nearly smashed my foot. Mother never went into the Enchanted Forest. Never. Then I saw the sword she was carrying, and if I'd still been holding the hammer, I'd have dropped it again.

Even from a distance, I could tell it wasn't an ordinary sword. It was about the same size and shape as the one I practiced with, but it shone too brightly and looked too sharp to be ordinary. Mother brought it over to me and set it down on top of the boards I'd been working on. "Don't touch it," she said, and went into the house.

I had a hard time following Mother's instructions. The more I looked at the sword, the more I wanted to pick it up and try a few of the passes Mother had taught me. It was such a beautiful weapon! Just looking at it made me shiver. But Mother always had good reasons for the things she told me to do, so I waited.

I didn't have to wait long. She came back almost immediately, carrying a sword belt and a sheath that I'd never seen before. They were old—so old that the leather had turned nearly gray—and very, very plain. I was disappointed; the sword deserved something more impressive.

Mother went straight to the sword and put it in the sheath. She relaxed a little then, as if she'd been worried about something. Mother almost never worried. I started wondering just what that weapon did. I didn't have much time to think about it, though. As soon as she had sheathed the sword, Mother turned and gave me her You're-not-much-but-you'll-have-to-do look. *I* started to worry.

Mother picked up the sword belt. "This is for you, Daystar." I reached for it, but she shook her head. "No, I'll do it this first time. Hold still."

She bent down and buckled the belt around my waist, then hung the sheathed sword on the belt. I felt a little strange letting her do all that, and my elbows kept getting in the way.

Finally she straightened up. "Now, Daystar, I have a few things to tell you before you leave."

"Leave?" I was shocked. Mother had never mentioned leaving before. It occurred to me that she'd said "you," not "we." I swallowed hard. "By myself?"

"Of course. You're sixteen; it's time you left, and I'm certainly not coming with you. Now pay attention." She gave me one of her sharp looks.

I paid attention.

"You have a sword, and you know as much as I can safely teach you. I don't want to see you back here again until you can explain to me why you had to leave. Do you understand?"

I nodded.

Mother went on, "Start with the Enchanted Forest. One way or another, things will happen more quickly there. Don't lose your sword, and don't draw it unless you need to use it. Oh, and watch out for Antorell. It'll take him a couple of days to get himself back together and find out where I put his staff, but once he does he'll try to make trouble again. All right?"

"But you haven't explained anything!" I blurted. "Why did that wizard come here yesterday, anyway? Why should he want to make trouble for me? And if he's so dangerous, why are you sending me—"

"Daystar!"

I stopped in midsentence.

Mother glared at me. "What happened to the manners I've tried to teach you?"

"I—I'm sorry, Mother," I said. "I was upset."

"Being upset is no excuse," Mother said sternly. "If you're going to be rude, do it for a reason and get something from it."

I nodded.

Mother smiled. "I know it's hard, and it's rather short notice, but this will probably be the best chance we get. I can't waste it just to give you time to get used to the idea of leaving home. Besides, if I tell you too much now, it could ruin everything. You'll just have to work things out for yourself."

I was more confused than ever, but I could see Mother wasn't going to tell me anything else. She looked at me for another moment, then bit her lip as if she wanted to say something and couldn't. Abruptly, she turned and walked away. At the door of the cottage, she stopped and looked back. "Good luck, Daystar. And stop wasting time. You don't have much of it." Before I could say anything, she disappeared inside.

I started off toward the Enchanted Forest. Mother's advice was always good. Besides, I was afraid she'd melt me or something if I hung around very long.

I didn't bother to follow the road. It isn't particularly useful, anyway—it disappears as soon as you cross into the forest. Or at least, it usually does. At any rate, I wanted to start with the section of the Enchanted Forest that I knew.

The Enchanted Forest comes in two parts, the Outer Forest and the Deep Woods. Most people don't realize that. The Outer Forest is relatively safe if you know what you're doing, and I'd gathered herbs there a few times.

I'd never gone more than an hour's walk from our cottage, and nothing particularly interesting had ever happened, but I'd always known that something might. The way things were going, I was pretty sure that this time something would.

I felt the little tingle on my skin that marks the border between the ordinary woods, where our cottage was, and the Enchanted Forest. Some people have trouble getting in and out of the Enchanted Forest, but I never did. I was feeling excited and adventurous, and maybe a little scared. I mean, for years I'd watched all those princes and heroes and so on go into the forest, and now it was my turn. I looked back over my shoulder to see if Mother was watching. The cottage was gone.

That shook me. You just don't expect the place you've lived in for sixteen years to vanish like that. I looked around. The trees were huge — much larger than the ones by our cottage. I couldn't reach more than a quarter of the way around the trunk of the smallest one. The ground was covered with dark green moss that ran right up to the bases of the trees and stopped short. I could see a couple of bushes, including one that had three different colors of flowers on it. Everything felt very dark and green and alive, and none of it looked familiar at all.

I shivered. This wasn't the Outer Forest. This was the Deep Woods.

I waited for a couple of minutes, but nothing happened. Somehow, I wasn't reassured. Being lost in the Enchanted Forest does not do much for one's peace of mind.

After a while I started walking again. I felt much less adventurous and considerably more scared.

I walked for a long time. Eventually I quit being scared, at least mostly. Finally I started looking for a place to rest; my feet hurt and I was getting very tired. I was careful, though. I didn't want to sit on a flower that used to be someone important. After about fifteen minutes I found a spot that looked all right, and I started to sit down. Unfortunately, I'd forgotten I was wearing the sword. It got tangled up in my legs and I sort of fell over.

Somebody giggled. I looked around and didn't see anyone, so I decided to get untangled first. I straightened my legs out and sat up, making sure the sword belt was out of the way this time. Then I took a second look around. I still didn't see anyone, but the same somebody giggled again.

"Sir or madam or—" I stopped. What was the proper honorific for something that wasn't male or female? I was pretty sure there was one, but I couldn't remember it.

"Oh, don't bother," said a high, squeaky voice. "I've never cared for all that fancy stuff."

I still didn't see anyone. "Forgive my stupidity, but I can't seem to find where you are," I said.

The giggle came again. "Down here, silly."

I looked down and jumped. A little gold lizard was sitting right next to my hand. He was about twice as long as my middle finger, and half of that was tail.

"Hey, watch it!" said the lizard. "You might hurt someone if you keep jumping around like that. Me, for instance. You big people are so careless."

"I'm very sorry," I said politely.

The lizard lifted his head. "You are? Yes, you are! How amazing. Who are you, anyway?"

"My name is Daystar," I said, bowing slightly. It was a little awkward to do from a sitting position, but I managed. Being polite to a lizard felt peculiar, but there are only two rules of behavior in the Enchanted Forest: Don't take anything for granted, and Be polite to everyone. That's if you don't live there. The inhabitants have their own codes, which it's better not to ask about.

"You're Daystar?" The lizard did something very tangled very quickly and ended up balanced on his tail. "So you are! Well, my goodness. I hadn't expected to see you around here for a while yet."

"You were expecting me?"

"Of course." The lizard looked smug. "I know everything that goes on in the Enchanted Forest. Absolutely *everything!* I've seen you in the Outer Forest. It was only a matter of time before you got this far, though I thought it would take longer. I'm Suz, by the way."

"Pleased to meet you," I said.

"You are?" The lizard leaned forward and almost lost his balance. "Yes, you really are! How positively extraordinary. Whatever are you doing in the Enchanted Forest?"

"I don't know," I said.

"You don't know!" The lizard did a back flip and scurried up onto a fat tree root, where he would have a better view. He balanced on his tail again and looked at me thoughtfully. "If you don't know what you're doing, why are you here?"

I thought for a moment. "Do you really know everything that happens in this forest?"

"Of course I do." Suz looked offended. An offended lizard is an interesting sight.

"I didn't mean to hurt your feelings or anything," I said hastily. "I just wondered if you could tell me where this came from." I touched the sword Mother had given me.

The lizard squinted in my general direction. "What? It's on the wrong side of you, silly. Bring it over where I can see it. If it came from the Enchanted Forest, I can tell you about it."

I lifted the sword, sheath and all, and twisted it around so it was on the same side of me as Suz. The lizard promptly fell over backward.

"Oh dear me my gracious goodness my oh," he squeaked. "Do you know what that *is*?"

"I wouldn't have asked you if I knew," I said. "It's a sword. I think it's magic."

"It's a sword! He thinks it's magic!" Suz ran around twice in a small circle, then did the tail-balancing trick again. "Where did you get it?" the little lizard demanded.

"My mother gave it to me. She got it out of the Enchanted Forest somewhere." I was getting a little tired of this. "Are you going to answer my question?"

"Your mother gave it to you. The Sword of the Sleeping King, that everyone in the world has been looking for for fifteen or twenty years, and *your mother gave it to you*." The lizard got so agitated he fell over again. "That isn't right. That isn't reasonable. My dear boy, that simply isn't done! Even in the Enchanted Forest there is a proper order for these things! Someone will have to notify them at the castle immediately. Oh, dear, what a stir this will cause!"

"I'm sorry, I didn't know. What's the Sword of the Sleeping King?" I'd never heard of it before, which rather surprised me. After Mother made me memorize all those pages of names and titles and peculiar weapons, I'd thought I knew the name of every magic sword in the world.

"You don't know?" The lizard froze in the middle of getting back up on his tail. He looked like a golden pretzel. "No, you don't! Oh, my. You'd better go to the castle at once. Kazul will know what to do with you. I'd better go there myself, right away." Suz untwisted and darted off into the undergrowth.

"Wait!" I shouted. "What castle? Who is Kazul? And why—"

The lizard looked back. "I don't have time for that! And even if I did, I couldn't tell you. You have to find out yourself. Magic swords always work that way. Don't you know *anything?*"

"Do you want me to recite the names of the Four Hundred Minor Swords of Korred the Spellsmith? . . . I know lots of things. I just don't know about this. How do I find out?"

"Follow the sword, silly," Suz said, and disappeared among the leaves.

In Which Daystar Is Polite
to a Bush and Makes a Friend

I didn't try to chase the lizard. For one thing, there wasn't much point in it. Suz was small enough to hide practically anywhere. For another, I didn't want to go running through the Enchanted Forest. People get killed that way, or enchanted, or other unpleasant things. Besides, I wanted to think.

I settled back against the tree and looked down at the sword, a little unhappily. "Follow the sword," Suz had said. But Mother had told me not to draw it unless I meant to use it, and I didn't think "following" it was the kind of use she meant. Besides, I wasn't sure I wanted to draw a magic sword in the middle of the Enchanted Forest, especially one I didn't know anything about. I decided to try something else.

I stood up and looked around. Over on my right there was a little gap in the trees, not enough to call a clearing, just a place where the trees were farther apart than usual. I went over to the middle of it and stood there while I tried to unfasten the sheath. That was a lot more complicated than it looked, and in the end I had to take the whole belt off. I wrapped the belt around the sheath and set it down in the middle of the open space. I backed up a couple of steps and sat down on the ground with the hilt of the sword close to me and the end of the sheath pointing away from me.

The woods had gone very, very quiet. I didn't like that, but after all the trouble I'd had getting out of the belt, I would have felt stupid if I'd just picked up the sword again without doing anything. Besides, I'd started setting up for a spell, and leaving things like that half-finished can be awfully dangerous.

I took a deep breath and spoke as steadily as I could:

> *"Sword of the Sleeping King,*
> *I conjure thee:*
> *By stream and starlight,*
> *By sun and shadow,*
> *By song and storm wind,*
> *Show me thy tale!"*

It was the simplest spell I knew—almost the only one, in fact. It's supposed to let the spell caster know more about the nature of whatever object is named in the first line of the chant. I didn't think the spell would work quite the usual way on a magic sword, but it wouldn't do any harm, and I was hoping to find out something useful.

I finished the spell, and everything was quiet for

about two heartbeats. *Fast* heartbeats. I was nervous. Then the world turned over.

That's what it felt like. The ground started shaking, and the part under the sword pushed up until it made a mound taller than I was. I didn't have much of a chance to look at it, though, because I was rolling all over the open space and trying to grab hold of something. Then everything went dark, and I was falling, and a huge, deep voice said solemnly, "All hail the Bearer of the Sword!"

And then it was over and everything was back to normal. I was lying on the ground in the Enchanted Forest, trying to dig my way through the moss. I stopped and waited. Nothing else happened, so I sat up and looked around. I was still sitting in the same not-quite-a-clearing, with the sword and sheath in the middle. The sword . . .

The sword was standing upright, half-buried in a knee-high mound that hadn't been there before. The blade was about a handspan out of the sheath, and it glittered when the sun got far enough through the trees to hit it. I stood up and walked over. The mound was covered with moss, just like the rest of the forest floor. It could have been there forever. I shivered, wondering how I was going to get the sheath out of the ground.

I put one hand on the hilt, intending to shove it back down into the sheath. When my hand touched it, my whole arm started to tingle. I jerked my hand away and stared at the sword. It just sat there. I reached out again, this time for the sheath.

As soon as I touched it, the sheath slid out of the ground. The belt was still wrapped around it, and no dirt clung to either of them. I touched the hilt again. My arm tingled, but this time I was ready for it, and I shoved the sword back into the sheath. Then I stuffed the sword belt under my arm and started walking. I was sure *somebody* must have noticed what had just happened, and I didn't want to be around when they came to find out what was going on.

I DIDN'T STOP AGAIN UNTIL midafternoon. By then I was hungry as well as tired. I hadn't brought any food with me, and even if I'd known how to get home it was much too late to go back for some. I sighed and sat down under another tree to rest and think, but I didn't get much thinking done. Mostly, I stared at the sword.

Finally, I gave up. Sitting under a tree wasn't going to teach me anything. I stood up and buckled on the sword belt. As I adjusted it, my hand touched the hilt of the sword again. *Three* little tingles ran up my arm before I pulled my hand away. I looked at the sword for a moment, then shrugged and reached for the hilt with my right hand, as if I were going to draw it.

As soon as my hand touched the hilt, I felt the tingling. This time, instead of letting go, I concentrated on the way it felt. I got three distinct impressions. One was a low sort of background vibration, like a kitten purring in its sleep; one was a deep rumble; and one was a bright buzz, like a bee in a jar. Almost as soon as I figured them out, they started to fade. In another minute they were completely gone, and they didn't come back.

I took my hand off the sword's hilt, then put it back. I didn't feel anything. I tried a couple more times, but whatever it was had stopped. Finally I gave up and started walking again. I wasn't getting anywhere trying to figure out the sword, and I had to find somewhere to spend the night.

At least I didn't have to worry about giants; they live farther east, in the Mountains of Morning. It occurred to me suddenly that I didn't know where I was. I might *be* in the Mountains of Morning. It wasn't a particularly cheerful thought. I started walking more quietly.

I'd been walking for nearly half an hour when I realized that I knew where I was going. Unfortunately, I didn't know where I'd be when I got there. It was very odd, and I was a little uneasy until I realized that I didn't *have* to go that direction. I could have turned around and walked the other way, or gone sideways. In fact, I did go sideways for a while, just to prove I could.

After that I felt better, so I stopped avoiding whatever it was and started walking toward it again. I wasn't going to get anywhere if I kept avoiding things, and I might miss something important. Besides, there isn't any way you can avoid *everything* in the Enchanted Forest. This way, at least I knew something was coming.

I was still walking very quietly when I heard somebody crying. I headed toward the sound, wondering what I was getting myself into. You can't just ignore things like that, especially in the Enchanted Forest. On the other hand . . .

I stopped, staring at a thick, prickly hedge. It was taller than my head and impossible to see through, much less to shove through. The crying was coming from the other side.

I bent over. The bushes were much too close together for me to crawl through them. I could make out sunlight and long red hair and a brown tunic on the other side, but not much else. I stood up and walked to one side, looking for a thin spot in the hedge. It wasn't long before I realized I was going in a circle. *Terrific*, I thought. *I bet it goes all the way around without breaking.* I kept walking anyway, just in case.

It didn't take long to make the full circle. I bent over and peered through the bushes again. Suz might be able to get through, but I never would. I stood up and tapped lightly on the outside of the bushes.

"Excuse me, please, but would you mind letting me through?" I asked as politely as I could.

The bushes rustled and pulled apart. I stared at them for a minute. I hadn't really thought it would work. The bushes rustled again. Somehow they managed to sound impatient.

"Ah, thank you very much," I said, and stepped through.

The hedge closed behind me with a prim *swish*, and I looked around. Inside the hedge was a circular clearing full of sunlight and the feel of magic. A red-haired girl in a brown tunic was lying at one side of the clearing. She sat up as I came in; her face was tearstained.

"Who are you?" she demanded fiercely, as soon as she saw me. "And what do you want?" She looked about my age, but I never have been very good at guessing how old people are, especially people who aren't in disguise or enchanted.

"My name is Daystar," I said. "I heard you, um, crying, and I wanted to see if I could do anything."

She looked at me suspiciously. "You just walked through that hedge? Ha! I've been trying to get out of here all day. It's not that easy. I bet you're a wizard." I noticed some scratches on her arms and some fuzzy places in the tunic where it might have caught on branches or trees.

"I'm not a wizard. Maybe it's easier to get in than it is to get out," I offered.

The red-haired girl sat back. "That could be true," she said a little less belligerently. She eyed me skeptically, and I tried to look trustworthy. "Well, you don't *look* like a wizard," she said at last. "Can you get out again?"

"I don't know," I said.

"Well, try!" she said. "No, wait. I'll stand next to you so I can get out, too. Then we'll both be rescued." She jumped to her feet. "What are you waiting for?"

"I'm sorry, but I don't really think I need to be rescued," I said. "I was looking for a place to spend the night and this seems pretty safe. I'm not sure I want to leave just yet. Besides, I don't know anything about you. Maybe I don't want to rescue you."

"Oh, rats." The redhead sat down again. "I thought you might be a hero. You can talk them into anything. Stupid creatures."

"Who are you?" I asked. "And why are you worried about wizards?"

"I suppose it won't matter if I tell you," she said after thinking for a minute. "They're chasing me. My name's Shiara," she added.

"Wizards are chasing you? More than one?" I was impressed. Wizards usually don't cooperate much, even the ones who belong to the Society of Wizards. At least, that's what Mother always told me. "What did you do?"

Shiara hesitated, then threw her hair back over her shoulder with a toss of her head. "I," she said defiantly, "am a fire-witch."

"You're a fire-witch?" Well, she had the red hair for it, but that doesn't always mean someone is a fire-witch.

She must have heard the doubt in my voice, because she scowled at me. "I *am* a fire-witch! I am!"

"I didn't say you weren't," I said hastily. That only seemed to make it worse.

"You don't believe me! But I am *so* a fire-witch! I am! I am!" By the time she finished, she was shouting. She glared at me, and her hair burst into flame.

That settled it. "I believe you, I believe you," I said. "Uh, shouldn't you do something about your hair?"

Shiara burst into tears and her hair went out.

I stood there feeling silly and useless. Finally I remembered my handkerchief. Mother made me carry one all the time, even to chop wood, so I actually had it with me. I pulled it out and offered it to her.

After a couple of sniffs, she took it and mopped her face, but she didn't say anything.

"I'm sorry," I said finally. "I didn't mean to make you mad."

"Well, you did," she snapped. She crumpled the handkerchief into a little ball and threw it at me.

I caught it and stuffed it back into my pocket. "I *said* I was sorry."

"I can't *help* having a temper," Shiara said crossly. "All fire-witches do."

"Really? I've never met one before. I've met heroes and princes, but no fire-witches. Does your hair always do that when you get mad?"

"No," she said. She looked like she was going to cry again.

"Why are the wizards chasing you?" I asked hastily, hoping it was a safer topic.

"I burned the Head Wizard's staff," Shiara said matter-of-factly.

My jaw dropped about a foot. A wizard's staff is the source of his power, and furthermore, most wizards store spells in them. Sort of an emergency reserve. A lot of the staffs get passed down from one wizard to the next, accumulating magic as they go. They're practically indestructible. Sometimes they get lost or stolen and then found in the nick of time under peculiar circumstances, but I'd never heard of one being destroyed before. And the Head Wizard's staff . . .

"You *burned* a *wizard's staff*?" I managed finally.

"You bet." Shiara's eyes glinted at the memory. "He deserved it, too. But the rest of them got mad. So I ran away while they were arguing about what to do with me."

"And you came to the Enchanted Forest? On purpose? Isn't that a little extreme? I mean, you could get, well, enchanted. Or killed or something. This place is dangerous."

"Having the whole Society of Wizards mad at you isn't exactly safe," she snapped.

I thought about it. She was right. "Why did you burn the Head Wizard's staff?" I asked after a minute.

"I didn't like him," Shiara said shortly. I got the distinct impression she didn't want to talk about it, so I decided to change the subject again. Besides, my feet hurt.

"Would you mind if I sat down?" I asked. "I've been doing a lot of walking today."

"Go ahead."

I moved the sword out of the way and sat down. This time I didn't fall over the sheath; I was starting to get the hang of it.

Shiara saw the weapon and frowned. "Are you sure you're not a hero or an apprentice hero or something?"

"I don't think I am," I said cautiously. "I'm not really sure."

"You're not sure? Don't you know who you are?"

I blinked. I'd never really thought about it that way. "I know who I *am*," I said. "I just don't know what I'm supposed to be *doing*. Except finding out what I'm supposed to be doing."

Shiara stared at me. "I don't believe it. Nobody comes to the Enchanted Forest without some kind of reason."

"What's yours, then? Besides running away from wizards." I was getting a little tired of people and animals and things not believing me.

"None of your business!" Shiara glared at me again. Then she jumped up and glared down at me. "I want to leave," she announced. "Right now."

"All right," I said. "But I thought you couldn't get through the hedge."

Shiara stamped her foot, and a little flame flared up from it. "I can't! Open it for me! Right now!" She was really mad, but at least this time her hair wasn't burning. I was glad. Watching someone glare at you with her hair on fire is a little unnerving.

"I don't want to open the hedge yet," I said reasonably. "I don't even know if I can. Besides, it would be dangerous. There are wolves in this forest. And it's getting dark. There could be nightshades out there already. That may not bother a fire-witch, but—"

"I hate you!" Shiara cried. She sounded like she meant it.

"Just because I don't want to get eaten by wolves or driven mad by a nightshade or something?" I said, puzzled. "What's wrong with that?"

Shiara just turned her back on me. I watched her for a minute, then sort of settled back on the ground. Things were getting very complicated. I was lost in the Enchanted Forest, with no food or water. I had a magic sword I didn't want to use because it did strange things to the ground. In another day or so I would probably have a wizard looking for me. I didn't have any idea how I was going to figure out why Mother wanted me to leave home. And then there was Shiara.

Fire-witches are rare. Nobody can learn to be one. You're either born one or you're not. They're very powerful. They can burn anything, of course, and fire doesn't hurt them at all. Fire-witches can learn almost any kind of magic there is. They're immune to most spells, too, which is why wizards don't like them. Fire-witches can even summon Elementals and get them to listen. Well, sometimes. And Shiara was a fire-witch. With enough power to burn a wizard's staff. The Head Wizard's staff.

I didn't think I wanted her to be mad at me.

I didn't know what to do about it, though. I didn't even know what I'd done wrong, and I wasn't at all sure what to do next. What do you say to a mad fire-witch?

Right about then I heard snuffling noises. I looked up. Shiara was crying again. I sighed and dug out my handkerchief.

"I don't mean to make you mad," I said as I watched her mop her face again. "I just keep doing it by accident. It'd make things a lot easier for both of us if you would tell me what I'm doing wrong so I can stop."

Shiara looked at me over the top of the handkerchief, which was starting to look sort of damp and wrinkled. "You want to talk to me? You're not scared?" She lowered the handkerchief and stared at me. "You mean it!"

"Of course I mean it," I said. "Why shouldn't I? And why should I be scared?"

"I guess I'd better tell you," she said with a sigh.

In Which They Meet a Wizard and Get Wet

The problem was, Shiara was a fire-witch who couldn't do anything. On purpose, I mean. Things happened when she got mad, and once in a while a spell worked for her, but most of the time she couldn't make anything happen, which was why she hadn't just burned her way out of the bushes before I got there. She didn't have very many friends because everyone was afraid of her. I could understand that. I mean, with a temper like hers and no way of telling what would happen when she lost it, people had reason to be nervous.

On top of that, everyone kept telling her all the things she ought to be able to do because she was a fire-witch. Like not worrying about nightshades. That was why she got mad at me. She was awfully sick of being told what fire-witches could do, especially when she couldn't, and she thought I was starting, so of course she lost her temper.

And then the Society of Wizards heard about this fire-witch who couldn't cast spells or anything. They decided it would be a great chance to find out more about fire-witches, so a whole bunch of them came and grabbed Shiara right out of the middle of town. Shiara didn't like it. She liked it even less when she found out they wanted her to stand in the middle of a circle of wizards while they threw spells at her to see what would work.

"I said no," Shiara told me. "And they said I didn't have any choice. That's when I burned the Head Wizard's staff. I don't like wizards."

"I don't blame you," I said.

She nodded and went on, "Anyway, it turned out that the wizards had brought me to the edge of the Enchanted Forest. So as long as I was here, I decided to see if there was somewhere in the forest I could find out how to use my magic. Only then I stumbled in here and I couldn't get out. I was afraid the wizards would catch up with me, and I was tired and hungry and mad, and I couldn't make my fire magic work enough to burn even a little hole in those bushes. That's why I was crying."

I wished she hadn't mentioned being hungry. Until then I'd almost forgotten that I hadn't eaten since breakfast. But there wasn't any food inside the hedge, and I wasn't going to try opening it. I'd already done enough experimenting for one day, and besides, it was getting dark.

"Your turn. What are you doing in the Enchanted Forest?" Shiara asked when I didn't say anything.

"I don't know," I said.

"How can you not know?" she demanded. "I told you why I came!"

So I explained about Mother and the wizard. Shiara was very interested.

"I want to meet your mother," she said. "After I learn how to use my magic. Do you think she would teach me how to melt a wizard?"

"I don't know."

Shiara thought for a minute. "I don't see how you can find out what you're supposed to be doing just by wandering around the Enchanted Forest."

"Well, *you're* planning to wander around until you find out how to use your magic, aren't you?" I said. "I don't think I really see the difference."

"I know what I'm doing," Shiara said. "That's the difference."

"If you knew very much about the Enchanted Forest, you wouldn't have gotten caught by this hedge."

Shiara scowled, then looked suddenly thoughtful. "Is it more dangerous to wander around the forest alone than with someone?"

"It depends," I said. "Two people attract more attention than one, but sooner or later everyone in the Enchanted Forest runs into something dangerous. And when you do get into trouble, it's sort of nice to have someone around to help."

"Why don't we stay together, then? After we get out of this stupid hedge, I mean. As long as neither of us knows exactly where we're going, we might as well wander in the same direction."

"All right." It sounded like a good idea, especially since it's hard to run into someone completely by accident in the Enchanted Forest.

Then Shiara made me describe Antorell in detail, and she decided that he wasn't one of the wizards who had kidnapped her. I wasn't sure whether that was good or bad. Shiara was nice when she wasn't mad, and I was beginning to like her. But if we were going to stick together, we would have two sets of wizards looking for us, and that didn't sound too good. Shiara was still curious, so I wound up telling her about the sword and the lizard and everything.

"The Sword of the Sleeping King," she said thoughtfully when I finished. "Well, it *sounds* important. Can you do that spell again? I'd like to watch. Maybe I could figure it out."

"I could do it, but I won't," I said. "Once was enough."

"You scared or something?" Shiara said scornfully.

"I'm not scared, I'm being sensible. That was no minor magic I set off. Are you *trying* to attract attention?"

"No, I suppose you're right. Will you let me see the sword, at least?"

"Sure, if you promise not to take it out of the sheath or say any spells at it or anything," I said. I stood up and started trying to unbuckle the belt. It was hard to do in the dark. Finally Shiara got tired of waiting and came and helped. It still took a while, and my elbows got in the way again, but finally we managed to get the sword belt off. Shiara took the sheath and squinted at the parts of the sword that showed.

"I can't see anything," she complained.

"There isn't much to see," I said. "Besides, it's dark. Maybe we should wait until tomorrow."

"I wanted to see it now. Oh, all right." She handed it back, hilt first. I took it and nearly let go again right away. The tingling was back, the one that reminded me of a bee, and it was a lot stronger than it had been before.

"Watch out!" Shiara said. "You almost dropped it."

"It's tingling again," I said.

"It is? Let me see." I handed the sword back, and Shiara touched the hilt. "I don't feel anything. Are you sure?"

"Of course I'm sure." I reached out and put my hand on the hilt, next to Shiara's.

"Ow!" I said, and Shiara went, "Oh!" and we both dropped the sword. We looked at each other for a minute.

"What did it feel like to you?" I asked finally.

"Like something pulling at me." Shiara eyed the sword warily. "You can have it back now. I don't want to look at it anymore."

I picked up the sword and put it back on. I still wanted to know what it was doing, but I wasn't going to mess around with it in the dark. Shiara and I talked a little, but we were both tired, and finally we decided to just go to sleep. We would have plenty of time to experiment in the morning if we still felt like it.

SPENDING THE NIGHT in the Enchanted Forest sounds awfully exciting, but it isn't really. Either you stay up all night so the wolves and nightshades and things won't get you and they don't, or you fall asleep and they do, or you find someplace safe and sleep there and never know. We slept all night—at least, I did—and when we woke up in the morning the hedge was still there.

By that time I was really hungry, and since there wasn't anything to eat inside the hedge I was ready to leave. So was Shiara. She was still worried about the Society of Wizards. We brushed most of the moss off our clothes, and I checked the sword, just to be safe.

"Will you quit fussing with that and come open this stupid hedge?" Shiara said.

I walked over to the bushes. They looked very dense and very prickly.

"Excuse me," I said to the hedge. "I would like to thank you for keeping the wolves and things out all night, and I would very much appreciate it if you would let us through now."

"That's the dumbest—" Shiara began, and the bushes rustled and parted. I grinned and stepped through. The branches shut behind me with a snap. "Ow!" said Shiara. I turned around. She was still on the other side of the hedge.

"What happened?" I yelled.

"What do you think happened? And you don't have to shout. I'm not that far away."

"Sorry."

"Make it open up again!"

"I'll try," I said doubtfully. I addressed the bushes again. "Excuse me, but you seem to have a friend of mine inside, and she can't get out. Will you please let her through?"

The bushes rustled smugly and didn't move apart at all. "I'd really appreciate it if you would let her out," I said. "She's nicer than you think."

The bushes rustled again. This time they sounded skeptical. They still didn't open.

"Well?" said Shiara's voice.

I sighed. "They won't open up. I'm afraid you'll have to apologize."

"Apologize? To a *bush?*" Shiara sounded outraged. "I won't! I'll burn this hedge to cinders! I'll—Ow!"

"I really think you'd better apologize," I said. "Otherwise you probably won't get out before the wizards come."

There was silence for a while. Finally Shiara said, "Oh, all right. I'm sorry I said you were a stupid hedge." She paused. "Now will you please let me through?"

Reluctantly, the bushes pulled apart. Shiara sighed with relief and stepped through.

She almost didn't make it. The bushes closed again so fast they caught a piece of her tunic.

"Hey!" she said. "Stop that!"

"I hate to mention this," I said as I helped Shiara work her tunic free, "but you really ought to be more polite."

"To lizards and bushes? Ha!" She jerked her tunic free and glared at the hedge.

"I mean it," I said. "It only gets you into trouble when you're not."

"I'm a fire-witch," Shiara said sullenly. "People are supposed to be polite to *me*."

"I thought you didn't like having everyone scared of you," I said. I turned to the bush. "Thank you very much."

The branches rustled politely. I turned back to Shiara, who was watching me with her mouth open. "If you act that way all the time, I don't think people would like you much even if you weren't a fire-witch. Goodbye." I turned around and started walking.

"Wait!"

I stopped. Shiara ran up beside me. "I—I'm sorry. I guess I'm not used to being nice to people."

"That could really get you in trouble in the Enchanted Forest," I said.

Shiara looked back over her shoulder at the hedge and shuddered. "No kidding. Well, I'll try."

"All right. Let's find something to eat."

That was easier to say than do. We found a bush that had some berries on it, but half of them were blue and half were red. I wasn't quite hungry enough to take a chance on them, and neither was Shiara.

"If my fire magic doesn't always work, my immunity to magic might not always work, either," she said. "I'd hate to turn into something awful just because of a few berries." I thought that was very sensible. We kept going.

Eventually we found a clearing full of blackberry brambles. It was so ordinary that it looked very odd sitting there in the middle of the Enchanted Forest. The berries were full of seeds, but we ate a lot of them anyway. I picked some extras and tied them up in my handkerchief for later. When we finished, we started walking again.

It wasn't a very exciting walk. The trees didn't get any smaller, the moss still covered the ground, and every once in a while there was a peculiar bush growing next to one of the trees. It would have gotten boring if Shiara hadn't been there. It was nice to have someone my own age to talk to. I'd never had any friends. Most people don't want their children getting close to the Enchanted Forest, so Mother and I had never had any visitors except the princes and heroes and so on. I told Shiara about living at the edge of the forest, and she told me about the town she lived in. I thought it was very interesting.

BY THE MIDDLE OF THE MORNING we were both hungry again. Blackberries don't stick with you for long. We stopped and ate the berries I'd saved in my handkerchief. They were squashed and messy, but they tasted fine. When we finished, we walked some more. It was a warm day, and by the time we saw the stream we were both very thirsty.

"Water! Oh, great!" Shiara said as we reached the bank. It was a small stream, ankle deep and a little too wide to jump. I could see the pebbles on the bottom. Shiara knelt on the bank and reached down.

"Wait a minute!" I said. "You shouldn't just drink that. You could turn into a rabbit, or lose your memory, or disappear, or something."

Shiara looked at me. Then she looked at the stream. "I don't care," she said finally. "I'm thirsty." She leaned toward the water again.

"But what if—Watch out!" I grabbed Shiara and pulled her away just as a huge swirl of muddy water came rushing down the stream. She scrambled back and stood up, and we watched the stream for a minute. It was now almost a river, deep and fast and angry.

Shiara looked at me. "Thanks."

"You're welcome. I guess we'll have to go back—" I started to turn back toward the woods and stopped. There was dark water on that side of us, too. We were standing on an island. A very small island. It was getting smaller every minute.

I stared at the churning water, and my hand went to my sword. I don't know why—most swords aren't any good against floods. As soon as I touched the hilt I knew that it wasn't in the nature of this particular stream to do this sort of thing. I didn't know how I knew, but I was sure someone was creating the flood.

Right about then I heard a chuckle. Not a nice chuckle. I was looking around for the chuckler when Shiara grabbed my arm. "Daystar! Over there!"

I turned. A man was leaning against one of the trees. He had blue robes and black hair, and he held a wizard's staff in one hand. I didn't like the way he was watching Shiara.

"Well, little fire-witch, I seem to have caught you again," he said.

"You leave me alone!" Shiara shouted. "Or I'll burn your staff, too."

The wizard chuckled again. He really had a nasty chuckle. "Oh, I don't think so. I've taken precautions, you see." He waved at the water that surrounded us and smiled patronizingly. "Or weren't you aware that fire magic won't cross water?"

"Magic may not cross water, but we can," I said. I was beginning to share Shiara's dislike of wizards. "Come on, Shiara. It can't be very deep."

"Where did you find the hero?" the wizard asked. Shiara just glared at him. The wizard laughed. I didn't like his laugh any better than his chuckle. "I should give him something to do, don't you think? A monster, per- haps. Heroes like monsters." He waved his staff in the general direction of the flooding stream.

The water on one side of our island bunched up and began to solidify rapidly. I didn't even have time to step back before the thing finished growing. When it was done, it looked sort of like a giant snake's head that dripped. The outlines kept changing because it was made out of water that wasn't completely solid, but it was pretty clearly a snake.

It lunged at me. I dodged, barely in time, and drew my sword. Shiara yelled, and steam puffed from the snake head. The snake didn't seem particularly hurt. Some of the stream water bunched up around it, but that was all. I heard the wizard laugh again.

"I'm afraid that won't work very well, young lady," he said. "You'd have to boil the whole stream away to get rid of my monster, and I don't think you can. Pity, isn't it? Be patient. You'll have your turn in another min- ute, and then the Head Wizard will owe me a favor."

The head lunged again. By now I was ready for it, but it was awfully fast. I dodged and struck at it with the sword, even though I wasn't sure what good it would do me to wound something that wasn't even alive.

The sword made a humming noise. I heard the wizard shout, and then a sound like an explosion. The snake head made a bubbly noise and collapsed in a wave of muddy water that swept over the little island Shiara and I were standing on, soaking everything. In another minute, the flood water drained away, leaving a lot of wet moss. And Shiara yelled again.

I whirled around. Shiara was pointing. It took me a second to realize what she was pointing at. It was the big tree that the wizard had been leaning against. A couple of short branches were lying at the foot of the tree. The wizard was gone.

In Which They Learn the Perils of
Inspecting a Wizard's Broken Staff

I stood where I was, panting and dripping. When I got my breath back, I went over to the tree. There was no sign of the wizard, except for the "branches" I'd noticed. There were three of them, and they weren't branches. They were pieces of a staff.

I looked at Shiara. "That's two wizards' staffs you've broken. They're really going to be after you now."

"I didn't break it," Shiara said indignantly. "You did."

"I did not," I said. We looked at each other for a minute.

"If neither of us broke it," Shiara said finally, "who did?"

"Me," said a voice. I looked up. A little man was sitting in the branches of the tree. He was about two feet tall and dressed entirely in green. His eyes were black and very bright, and his ears were slightly pointed. He had to be an elf.

"I think you mean 'I,'" I said automatically.

"I shouldn't wonder if you're right." The elf tilted his head to one side. "Does it matter?"

"Can you get down from that tree?" Shiara said. "You're giving me a crick in my neck."

The elf looked from me to Shiara and back to me again. "Introduce me to your charming companion."

"Oh, excuse me," I said. I told the elf our names and thanked him for taking care of the wizard. I was a little curious about that. I'd never met an elf, but they didn't have a reputation for altruism. I wasn't sure I wanted to trust one, either. Elves can be very tricky.

"You're welcome," the elf said. "I've never cared much for wizards. Unfortunately, it's very difficult to do anything permanent to them. This one will be back in a day or two."

"If there is anything we can do for you in return, I would like to hear what it is," I said. If someone in the Enchanted Forest does you a favor, you have to offer to do one for them. Well, you don't have to, but if you don't, things seem to go wrong a lot after that. You have to be careful, though. If you promise to do a favor before you hear what it is, you can end up in more trouble than you started with. I wasn't going to promise anything without finding out first what I was promising.

"Consider the debt canceled," the elf said politely. I thought he sounded disappointed, and I didn't like the way he was looking at my sword. Suddenly I was very glad Mother had told me about making promises in the Enchanted Forest.

"Thank you," I said. "You did a very neat job." He had, too; the staff had been sliced cleanly into thirds. I began to wonder how he had done it. I hadn't thought elves were powerful enough to break a wizard's staff. I didn't want to offend him by asking about it, though.

"You may have the staff, if you want it," the elf said, waving at the pieces.

"What good is a busted wizard's staff?" Shiara asked. "You can't *do* anything with it."

"Nonsense," said the elf. "Wizards' staffs are just as powerful in pieces as they are whole, and they're fairly easy to put back together. Please, take it with you."

I didn't like the way he kept suggesting that, though it sounded reasonable enough. "Are you sure you don't want it?" I asked finally.

"What would an elf do with a wizard's staff? If you don't take it, I'll just have to get rid of it somewhere."

That sounded reasonable, too, but I wasn't going to commit myself. He was too insistent. "Thank you for the suggestion," I said. "We'll think about it."

"Do," the elf said. His black eyes twinkled. "Perhaps I'll see you later. Goodbye." Before I could say anything he had disappeared into the treetops. Elves move very quickly.

"What was that about?" Shiara demanded.

"I don't know about that elf," I said slowly. "I think something funny is going on. He was trying too hard to get us to take that staff."

"Well, we have to do something with it," Shiara said.

"Why?" I said. "*We* didn't break it. And I don't want to mess with a wizard's staff, even a broken one."

Shiara frowned. I made a gesture toward the pieces and realized that I was still holding the sword in my hand. I started to put it back in its sheath, then stopped. The sheath was as wet as everything else I was wearing. I couldn't put the sword in that. I mean, not all magic swords are rustproof, and even if you have one that is, putting your sword away without cleaning it is a bad habit to get into. I checked my pockets, just in case, but even my handkerchief was wet.

"Shiara, do you have anything—no, you wouldn't, you were in the middle of that stream, too."

"What? What are you mumbling about?" Shiara said.

"I need something to dry off my sword," I said. "Everything I have is soaked. But you're just as wet as I am . . ." My voice trailed off, because right then I really looked at her, and she wasn't. Wet, I mean. Her shoes were steaming a little, but her hair and her clothes weren't even damp.

"Fire-witches dry off fast," Shiara said in a smug tone.

"Then can you give me something to clean my sword?" I asked. "Everything I have is soaked."

"What does that have to do with the wizard's staff? Oh, give it here. I'll fix it." She held out her hand a little reluctantly. I could see she didn't really want to take the sword. After what had happened the last time she'd touched it, I couldn't blame her.

"That's all right, I'll do it," I said. "It's my job. All I need is something dry to wipe it with."

Shiara glared at me. "All I have is my tunic, and I am not going to take it off just so you can dry your stupid sword! If you won't give it to me, it can rust."

My face got very hot. "I, um, I'm sorry, I didn't mean . . . I mean, I didn't think . . ."

"Oh, shut up and give me the sword."

I held it out. Shiara took it a little gingerly, but neither of us felt anything unusual. While she wiped it dry on the front of her tunic, I walked over to the stream. I was pretty sure, now, that the water was safe to drink. I'd swallowed some of it when the wizard's wave hit me, and nothing had happened to me yet. I bent over and took a drink.

The water was clean and cold, with just a hint of lime. It tasted awfully good, though I prefer lemon-flavored streams myself. I think I like lemon because Mother and I got most of our drinking water from a lemon-flavored stream just inside the forest. It was much nicer than the well water we used for washing, even if it was more work to haul the buckets that far.

Shiara came over just as I finished. She looked at me for a minute, then handed me the sword. "Here." I took it, and she sat down and started trying to drink out of her cupped hands. Most of the water ran out, but she kept trying.

I stood holding the sword and wondering what I was going to do with it. I mean, walking through the Enchanted Forest with a sword in your hand is just *asking* for trouble. On the other hand, I couldn't put it away until the sheath dried out, and that would probably take hours.

Shiara finished drinking and sat up. "Now, what are we going to do about that wizard's staff?"

Neither one of us wanted to take it with us. Shiara

suggested hiding the pieces before we left, and finally I agreed. We walked back over to the tree. I started to put my sword down, then changed my mind. One of the easiest ways of losing important things in the Enchanted Forest is to put them down while you do something else. Then you have to go to all the bother of finding whoever took your things before you can get on with whatever you really want to do. I shifted the sword into my left hand and looked around for the nearest piece of staff.

"Daystar! Come see!" Shiara was waving a piece of the staff to attract my attention.

"You really shouldn't do that," I said as I walked over. "You might set off a spell or something. This used to be a wizard's staff, remember? We ought to at least *try* to be careful."

"Yes, but look what it did," Shiara said, pointing. I looked down. There was a brown patch in the moss, just the size and shape of the stick Shiara was holding. I bent over and looked more closely. The moss was so dry and brittle that it turned to powder when I touched it.

"But this is the Enchanted Forest," I said to no one in particular. "You aren't supposed to be able to *do* things like this."

"Well, this wizard's staff did," Shiara said. "I bet it'll do it again, too." Before I could stop her, she laid the stick down on the moss. She picked it up almost immediately. The moss underneath it was brown and dead.

I stared. "I don't like this," I said. There aren't very many things you can be sure of in the Enchanted Forest, but I'd never seen a dead plant there, not even in the

Outer Forest. The whole place felt too alive to put up with that sort of thing. "I wonder if all wizards' staffs do that."

"I don't know about other staffs, but we can check the other pieces of this one," Shiara said. She walked toward one of the other two sticks. I sighed and started for the last one.

"This one's the same," Shiara reported after a minute. "What about yours?"

"Just a minute," I said. I bent over and picked it up in my right hand . . .

When I woke up, Shiara was dripping water on my face. "You can stop now," I said. "I'm wet enough already."

Shiara shook her head. "Are you all right? I mean, you're not enchanted or anything, are you?"

I thought about it for a moment. "I don't think so, but if I am, we'll find out pretty soon." I sat up and realized I'd been lying on the moss at the foot of the tree. "What happened?"

"How should I know? One minute you were standing there with that sword, and then there was some kind of explosion and when I turned around you were lying here and that piece of the wizard's staff was over there, burning. I don't think anyone's going to put that staff back together again. It was the middle piece." Shiara scowled. "But I think you were right about that elf."

"Where's my sword?" I asked. All of a sudden I was sure someone had taken it while Shiara and I weren't paying attention.

"In your hand," Shiara said. She sounded a little exasperated. "You wouldn't let go of it."

I looked down. My left hand was still clenched around the hilt. When I relaxed my hand, the fingers started to tingle. I'd been holding on so tightly that my hand had fallen asleep.

Well, at least I hadn't lost it. I started to shift the sword back to my right hand, then stopped and swallowed hard. The hand was burned black. I couldn't even feel it. I looked away, feeling sick. Shiara was staring, too.

"Daystar, I didn't notice, I was so worried about waking you up I didn't even see—" She stopped. She tilted her head back until she was looking up the tree trunk, and her eyes flashed. "I'm going to find somebody who can fix this," she said grimly. "And then I'm going to find that stupid elf and make him sorry he ever mentioned that wizard's staff." The way she said it made me very, very glad I wasn't an elf, particularly the elf she'd be looking for.

"It doesn't really hurt or anything," I offered. As soon as I said it, my arm started to throb. Not the hand; it was my wrist and arm that hurt. As far as I was concerned, that was more than enough.

"That's bad," Shiara said. She looked worried. "I know a little about burns, from the times when I . . . Are you sure you can't feel anything?"

"Not in my hand," I said. "And I'd really rather not talk about it. It might help me not notice the way my arm feels."

"Well, let me look at it, then, and I won't have to ask questions," Shiara said.

I stuck my right hand out in her direction and stared

at my sword for a couple of minutes. I didn't succeed in ignoring the sensations that were coming from my arm, but I tried awfully hard. Finally Shiara said, "You can put it down now." I looked back in her direction.

"It's bad," she said. "I don't know what to do for it, either. We have to find help, and pretty soon, too. There has to be someone in this forest who knows something about healing. Can you walk?"

"My legs are all right," I said. I started to stand up and discovered I was very dizzy. I made it on the second try, but only by using the sword as a prop.

Shiara picked a direction and we started walking. After about twenty steps I stopped worrying about which way we were going and concentrated on walking and hanging on to the sword. It was hard; I really had to work at it. I was still dizzy, and I was beginning to feel cold, too—all but my arm, which felt as if it were on fire, and I wondered whether the wizard's staff had done more than just burn my hand.

I don't know how far we went before we stopped. By that time, Shiara was holding my good arm, trying to help me walk. She couldn't help as much as she might have, because she had to keep out of the way of the sword. As soon as we quit walking, I sat down.

"Daystar, are you sure you can't put that sword away yet?" Shiara asked. "It gets in the way a lot."

"The sheath is still wet," I said hazily.

"Well, can we at least put the sheath in the sun so it'll dry faster?"

I looked around, feeling sort of lightheaded as well as dizzy. On top of everything I was getting thirsty. "We can't do that," I said. "The cat has the only patch of sun around here."

"What cat?"

"That one." I pointed at the large, dignified, black-and-white cat that was cleaning its face in the middle of a puddle of sunlight. It didn't even strike me as odd that I hadn't noticed it until I started talking about it.

Shiara turned her head. As soon as she looked at it, the cat stopped washing itself. It stared at her for a minute, then stood up. The tip of its tail twitched three times, and it turned around and started walking away. After a minute, it stopped and looked back over its shoulder. It was obviously waiting.

Shiara jumped up. "Come on, Daystar. We're going to follow the cat. I think somebody sent it."

"That doesn't make sense," I said, but I wasn't in very good shape to argue. Eventually, Shiara got me back on my feet. The cat was still waiting for us, but as soon as we moved in its direction it started walking again. I decided Shiara was right and concentrated on walking.

I don't know how far we followed the cat. It seemed like a long way, but anything would have seemed like a long way at that point. My arm hurt, and every muscle in my body felt shaky. I never quite dropped the sword, but a couple of times I came close. After a while I stopped thinking about it.

Finally Shiara stopped moving.

"I was about ready for another rest," I said fuzzily. "Is the cat still around?"

"This isn't a rest," Shiara said. "We're here."

I looked up. We were standing in front of a neat gray house with a wide porch and a red roof. A wisp of smoke was coming out of the chimney, and whatever was cooking smelled delicious. Over the door was a black-and-gold sign in block letters that read, "NONE OF THIS NONSENSE, PLEASE."

I'm going to like whoever lives here, I thought.

The door of the house was closed, but the black-and-white cat jumped up on the porch and scratched at it. A moment later, the door swung partway open and the cat disappeared inside.

In Which They Meet a Witch

We stayed where we were for a minute, waiting. I don't think either one of us really knew what to do next. A few seconds after the cat vanished, the door opened the rest of the way and the owner of the house appeared.

She wore a very loose black robe with long sleeves and a small pair of glasses with rectangular lenses. She was considerably shorter than I was, though she obviously wasn't a dwarf; she managed to look down her nose at both of us anyway. Standing on the porch helped, I think. "It's about time you got here," she said.

"Do you know anything about healing?" Shiara demanded.

"Of course I do, or I wouldn't have sent Quiz out to get you," said the woman.

"Quiz?"

"The cat. Do you plan to stand there all day? I certainly can't do anything for you while you're outside."

So we went inside. The porch steps didn't creak.

Neither did the porch, and the hinges of the door didn't squeak at all. I didn't think they would dare.

The inside of the house seemed to consist of a single large, airy room full of cats. I counted five before I stopped. Several of the cats had furniture under them, and there was a table in the middle of the room and another door next to the stove in the corner.

The woman in the black robe shooed two cats off of chairs, and Shiara and I sat down at the table. Shiara looked at me. "You can put that stupid sword down now. No one's going to take it."

"No." I didn't know why I wanted to hold on to the sword, and I didn't have enough energy to explain it if I had known. I just knew I wanted it in my hand.

"Sword?" said the woman in black. "Oh, *that* sword. It's quite proper of you to keep it for now. If I may see your hand?" She came over next to me and examined my right arm while I carefully didn't watch. Oddly enough, it didn't hurt when she touched it. After a minute or so, she nodded.

"Just as I thought. This could have been very bad, but you got here in plenty of time." She went over to a cupboard by the stove and took out a piece of something that looked like dried vine. She brought it back to me and tied it around my arm, muttering something as she did. Suddenly my head wasn't fuzzy anymore.

"That should take care of things for the time being," she said, "and in a little while I can take care of the magic. Then we can pack the burns with salve. Would you like some cider while you wait?"

I nodded.

Shiara frowned. "Can't you do anything right away?"

"I have done something," the woman said. She set three mugs on the table, all different. "Several things, in fact. I sent Quiz out to bring you here, and I have stopped the damage from spreading. I have also made gingerbread, which should finish baking any minute now."

"Gingerbread?" Shiara blinked. "Daystar is hurt! Why are you baking gingerbread?"

"For you to eat," the woman said. "Why, were you expecting me to make a house out of it?"

"Well, no, but—Oh, never mind the gingerbread! How did you know to send a cat out for us? Who are you, anyway?"

The woman looked through her glasses. "I know a lot of things. I'm a witch. My name is Morwen. And you?" She stopped. The cats looked at us.

"Pleased to meet you," I said. "This is Shiara, and I'm Daystar."

"Why do we have to wait?" Shiara asked again.

"Mixing magic and cooking is *never* a good idea," Morwen said. "Don't worry, the gingerbread won't take much longer." She got out a large jug and began pouring the contents into the mugs. "There!" she said as she set the jug down. "Help yourselves. I'll be back in a minute."

Morwen went over to the second door and opened it. I got a glimpse of a small yard with a square garden, a well, and two more cats. Then the door closed with a swish of black robe. I stared at my mug, wondering how I was going to pick it up without putting my sword down. Then I heard a sniffle and turned my head. Shiara was not crying. Much.

"What's wrong?" I said.

"It's all my f-fault!" Shiara said miserably. "If you hadn't been with me, you wouldn't have run into that wizard at all, and if I hadn't insisted on hiding that stupid staff, your hand wouldn't have gotten . . ." Her voice trailed off into snuffles. I sighed.

"If you want my handkerchief, you'll have to get it out yourself," I said. "And it's probably still pretty wet. But you can have it if you want it."

That made Shiara look like she was really going to burst into tears. Fortunately, just then the door opened and the witch came back in. When she saw Shiara, she set down the plants she was carrying and produced a large black handkerchief from somewhere inside her sleeve.

"That is *quite* enough of that," she said, handing the handkerchief to Shiara. "It does nothing constructive, it makes everyone else feel bad, and it is extremely self-indulgent. Drink your cider. You'll feel much better."

Just then one of the cats made a loud noise, sort of a cross between a purr and a meow. "Good, the ginger-bread is done," Morwen said. She got it out of the oven and gave us each a piece. Shiara looked much better by that time, even if she still didn't seem really happy.

Morwen put a large pot of water on the stove and then started sorting through the plants she had brought in. After a minute, she frowned.

"Two sprays or three?" she muttered. "I suppose I'd

better look it up." She put the plants down and went out again. A few seconds later, she came back holding a book. I saw a roomful of shelves behind her before the door closed.

I blinked. My head didn't feel fuzzy, but I was sure that a minute ago that door had led out to the yard. I looked around the room, but there weren't any other doors, except the one we'd come in through. Finally I decided to ask.

"Excuse me, Morwen, but would you mind telling me where that door leads?"

Morwen stuck a finger in the book and looked up. "Wherever I want to get to. What good is a door if you can't get somewhere useful by walking through it? Within reason, of course." She went back to the book.

I thought about it for a minute. Then I decided not to think about it. I was afraid it was going to make sense. Instead, I looked at my cider and gingerbread. I was just about ready to put the sword on the floor so I could eat when Morwen set the book down next to the plants and looked over at me.

"Daystar, you aren't—Oh, of course, you're still holding the sword. No, don't put it down yet. This will only take a few more minutes." She picked up a handful of plants. "Come here, please, both of you."

We got up and walked over. Morwen had me stand next to the stove, holding the sword across the front of my chest so that the tip of it rested on the pot of water. Shiara was behind me, with one hand on my right arm just above the dried vine. It took a while before Morwen was satisfied with our positions, but finally she stepped back. "Very good. Stay just like that until I'm finished, please."

She reached inside one of her sleeves and brought out a silver knife. She dipped the knife in the pot of water, then began muttering over the plants she was holding. Immediately, all the cats jumped down onto the floor and formed a half-circle around the stove, with Morwen and Shiara and me in the middle. They just sat there with their eyes glowing and only the tips of their tails moving, in tiny twitches. Suddenly, there was a sizzling noise from my right. The water was boiling.

Morwen gave a shout. Then she held the plants high over her head and said loudly,

> *"By the darkness of the stone's heart,*
> *By the silence of the sea's tears,*
> *By the whisper of the sky's breath,*
> *By the dawning of the star's flame,*
> *Do as I will thee!"*

Just as she finished she threw the plants into the boiling water.

A cloud of steam puffed out of the pot, smelling of herbs and magic and gingerbread, and I sneezed. The steam spread out around me and got thicker. It smelled more and more like herbs and magic and less and less like gingerbread. My right arm started to ache, and my left arm started to tingle. The ache got stronger, but it stayed where it was; the tingle spread. In another second or two I was tingling all over, except for the arm that was aching.

By now the steam was so thick I couldn't see anything, but I could still feel Shiara's hand and the vine Morwen had tied around my arm. For what seemed like a long time, nothing else happened. Then one of the cats yowled. I saw Morwen's hand, the one holding the silver knife, come out of the mist.

"In the King's name!" Morwen's voice said, and the knife cut the vine from my arm and pulled it away.

My sword flashed once, very brightly. Most of the steam settled on my right arm and turned black. The ache started to creep upward, and something that felt like lightning or wind ran up my left arm and down my right one. I heard Shiara gasp. The black steam stuff dropped off my arm into a slimy blob on the floor. My right arm stopped hurting, and my other arm stopped tingling, and everything felt normal again. I let my breath out and looked around.

Morwen was looking in my direction with an expression of extreme distaste. "That," she said, "was an exceptionally nasty wizard. He deserves what's coming to him."

"What's coming to him?" Shiara asked hopefully.

"I don't know, but he certainly deserves it," Morwen said. "Anyone who would keep a spell like that in a staff . . ." She shook her head and looked down. "I do hope it doesn't disagree with the cats."

I followed her gaze. The cats had formed a small mob and were playing with something I'd rather not describe in detail. I looked up again very quickly and took a step backward. I bumped into Shiara and remembered that Morwen had said not to move until she was finished. "I'm sorry," I said to both of them.

"It's quite all right. You can sit down again now," Morwen said. "And if you don't want to put your sword in your sheath, you can lean it against the wall. You won't need it for the time being."

I followed Morwen's instructions and sat down at the table again. I didn't realize until I reached for the gingerbread that although my right hand felt better it didn't *look* any better. I didn't have time to worry about it, though, because Morwen was already standing by my chair with some oily-looking salve and bandages. She worked on my hand while I ate gingerbread and cider left-handed. We finished about the same time, and I thanked her.

"You're welcome," Morwen said. "Now, perhaps you would explain how you got into such an uncomfortable situation? I have a general idea, but I would appreciate a few details."

I told her about the wizard and the elf, and then Shiara explained how the staff had exploded.

"Of course the staff exploded!" Morwen said severely. "That sword doesn't like wizard's staffs. Next time, make sure it's sheathed before you touch one."

"I knew it!" Shiara said angrily. "That elf was *trying* to get Daystar hurt!"

"Not necessarily," Morwen said. "He may simply have been trying to make sure the wizard found you again. If you'd taken the pieces of the staff with you, the wizard would have had no trouble locating you once he got himself back together, because the first thing he'd do would be to look for his staff."

"If that elf wanted the wizard after us, why'd he get rid of the wizard in the first place?" Shiara objected.

"I doubt that he did," Morwen said calmly. "It's more the sort of thing the sword does. I wouldn't depend on it in the future, though, particularly since you still haven't learned how to use it properly."

I wanted to ask more questions about the sword, but I was pretty sure Morwen wouldn't answer them. "What if the wizard couldn't find his staff when he came back?" I asked instead.

"Wizards always know where their staffs are. And it's almost impossible to keep wizards away from their staffs for any length of time. One can slow them down a bit by putting the staffs somewhere hard to get at, but they usually manage in the end."

"That's why Mother hid Antorell's staff!" I said.

"I shouldn't wonder," Morwen murmured. "Now, I strongly suggest that you rest for a while, Daystar, and while you are doing so I will talk with Shiara in the library." She stood up and nodded to me.

Shiara frowned and opened her mouth to say something. Then she looked at me and seemed to change her mind. "All right," she said.

Morwen went to the door, followed by Shiara and most of the cats. It was the room of books again. Trying to be careful of my bandaged right hand, I lay down on a bench that had had three cats on it before they went into the library with Morwen. I fell asleep almost immediately.

WHEN I WOKE UP, I could tell by the way the sunlight was slanting in through the windows that it was late afternoon. There wasn't anyone else in the room, except for the black-and-white cat who had led us to Morwen's house. It was sitting in the middle of the table, washing its tail.

"Hello," I said. "And thank you very much for bringing Shiara and me here."

The cat looked up briefly, decided I was uninteresting, and went back to cleaning its tail.

I shifted a little; the bench was hard. I felt much better than I had when I lay down. Then the back door opened—this time it was the door to the yard—and Morwen came in.

"You're awake. Good. Shiara has been waiting for you."

I sat up just as Morwen saw the cat on the table. She frowned at it. "Child of Scorn," she said sternly, "you are *not* allowed on the table."

The cat looked at Morwen. Morwen looked at the cat. After a minute, the cat jumped down to the floor, where it did its best to pretend that the floor was exactly where it had wanted to be all along. Morwen shook her head.

"You'll have to excuse the Grand Inquisitor. He knows he did me a favor when he brought you here, and he's inclined to take advantage of it. I would have sent Cass, but I was afraid you wouldn't pay attention to her."

"Cass?"

"Cassandra." Morwen nodded at a small gray cat that I hadn't noticed before. "She has much better manners than Quiz, but she tends to be overlooked. Nobody overlooks Quiz."

I studied the cats. They both ignored me. I glanced back at Morwen. "I don't think I've thanked you yet for —for fixing my arm." I wasn't really sure what else to call whatever she'd done.

"Yes, you have," Morwen said. "And if you insist on repeating yourself, you'd better wait until you take the bandages off tomorrow. Time enough for thanks if it's healed properly. Not that I have any doubts, mind, but it's better to be sure."

"All right," I said. "Did you say Shiara was waiting for me?"

Morwen went over to the stove. "Yes, I did. She's out by the garden," she said over her shoulder. She reached up and lifted a large kettle down from a hook on the wall.

"Thank you," I said. I got up and opened the back door. There was a room on the other side, with a bed and a large bookshelf and, of course, a cat. I shut the door and tried again. This time I got the library. Morwen had more books than anyone I'd ever heard of. I shut the door and looked back at Morwen.

"How do I get out to the garden?" I asked.

"Through the door," Morwen said without turning. "Just be firm. Sometimes it's a little contrary with strangers, but that won't last long."

I turned back, wondering how to be firm with a door.

I opened it again. Still the library. I closed it, wondering how long it would take me to get to the garden. I didn't really want to spend the rest of the afternoon opening and shutting Morwen's door, but what else could I do? I sighed and opened the door again.

This time it worked: The door opened onto three steps going down into the yard. I went through quickly, before the door could change its mind. Shiara was sitting on a stone bench by the corner of the house. She looked a lot happier than she had earlier, but all she would say was that she'd been talking to Morwen.

"She's been showing me some things," Shiara said. "And she's going to give me a kitten."

"That's nice," I said. Actually, I wasn't sure it would be a good idea to have a pet with us while we wandered around the Enchanted Forest. On the other hand, if it was one of Morwen's cats, it could probably take care of itself.

Shiara and I sat and talked for the rest of the afternoon. I discovered that somehow she and Morwen had decided that we would be spending the night here. Shiara was very pleased about it. Evidently Morwen had promised to show her some interesting magic. I wasn't sure we should stay, even though I liked Morwen. After all, neither of us had ever met her before. I had to admit, though, that it sounded a lot better than sleeping out in the open. We were still discussing it when one of the cats came to bring us in to dinner.

In Which Daystar Makes a Mistake

Dinner was a stew that smelled and tasted awfully good, though it didn't look like much. Morwen had made a large pot of the stuff. Half of it she put in a big pan and set on the floor for the cats, and the rest we ate. By the time we'd finished, we had decided to spend the night with Morwen and the cats.

I was a little worried, at first, about what to do with the Sword of the Sleeping King. I didn't want to leave it leaning up against Morwen's wall all night. Finally, I decided to keep it with me. It wasn't that I didn't trust Morwen, but Mother had given the sword to me and it was my responsibility. Once that was settled, I started wondering where Shiara and I were going to sleep.

I shouldn't have worried. Morwen had several extra bedrooms behind her magic door, and she simply put each of us in one of them. By that time I was starting to wonder how many rooms she had in her house and where she kept them all when they weren't needed.

That isn't the sort of question you ask people in the Enchanted Forest, though. So I didn't.

Besides, I was tired again. As soon as Morwen showed me to my room, I stuck the sword under the bed and went to sleep. I was pretty sure the sword would be safe there.

I was right, too. When I woke up in the morning, a cat was asleep on top of it.

After breakfast, Morwen took the bandages off my hand. The burns were gone and it felt fine, but she examined it carefully anyway. When she was finished with my hand, she helped me get my sword belt on. The sheath was dry, so I put the sword back in it. While I was doing that, Morwen produced a couple of bundles and a small black kitten with one white paw. She gave Shiara the kitten and one bundle and turned to me.

"This is for you," she said, handing me the other bundle. "It should make your travels a little easier. Now, come outside."

She opened the front door and went out onto the porch. I let Shiara leave next and started to follow her, but one of the cats darted in front of me and I nearly tripped. I had to grab for the door frame to keep my balance.

"Watch out!" Shiara said, then, "Daystar! What's the matter?"

I almost didn't hear her. I was staring down at my sword. My hand had brushed it when I'd tripped, and I'd felt the tingling again. Only this time there was even more of it. I reached over and took the hilt in my right hand. The rumbling tingle hadn't changed, but the buzzing tingle and the purring tingle were considerably stronger than they had been, and they'd been joined by a brisk vibration I hadn't felt before. I concentrated on the new feeling, trying to figure out where it had come from, and found myself looking at Morwen.

I looked back at the sword. I hadn't let go, and my arm was still tingling. I tried to pick out one of the other vibrations. Suddenly I was feeling mostly the purring tingle and looking out into the woods. I blinked and tried again. This time I got the buzz, and I was staring at Shiara. Suddenly I understood.

"It's magic!" I said.

"Of *course* it's magic," Shiara said. "Honestly, Daystar—"

"No, I mean that's what it does," I said. "The Sword of the Sleeping King finds magic!"

"Among other things," Morwen said in a satisfied voice.

"Finds magic?" Shiara said skeptically.

"That's what the tingling is," I said. I was completely sure of myself, though I didn't know why. "Different tingles mean different kinds of magic, and the tingles get stronger when the sword gets closer to the magic." I looked at Shiara. "No wonder it gave me such a jolt when we both touched it at the same time."

Shiara had been reaching for the hilt, but she pulled her hand back hastily. "If the sword finds magic, how come I couldn't feel anything until you touched it? And if the tingles are the way it finds things, why can't you feel them all the time?"

"I don't know," I said. The tingling was fading again, the same way it had when I held onto the sword before, so I let go of the hilt.

Morwen considered me through her glasses. I couldn't tell what she was thinking from her expression. Finally she nodded very slightly. "I see. There is considerably more to you than I had expected, Daystar," she said in a thoughtful tone.

I was still trying to figure out what that statement meant when Morwen turned away and said briskly, "However, it is time for you to be going. You see those two trees? Walk straight between them and keep on until you get to a stream, then follow the stream northward. You'll get to something eventually, and you should be able to figure out what to do from there."

My eyes turned in the direction Morwen was pointing. It was the same way I'd been looking when I'd been concentrating on the purring tingle from the sword. I looked back at Morwen.

"Exactly," Morwen said.

"What?" said Shiara.

"Let's go," I said. I was feeling a little unsettled by the whole thing, and I didn't want to talk about it anymore. Shiara scowled, but she didn't insist on an explanation.

We said goodbye and thank you to Morwen and started walking toward the trees. Shiara carried the kitten for a while, but pretty soon the kitten decided it wanted to walk. We slowed down a lot after that, until the kitten got tired enough to let Shiara pick it up again without scratching her.

Shiara and I spent most of the walk talking. I hadn't realized how little she knew about the Enchanted Forest, and I wound up telling her a lot of things. Like about being polite to people and why you shouldn't promise things without knowing what they are first.

Morwen hadn't told us how far away the stream was, and eventually I started wondering how much longer it would take us to find it. I was also curious about where we were going. Right about then, I noticed that the trees we were walking past were larger than the ones I'd seen the previous day. At least, I *thought* they were larger. I studied them as we walked, trying to decide whether it was my imagination or whether they really were larger. I was just getting ready to mention this to Shiara when I heard a cough. I stopped and looked around.

"Ahem," said a voice.

This time I located the speaker. It was the little gold lizard, Suz. He was sitting on a branch at just about eye level, watching me.

"Oh, hello, Suz," I said. Shiara looked around. I nodded toward the lizard and said, "Shiara, this is Suz. You remember, I told you about him. Suz, this is my friend Shiara."

The lizard ignored the introduction and continued staring at me. "Why," he demanded in an aggrieved tone, "didn't you tell me Cimorene was your mother?"

"You didn't ask," I said.

Suz looked at me reproachfully. "It would have saved me a great deal of trouble if you'd mentioned it."

"I'm sorry," I said. "I didn't know it mattered."

"You didn't?" Suz ran down the branch and peered

at me. "No, you really didn't! How amazing. I can't understand how it happened."

"What are you talking about?" Shiara said.

The lizard appeared to see her for the first time. He leaned outward in Shiara's direction and I thought he was going to fall off, until I saw that his tail was wrapped tightly around a sturdy twig on the far side of the branch. "You've brought someone with you? Dear me, this will never do. Who is this?"

"I've already introduced you once," I reminded him. "You weren't listening."

"You did? Yes, of course, you did. How perfectly dreadful." Suz ran around the branch very fast, and for a minute I was afraid he was going to try to stand on his tail. If he did, I was sure he'd fall off, because the branch wasn't very wide.

"What's so dreadful?" Shiara demanded. "There's nothing wrong with me."

"No, of course, there isn't. Oh, dear, Kazul will be terribly unhappy about this."

"Who is Kazul?" I asked.

Suz looked at me in astonishment. "You don't know? No, you don't. I haven't told you yet. Kazul is who you're going to see." He cocked his head to one side as if that explained everything.

"Why should I want to see Kazul?" I asked. "And why should he care about me, or Shiara, or anything?"

"She," Suz said. "And of course you want to see her. You have the Sword of the Sleeping King, don't you? I'm afraid she'll be dreadfully upset if you bring someone with you, though."

"Well, I'm not going to leave Shiara alone in the middle of the Enchanted Forest," I said firmly.

"No, no, you couldn't possibly do that," the lizard agreed. "That wouldn't be right at all. Dear me, whatever are we going to do?"

"You don't have to worry about me," Shiara said indignantly. "I'm a fire-witch. I can take care of myself."

"You are?" Suz turned his head and looked at Shiara so intently that his eyes crossed. "You really are! How convenient! Everything's quite all right, then. Kazul won't mind a fire-witch at all."

"Who," I said very slowly and carefully, "is Kazul?"

The lizard stared thoughtfully at me for a long time. "I don't think I ought to tell you any more," he said at last. "You're quite safe, you really are, but it wouldn't do at all for Kazul to lose her temper with me. Oh, dear, no."

"Quite safe? In the middle of the Enchanted Forest, with wizards after us?" Shiara said sarcastically. "You're crazy."

"I am? No, I'm not at all! How very rude." He turned his back, looking extremely offended. Shiara stared at him. As I said, an offended lizard is an interesting sight.

I sighed. "Shiara."

Shiara looked at me. I just stood there. After a minute, she looked down. "Well, it *is* dangerous to be out here, even if you do have that stupid sword," she said defensively. "What's wrong with saying so?"

"It wasn't very polite," I said. "And you promised you'd try."

Shiara glanced up at me, then sighed. "Oh, all right. I'm sorry, Suz."

The lizard twisted his head around. "You are?" He ran around the branch again and peered at her upside down from underneath the limb. "No, you're not at all. How disappointing. I accept." He ran back up on top of the branch.

"Accept?" Shiara said.

"Your apology," the lizard said with dignity. A dignified lizard looks even odder than an offended one.

"Oh." Shiara looked at Suz doubtfully.

"If you won't tell us who Kazul is, will you at least tell us how to find her?" I asked hastily. I didn't want Shiara to say anything that would offend Suz again, and she looked like she was going to. Besides, I was curious.

"You won't have any trouble," the lizard assured me. "Just head for the castle. Kazul will—" He broke off in midsentence, staring at the kitten Shiara was holding. "What is that?" he asked disapprovingly.

"A kitten," Shiara said. "What does it look like?"

"You're sure it's under control?" Suz seemed a little nervous. I looked at the kitten. It was watching Suz with a great deal of interest.

"What do you mean, under control?" Shiara said. "She's a perfectly well-behaved kitten. Morwen wouldn't have given her to me if she wasn't."

"Cats are not—Did you say Morwen?" Suz peered at Shiara.

"Yes, I said Morwen. Can't you finish a sentence?"

Suz ignored her. "You've been to see Morwen? I

didn't know that. Oh, dear me, I must be dreadfully behind. Why, all sorts of things could be happening that I don't know about! How perfectly dreadful. I must really get back to work at once. Oh yes, indeed I must."

The lizard ran down the branch and disappeared behind the tree trunk. "Wait a minute!" I said. I ducked around the back of the tree, but Suz was nowhere in sight. I shook my head and went back to where Shiara was standing.

"He's gone again," I said. "And he still hasn't told me what castle he's talking about."

"So what? Nobody else has told us anything either." Shiara glared at the branch where Suz had been sitting. "I don't think *he's* very polite. He didn't even say goodbye."

"He keeps going off like that," I said. "I think that's just how he is."

"Well, I can't say I'm sorry he left," Shiara said. "Come on, let's find that stream Morwen was talking about. I'm thirsty."

We started walking again. Shiara put the kitten down, and we took turns keeping an eye on her. She had a marvelous time jumping on leaves and attacking bushes while Shiara and I talked about what Shiara was going to name her. Finally she decided on Nightwitch. I didn't think that was a very good name, but Shiara liked it, so I didn't say anything.

By the time we found the stream, Shiara and I were tired and hungry as well as thirsty, so we stopped. We each took a drink, and then we sat down and opened the bundles Morwen had given us. Just as I had expected, there were packets of food right on top—meat pies and apples and gingerbread. Shiara and I each ate some, and we gave one of the meat pies to Nightwitch. There was a little left over, so we wrapped it up and put it back in my bundle before we started off down the stream.

We stayed as close to the bank as we could. It's easy to get lost in the Enchanted Forest, especially if you don't really know where you're going. If we got out of sight of the stream, we might never find it again.

In a couple of places the trees grew in thick clumps, right up to the water's edge, and we had to choose between wading and going around. I didn't like the dark look of the forest near the tree clumps, and the water was only ankle deep, so we waded. Nightwitch did *not* approve.

The forest got darker as we went along. I was sure, now, that the trees were bigger, and they were certainly closer together even when they weren't growing in tight clumps. We spent more and more time in the stream, but the water wasn't very cold and the pebbles on the bottom were smooth, so it wasn't particularly unpleasant. Even so, I was glad when the woods started to open up again.

Then I saw the clearing a little ahead of us. A minute later, I saw the person sitting in it.

She was a princess. She had to be. Her hair was long and golden and not tangled at all, and her eyes were very blue, and her skin was very white, and she was very, very beautiful. One dainty foot was peeping out from under her blue silk gown. Her hands were folded in her lap, and she was looking at them with a sad expression.

Shiara poked me. I realized that I was standing in a stream with my shoes in one hand and Morwen's bundle in the other and my mouth hanging open. I swallowed and waded over to the bank. I wanted to put my shoes back on before we got any closer. I had seen at least two princesses before, that I knew of, but both of them were enchanted and hadn't looked at all like their usual selves when I met them. When I finished with my shoes, the Princess was looking in our direction.

I stood up hastily and hurried toward her. Shiara followed. As soon as I was within speaking distance, I stopped and bowed. The Princess smiled sadly.

"I bid you such poor welcome as I may," she said in a musical voice. "Alas! That I can offer you no refreshment. For I am in great distress."

"I'm sorry to hear that," I said. "Is there anything I can do to help?"

"I fear not," said the Princess. "For you are as yet a youth. Alas! and woe is me! For I am in great distress."

"All right, all right. So tell us about it," Shiara said. She sat down on the ground and looked at the Princess expectantly.

I frowned. I didn't think that was the proper way to address a princess, though I wasn't positive. Mother had taught me a lot more about dragons than she had about princesses.

"You are kind to inquire of my sad tale," the Princess said. "It is not long to tell. My father was a king, much beloved of his people, and I his only daughter. Being lonely after my mother's death, my father remarried, to a woman comely but proud, and under her influence have I suffered these seven years. And now the King my father is dead, and my stepmother hath cast me out, to wander alone and friendless through the world. Alas! For I am—"

"In great distress. We know. You said that before," Shiara said. "Why didn't *you* throw *her* out when your father died? It would have saved you a lot of trouble."

The Princess's blue eyes filled with tears and she bowed her head. "'Twas not within my power to work harm against her, alas. And now I seek some prince or hero who will take pity on my destitute state and return me to my proper place. Woe is me! That I should be without help in such distress."

"Sounds like a lousy excuse to me," Shiara muttered under her breath. Fortunately, the Princess didn't hear.

"I'm afraid we can't help you get your kingdom back," I said. "I'm very sorry. But if there's any other service I can do for you, I'd be happy to try."

"Daystar!" Shiara's voice was horrified, and suddenly I realized what I'd said. I swallowed. At least I'd only promised to try.

"There is one thing," the Princess said. She raised her head, and her eyes were very bright. I went cold. The Princess smiled sweetly.

"Give me your sword," she said.

In Which There Is a Good Deal of Discussion

I stared at the Princess. Then I shut my mouth and swallowed again, hard. *Mother isn't going to like this at all*, I thought. I was just about to draw the sword and give it to her when Shiara said, "Wait a minute, Daystar."

I stopped and looked at her. She looked at the Princess. "Daystar hasn't got a sword."

"What?" the Princess and I said at the same time. The Princess frowned. "I am not blind, to be so easily deceived. See, there it is." She pointed to my scabbard.

"That," said Shiara triumphantly, "is the Sword of the Sleeping King. So it belongs to him, not to Daystar, and Daystar can't give it away."

The Princess looked very puzzled. I thought for a minute. Shiara was right, but she was wrong, too. I mean, it was obvious what the Princess had *meant*, even if she hadn't said it right. I sighed and reached for the hilt.

Shiara turned on me. "Daystar, what are you doing?"

"Giving her the sword," I said, tugging at it. The sword wouldn't come out of the sheath. "You know as well as I do what she meant."

"Well, if all those wizards and sorceresses can be picky about the way people say things, why can't you?" Shiara was so mad I expected her hair to start burning any minute. "You can't even get it out of the sheath! You only said you'd try to do what she wanted. Well, you've tried. Isn't that enough?"

I sighed. "I'm sorry, Shiara, but it's my sword, and I'm not a wizard. I just have to do it."

"Daystar, you . . . you . . ." Shiara gave up and just glared.

I tugged at the sword again, and Shiara turned her back. The Princess still looked puzzled. I shook my head and unbuckled the whole sword belt. I stared at it for a minute, then held it out toward the Princess. "Here. Take it." My voice seemed too loud, and I realized that the woods had gotten very quiet. The Princess smiled and took hold of the scabbard. I let go of the sword.

There was a rumbling noise, and the Princess said, "Oh!" very loudly and dropped the sword belt. The point of the scabbard hit the ground, and there was another rumble, and an enormous geyser of water shot up into the air.

I saw the Princess cringe, and Shiara fell backward. Then I couldn't see anything but white spray. A voice said, "All hail the Holder of the Sword!" The words echoed hollowly around me as the fountain vanished.

Shiara and the Princess were both staring at me, wide eyed. All of us were dripping. The sword was standing upright in front of me, in the middle of a pool of water about four feet across. It was about halfway out of the sheath, and the blade shimmered in the sun.

The Princess burst into tears. "I knew not that this weapon was of such potency," she said between sobs. "Alas! For I cannot hold the sword, and who now will be my help? Alas, and woe is me!"

"You mean you don't want the sword anymore?" Shiara demanded.

The Princess nodded. She was weeping too hard to say much.

"And Daystar can have it back now?"

The Princess nodded again. She was still weeping.

I sighed and dug out my handkerchief. It was wet. I squeezed it out and offered it to the Princess anyway. She took it without thanking me and cried some more.

"What am I to do?" she kept saying. "Who now will be my help? Alas! For I am in great distress!"

"Oh, help yourself," Shiara said crossly. "Daystar, are you going to take that stupid sword?"

I hesitated, then reached out and took hold of the hilt. The blade flashed once, and a brief shock ran through me as the hilt came to rest. I ignored the feeling and pulled at the scabbard. It came free almost at once, and the water closed silently behind it. I took a closer look at the bottom part of the sheath. I wasn't even surprised when I saw that it wasn't wet.

I looked up. The Princess had just about stopped crying. I looked at the sword. Then I looked back at the Princess. "Are you sure you don't want this?" I asked finally.

"Daystar!" Shiara sounded like she wasn't sure whether to be mad or horrified.

The Princess didn't seem to hear her at all. "I cannot take it!" she cried. "Oh, indeed, I cannot! Alas! That I am so helpless in my time of need!"

"Well, if you didn't want the sword, why did you ask for it in the first place?" Shiara said angrily.

"I fear I have deceived you," the Princess said tragically. "Yet I myself have been misled. Alas! I beg of you, forgive me! For indeed, I am—I am in great distress."

"Distress? Ha!" said Shiara. "You better tell us the truth, right now, or you'll find out what distress is."

"Shiara—" I began.

Shiara turned. "You shut up. You obviously don't know anything about handling princesses, so let me do it. Now," she said to the Princess, "explain. And it better be good."

"I am a king's daughter," the Princess said. "My father would have me wed the prince of a neighboring kingdom, to bring us wealth. Yet I could not, for I love not him but another. My father listened not, for all my pleading, so my love and I fled into the forest. We wandered far, and great was our suffering, yet were we happy, for we had each other. But I, being unused to travel, became tired, and my love at last set me here and bade me wait for him. And here have I stayed these two long days, and I fear me some evil may have befallen him. Alas! That we are parted!"

"What," said Shiara, "does all this have to do with Daystar's sword?"

The Princess sighed again. "I was seated here, as

you see me, bewailing my bitter fate, when lo! a man appeared, most wise and powerful of aspect. He told me my love was imprisoned by a mighty sorceress, and at that news I wept bitterly. Then he bade me desist from my grief, for the means of delivering my love was at hand, to wit, a sword most magical. And he himself made promise of aid, if I would but attain the sword. And this have I attempted, and I have failed. Alas, and woe is me!"

"I don't think I understand," I said. "Why didn't you tell us this to begin with?"

The Princess began to weep again. "My unknown friend instructed me in what I was to say and told me that all would be well once I had the sword in my own hands. And in this he deceived me, for the touch of the sword burns so that I cannot hold it. And the cause is that I deceived you, and tricked you into offering me the sword, and the sword knew, and it will not abide in my hand, and now am I utterly without hope."

"What did this person look like?" Shiara asked unsympathetically. "The one you were going to give the sword to."

The Princess seemed a lot more interested in explaining how wise and powerful and helpful the man had been than she was in giving a simple description, but eventually we managed to get some idea what he looked like. Tall, dark haired, blue eyed, and carrying a staff—

"It sounds a lot like Antorell," I said finally.

"Antorell?" Shiara asked.

"The wizard that Mother melted. She said he might try to make trouble for me in a day or two."

"Oh, great. All we need is another wizard looking for us."

The Princess didn't seem to be following the conversation at all. "Alas!" she said finally. "There is nothing left for me but grief. I have no means now to save my love, so I shall die with him. I shall fling myself in yonder stream and make an end."

"You are even dumber than Daystar," Shiara informed her. "That stream isn't deep enough to drown in. You'll only get wet. Besides, if that stupid wizard lied about the sword, how do you know he didn't lie about your love? Who is this person you ran off with, anyway?"

"He is a knight," the Princess said, her eyes lighting up. "Poor in goods, yet rich in spirit, of most pleasing aspect. His eyes are a hawk's, his arms are mighty, and his sword is bright and—"

"He sounds like he can take care of himself," Shiara said. "I don't think you have to worry about him."

Shiara's words had a marvelous effect on the Princess. "Truly, you believe this?" she said, and her face lit up even more. "Then here will I await his coming, for surely he will return to me. Ah, joy! That we shall soon be once more together!"

Shiara looked disgusted. "I'm sure you'll be very happy. Come on, Daystar, let's go." She stood up.

"I don't think we should leave her here by herself," I said.

"Daystar, you're impossible!" Shiara was still mad. "She tried to trick you! Besides, she's been here two days already, and nothing's happened to her yet."

"Alas! I did indeed attempt to deceive you," the Princess said. "And for that I beg forgiveness. Yet consider my unhappy plight, and be not harsh with me."

"Oh, shut up," Shiara told her.

"What if Antorell comes back?" I said. "Somebody ought to take care of her. Besides, I made a promise."

"Well, I didn't!" Shiara said. "And I'm not going to sit here doing nothing just because of a stupid princess! I'm leaving."

"You can't do that!" I said. I was really upset. Shiara didn't know very much about the Enchanted Forest, and she was going to go tramping off into the middle of it with no one but Morwen's kitten. I couldn't let her do that, but I couldn't leave the Princess sitting there alone, either.

"Want to bet?" Shiara said. She picked up the bundle Morwen had given her. "Come on, Nightwitch. Let's go."

"Nightwitch? What an unusual name for a cat," said a new voice.

Shiara stopped and both of us turned. An old man was standing at the edge of the clearing, in front of a clump of scruffy lilacs that were almost tall enough to be considered trees. His beard and what was left of his hair were quite white, and he was stooped over and leaning on a staff. Even without the way my skin prickled, I knew he was a wizard.

The Princess was the first to recover from the

surprise of seeing him there. "Ah, sir, have pity on my sad state!" she said. "Have pity, and if you have seen a knight, bright armored, hawk eyed, most fair and pleasing in speech and semblance, then tell me speedily where he may be found. For he is my love, and we are parted, and thus am I in great distress! Alas!"

"That's quite all right, my dear," the wizard said in a kindly tone. "You've nothing to worry about. In fact, he should be here before very much longer. That's why I hurried. Just sit there and wait quietly, like a good girl."

"Oh, joy! Oh, bliss!" said the Princess rapturously. "To be with my love again!" She started happily explaining how strong and handsome and generally wonderful her missing knight was. Since she didn't seem to be speaking to anyone in particular, the rest of us ignored her.

Shiara, Nightwitch, and I were edging backward. I had my right hand on the hilt of my sword, and my whole side was tingling with the feel of the wizard's magic. The wizard noticed us and smiled.

"Take your hand from your sword," he said, looking at me. "I am not here to engage in a vulgar physical contest with you."

"Are you from the Society of Wizards?" Shiara demanded. Her voice sounded a little shaky, but I don't think anyone who didn't know her would have noticed.

"No," the wizard said. "Why? Are you looking for one of them?"

"Then why are you here?" I said.

"Why, to assist you," the wizard said.

"Assist *us?*" Shiara said. "But you're a *wizard!*"

"I am not at all concerned with your baseless prejudices," the wizard told her. "I have come to offer to help your companion, and I will thank you to cease interfering."

I stared at him. "I don't want to be impolite," I said before Shiara could say anything else, "but why do you want to help me?"

"Why, because you deserve it, of course," the wizard said. "You made a foolish promise to this other young lady," he went on, nodding toward the Princess, who was still talking to the air. "You could have gotten out of it several times, but you refused to behave dishonorably. I think that is deserving of a reward."

"Thank you very much," I said. I didn't really know what else to say. After all, there are people in the Enchanted Forest who go around rewarding heroes and princes for noble deeds. Why else would all those heroes come here?

"Well, what would you like?" the wizard said after a moment.

"Like?"

"As a reward." He sounded a little impatient.

I thought about it for a moment. "I appreciate the offer," I said finally. "But I really don't need anything. Thank you very much all the same."

"What? Isn't there anything you want?" he asked sharply. He didn't look nearly as friendly as he had at first.

"No, I don't think so," I said.

For a moment the wizard looked very disconcerted. Then he seemed to relax a little. "Perhaps I did not make myself clear enough," he said. "You need not ask for something material. Information will do just as well. The word for *sorcery* in the tongue of the giants, or the location of the Well of Silver Storms, where the unicorns drink. There must be something you want to know, even if there is nothing you want to have."

The only thing I wanted to know was what I was supposed to do in the Enchanted Forest. Somehow, I didn't think Mother had told him. "No," I said. "I don't think there is anything."

The wizard looked at me, and his eyes narrowed. "Come, come! You need to know the name of your father, do you not?"

"No," I said, puzzled. I'd wondered about my father a few times, but I'd never asked Mother about him. She would have told me if she'd thought I ought to know. And I certainly couldn't think of any reason why I *needed* to know. "Why should I?"

"You're looking for him, aren't you?" the wizard snapped.

"No, not really." That might be one of the things Mother wanted me to do, but it certainly couldn't be the only one. Furthermore, I couldn't see how knowing his name would help much, even if I were looking for him. In the Enchanted Forest, looking for someone usually isn't the best way of finding him. You're much more likely to run into people by accident.

"You aren't? Then you must know! She *told* you! Who is it?"

"I thought *you* were going to tell Daystar that," Shiara said. "Don't you know?"

"Silence, fool! I have waited too long for this." The wizard turned back to me. "You will tell me now or regret it deeply: Who is your father?"

"I don't know," I said. "And if I did, I don't see why I should tell you."

"There are other ways of learning what I wish to know," the wizard said. He straightened abruptly. The Princess squeaked and fell silent. Nightwitch hissed. Shiara started edging backward again. And the wizard changed.

He got a little taller and a lot younger; his beard and hair darkened and filled in. His eyes changed from brown to blue, but they still glared.

"Antorell!" I said, and drew my sword.

The steel rang as it came out of the sheath, and the blade shimmered and flashed in front of me. It made the whole clearing seem brighter. Antorell's lips curled into a sneer.

"Fool! What use is a sword against a wizard?"

He raised his staff, and a globe of green light appeared at the lower end of it. A thread of green, dark and bright as the shine of a snake, reached out toward me from the staff. I raised the sword.

The green light touched the Sword of the Sleeping King. The sword hummed a little and the ray of light vanished, and that was all.

Antorell frowned, and another, larger ray of green reached out. This time, the humming was a little louder, and the light around the end of Antorell's staff vanished, along with the ray touching the sword. The jangling feeling lessened a little. I was considerably relieved. Antorell looked shocked.

"You cannot! Not possibly! That sword can't . . ." His eyes moved to my face, then back to the sword, and he took a deep breath. "So! She must have known all along. But now I will have that weapon. I *must* have that weapon!"

"No," I said. "Mother wouldn't like it."

Antorell's eyes narrowed. "Cimorene has had her way long enough. If you will not give me that sword, I will take it." He started to raise the staff again.

The lilacs behind Antorell rustled noisily, and the wizard shifted. "You, there!" he called over his shoulder. "Show yourself at once!"

"*Ach—ach—*" said someone behind him, and the tops of the lilacs rustled again. I looked up at them, wondering how tall whoever-it-was was. The branches that were rustling were a good ten feet off the ground.

Antorell frowned and turned around, raising his staff. "I will teach you to interfere—"

The angry look on Antorell's face changed abruptly to one of mingled surprise and fear. He stepped backward very quickly and waved his staff through the air in front of him.

"*Achoo!*" said the voice, and an enormous ball of fire demolished the lilacs and enveloped Antorell. The wizard screamed and disappeared, and we could see the person who had been behind the bush.

It was a dragon.

In Which They Meet Their First Dragon

I t was about twelve feet tall, which is not very large, as dragons go. But it was definitely a dragon. It sneezed again, which took care of the remains of the lilac bush, and slid forward over the ashes into the middle of the clearing. The Princess fainted.

I put my sword away. Walking through the Enchanted Forest with a drawn sword is bad, but talking to a dragon with a sword in your hand is much worse. Fortunately, the dragon hadn't noticed it yet. As soon as the sword was sheathed, I looked up again, and my stomach went hollow.

The dragon was eyeing Shiara, and I didn't like the gleam in its eyes. I didn't like the militant way Shiara was glaring back, either. There wasn't very much I could do, though. You just don't interrupt a dragon when it's busy with something else. They don't like being distracted.

The dragon slid closer and bent its head until it was staring at Shiara from about a foot in front of her face. Shiara jumped. The dragon blinked.

"Are you a princess?" it asked hopefully.

"No. I'm a fire-witch," Shiara said. "And if you bite me, I'll burn your nose off."

"Oh. I thought you were a princess." The dragon lost interest in Shiara. It looked around the clearing again and saw me. Its head moved over in my direction.

I bowed. "Sir or madam," I said, trying to recall all the proper ways of addressing a dragon, "I offer you greetings in the name of myself and my companions, and I wish you good fortune in all your endeavors."

"I beg your pardon?" said the dragon. Its voice reminded me of one of those wooden wind instruments, the deep kind that you have to stand on a chair to play. It eyed me doubtfully. "Are *you* a princess?"

"I—" I stopped and stared. Dragons just don't beg people's pardon. Then I realized that this must be a very young dragon, and I relaxed a little. Dragons don't usually insist on formality until they get old enough to decide which sex they're going to be. "I'm very sorry, but I'm afraid I'm not a princess. My name is Daystar, and I'm very pleased to meet you."

The dragon sat back. "I had no idea princesses were so hard to find." It blinked and seemed to look at me for the first time. "I'm sorry I burned your bush, but I couldn't help it."

"Oh, please don't worry about it," I said. "It really doesn't matter in the least."

"It was the wizard," the dragon said confidentially. "I'm allergic to them. All dragons are."

"I'm sorry to hear that," I said.

The dragon looked at me. "You're very polite,

Daystar." Its head swiveled back toward Shiara. "Say
—you weren't polite at all!"

Nightwitch poked her head out from behind Shiara's ankle and hissed. The dragon started and then
peered down at the kitten. "You aren't polite, either," it
said.

I nudged Shiara. "Offer to do something for him," I
hissed.

"What? Why?"

"If you insult a dragon, you have to do him a favor," I said. "Hurry up!" If she didn't say something
quickly, the dragon would probably eat both of us. Unfortunately, the dragon might eat Shiara anyway. The
favor most dragons want is dinner. I couldn't tell Shiara
that, though, without offending the dragon. I wondered
whether I could talk the dragon out of eating us, if it
came to that. I didn't think so. Dragons are stubborn.

The dragon's eyes glittered. Shiara looked at it. "Can
I do anything for you?" she asked finally. She sounded
a little sullen, but dragons aren't very good at tone of
voice. Besides, it's the offer that counts.

"Find me a princess," the dragon said promptly.

I breathed a very quiet sigh of relief. I didn't think
there was a polite way to kill a dragon, and I hadn't
been able to think of any other way of stopping it from
eating Shiara and me if it wanted to. It was nice to know
I wouldn't have to try.

"You want a princess?" Shiara looked thoughtful.
"Why?"

"Dragons are supposed to have princesses," the
dragon explained. "I can't be considered a proper

dragon until I have one. But I've been looking for two days, and I haven't seen even a *smell* of a princess, and I'm tired of it. So you do it."

"You aren't going to eat her or anything, are you?" Shiara asked.

"Eat her?" The dragon sounded horrified. "And waste a perfectly good princess? Of course not! There aren't enough of them to go around as it is. What kind of barbarian do you think I am?"

"Well, I've never met a dragon before," Shiara said. "How was I supposed to know? I didn't mean to hurt your feelings."

"All right," said the dragon. "But you have to get me a princess. It doesn't have to be a large one."

"Do you want any particular kind of princess?" Shiara asked. "I want to be sure you'll be satisfied."

"Oh, young and beautiful, of course," the dragon said. "Are there other kinds?"

"There are enchanted princesses," Shiara pointed out. "Especially around here."

"That's right. Say, maybe that's why I haven't found one!"

"I wouldn't be surprised," Shiara said. "But will you take an enchanted princess?"

The dragon thought for a minute. "No, I don't think so. Spells make things too complicated."

"And does it matter how long it takes me to find her?" Shiara went on.

The dragon considered. "I don't want to wait too long, but I really don't want to be unreasonable, either. How about a week? You bring the princess here by a week from today, otherwise you owe me another favor." It licked its lips with a long red tongue.

"That sounds reasonable," Shiara said. "But what if I'm early?"

Suddenly I realized what Shiara was planning to do. I edged around the clearing, toward where the Princess was lying, but I wasn't quite fast enough.

"The earlier the better," the dragon said.

"Then, there's your princess!" Shiara said, and pointed.

"My, you do work fast," the dragon said. It turned and looked at the Princess. "She's certainly beautiful enough, but are you sure she isn't enchanted?"

"I'm quite sure," Shiara said.

"Then why is she asleep in the middle of the day? I didn't think princesses were nocturnal creatures."

"She just fainted when she saw you," Shiara said reassuringly. "It's nothing to worry about. It happens to princesses all the time. Will she do?"

"Quite well." The dragon nodded. "You're very prompt. Thank you very much."

Shiara nodded. I waited until the dragon turned away, then I frowned at Shiara.

"Why did you do that?" I whispered. "That was a terrible thing to do!"

"Would you rather I got eaten?" Shiara whispered back. "*She* won't get eaten. The dragon said so. And I bet it won't want her for long. Dragons are smarter than some people."

I didn't know what to say to that, so I looked back at the dragon. As it bent its head to inspect the Princess more closely, the Princess opened her eyes. She gave a small scream, and the dragon frowned.

"You don't have to be frightened," it said. "Really. You're my princess now, and I'm going to take proper care of you, and you can clean my scales and cook for me. I believe that's the standard arrangement."

The Princess burst into tears. The dragon pulled back, eyeing her uncomfortably. "Did I say something wrong?"

The Princess just cried harder. "Alas! Ah, woe is me! So recently was I happy, awaiting the coming of my love to rescue me from this dismal forest! And now am I a prisoner of a monster, and when my love arrives he will be eaten by this awful beast, and I abandoned to my fate! Alas, that I should come to this!"

The dragon looked considerably taken aback. It turned to Shiara and me. "*This* is a princess?"

"Yes, she is," I said, and Shiara nodded.

The Princess had heard the question, too, and she raised her head. "Indeed, I am a princess, and the daughter of a king, and see to what misery I have been brought!" she said tragically. "Alas, the day I left my father's house! Yet would I flee again, and endure with patience all the trials and woes which have come upon me, only to be with my love once more!"

The dragon backed up a pace. "Are you *sure* this is a princess?"

"Alas! Now even my birth is doubted, and to whom shall I turn in my distress? Ah, pity my sad state! For I am alone and friendless, and parted from my love. Ah, woe! That ever I let him leave my side! For he is mighty among men, most brave and fearsome in battle, and of a fair and pleasing appearance in all things, and he would not leave me thus, did he but know my fate." She went back to crying.

"If this *is* a princess, I'm not sure I want one after all," the dragon said. It looked at the Princess speculatively. "Maybe I could eat her instead."

"Ah, help!" said the Princess.

"I really don't think you should eat her," I said. "After all, you did say you wouldn't."

"That's right, I did." The dragon looked at the Princess, who was crying again, and sighed. "Nobody told me princesses were like this," it said in an aggrieved tone. "And who is this love she keeps talking about?"

"We haven't met him yet, I'm afraid," I said. "She says he's a knight that she ran away with because her father wanted her to marry someone else."

"A knight?" The dragon backed up a little farther. "I don't think I'm ready for knights yet. They're so unpredictable. I don't suppose you could find me a princess without a knight?"

"All really good princesses have knights," Shiara said firmly. "And you wouldn't want a second-rate princess, would you?"

"All of them?" the dragon asked plaintively.

"Well, not all of them," I said. "Some of them have princes instead."

"Princes are much worse than knights," Shiara said thoughtfully. "They have magic rings and sorceresses for godmothers and things like that. With knights you only have to worry about their armor and weapons, and maybe once in a while an enchanted sword."

"My love has no need of magic!" the Princess broke in indignantly. "For he is most strong and skilled, and never has he been beaten in combat with sword or spear. Woe that he is no longer at my side!"

"I don't like the sound of this," the dragon said uneasily. "Maybe if I just—"

There was a loud crash from the bushes at the edge of the clearing, and then a rather tinny-sounding voice said, "What ho! A dragon?"

The Princess stopped crying very suddenly and sat up quite straight. "Hark! My love approaches! Now shall you see his prowess for yourselves!"

There were more crashing noises. The dragon backed up again, looking nervous. A moment later a knight in a dented suit of armor fell through the middle of the thickest clump of bushes, right in front of the dragon.

"On guard, monster!" the knight said as he picked himself up. "Prepare to die!" He pulled out a sword and waved it at the dragon. Well, actually, he waved it a couple of feet to one side. His helmet had slipped a little, and evidently he couldn't see very well. The dragon looked at him, and then back at Shiara.

"*This* is a knight?" it said.

"My love is the bravest and best of knights!" the Princess cried.

"If this *is* a knight, maybe I can handle him after all," the dragon said. "He doesn't look so bad."

"Ah, hideous reptile! No longer do I fear you, for my

love will defend me! Yea, he will defend me even unto death!"

"Now, wait a minute, Isabelle," the knight said. He pulled off his helmet, looked at it disgustedly, and threw it on the ground behind him. "I'm perfectly willing to kill dragons for you, but who said anything about dying?"

"You are my knight, and my brave love!" the Princess said dramatically. "Oh, save me from this awful monster, who would carry me off and eat me!" She sprang up and threw her arms around the knight.

"It's going to be a bit difficult for me to save you if you hang about my neck like that," the knight said apologetically. "It's quite awkward. If you'll just sit down, I can see about doing this properly."

The Princess only hung on to him more tightly, which made his aim almost as bad as it had been when he was wearing his helmet crooked. The dragon was watching them closely, and its eyes were starting to glow. "You certainly aren't very polite," it said.

"My love is the soul of courtesy!" the Princess said from behind the knight. "For he is a knight most gentle and well spoken, much given to—"

"I say, Isabelle, must you go on like that?" the knight said. "It's embarrassing. Do, please, sit down and let me fight the dragon. Then you won't have to worry about being eaten, you know."

The Princess gave a small scream. "Alas!" she said in a quavery voice. "Behold my sad state! For now must I watch a bloody battle, and perhaps see my love slain before my eyes, and become a captive of this monster."

"This is ridiculous," said Shiara, and before I could stop her she marched over to stand between the dragon and the knight. I followed her, hoping I could get her out of trouble if I had to.

"Ah, save me!" the Princess said as we got closer. I wasn't sure whether she wanted to be saved from the dragon or from Shiara.

Shiara glared at her. "You shut up," she told the Princess. "You've caused enough trouble already."

"I say," said the knight. "If we're going to discuss politeness—"

"We aren't," said Shiara. "We're going to discuss battles. Battles between dragons and knights. Why do you want to fight this dragon?"

"Knights are sworn to do battle with the beasts that ravage the fields, carry off innocent maidens, and generally make a nuisance of themselves," the knight said. He sounded as if he were reciting something, and he didn't look very pleased about the idea, but the Princess nodded approvingly.

"Well, this dragon isn't ravaging anything, and it doesn't even want your stupid princess," Shiara said.

"I do, too!" the dragon broke in. "If I'm not going to carry her off I could eat her, after all. And if I fought a knight no one could say I'm not a proper dragon, even if I don't have a princess."

"I really don't think that's a good idea," I said. "Princesses aren't all that common, after all."

"Besides, you promised me you wouldn't," Shiara said.

"I did not!" the dragon said. "I only said I wouldn't

waste a perfectly good princess, and this one's not so great. Eating her wouldn't be much of a waste."

"I don't think that would be very polite," I said. "Especially when you've talked to her this long without bringing it up. You really ought to ease into these things gradually, you know."

"Are you sure?" the dragon said.

I nodded.

"Oh, all right," said the dragon. "I won't eat her, then. But couldn't I fight the knight anyway? Just for practice?"

"I say, that sounds like an excellent idea," the knight said, brightening perceptibly. "A sort of exercise for both of us."

"A tourney!" the Princess cried. "Oh, brave and clever, to think of such a thing!"

The knight looked pleased. So did the dragon. It nodded, then whispered to Shiara, "What's a tourney?"

"It's like a battle, only no one gets hurt. Usually."

"Not even a little?" the dragon said. The knight started looking worried again.

"Of course not!" Shiara said to the dragon. "It's a show of skill."

"If you were trying to hurt each other, it wouldn't be a tourney," I added. Actually, it wasn't going to be a tourney anyway. There are very specific rules about what a tourney is, and a practice fight between a dragon and a knight just doesn't qualify. I decided not to say so.

"Oh, all right, then," the dragon grumbled. "I don't know why I'm letting you talk me into this. How do we start?"

In Which There Is a Fight, Sort of, and
They Find Out Where They Are Going

The hardest part was getting the dragon and the knight to agree about rules. The Princess was no help at all. She kept talking about the marvelous tourneys she'd seen, and which knights had been wounded. Whenever she did, the dragon would start looking at the knight, and pretty soon it would want to know why it couldn't bite off one of the knight's arms, or at least a hand. The knight would get worried, and the Princess would start crying, and Shiara and I would have to talk the dragon out of it. As soon as the dragon agreed, the Princess would cheer up and start talking about tourneys again.

Finally, Shiara told the Princess to shut up. It wasn't very polite, but it worked. Well, sort of. The Princess didn't stop talking, but as long as she was complaining about Shiara and not talking about tourneys we didn't have any more problems getting the dragon and the knight to agree.

When we finally decided on the rules, we had to draw a circle in the middle of the clearing for them to fight in. It was harder than it sounds. For one thing, a circle has to be pretty big if a dragon is going to fit inside it, even if it's a small dragon. Also, the moss in the Enchanted Forest grows awfully fast. By the time we finished drawing the circle, the first half of it had already disappeared. Shiara watched for a minute, then looked at the knight.

"Are you sure you *have* to have a circle to fight?" Shiara said.

"I really do think so," the knight said apologetically. "It wouldn't be a proper tourney without it, don't you see."

"I'm sick of proper dragons and proper princesses and proper tourneys," Shiara said under her breath. Fortunately, the dragon didn't hear her.

We started redrawing the circle, trying to make the line wider this time. The knight scratched at the moss with his sword. Shiara used a stick. So did I; I didn't think Mother would approve if I used the Sword of the Sleeping King to cut moss. Nightwitch and the dragon sort of dug at the ground. The Princess sat under a tree.

Eventually we finished, and the knight and the dragon stepped inside the circle. "Well, what are you waiting for?" Shiara demanded.

"Someone has to say, 'go,'" the knight said in a reasonable tone.

"Go!" I said quickly.

Shiara gave me a disgusted look, but she didn't say anything, because as soon as I shouted, the dragon and the knight got started. They were fairly evenly matched. The dragon was much larger, of course, and it had a very good sense of timing, but it didn't have much experience. The knight was wearing armor, which helped, and he was obviously used to fighting, but he was a little awkward most of the time. They were both good at dodging, though, and they each managed to take three or four swings without hitting the other. The dragon was just starting to take another swipe at the knight when a little tree sprouted up in front of him and hit him in the nose.

I was surprised. I mean, even in the Enchanted Forest, trees don't usually grow that fast. The dragon was even more surprised than I was. It sort of reared back, and its tail came around very fast to balance it. Nightwitch was a little too close and had to scramble back out of the way.

"Hey, watch out!" Shiara said.

The dragon jumped and swung around, looking as if it expected another tree to pop up behind it. Its tail swung in the other direction, and the end of it caught the knight right in the middle of his chest plate as he was trying to back out of the way. The dragon yelped, the Princess screamed, and the knight fell over backward into the pool of water that my sword had made when the Princess had tried to take it.

Evidently the pool was a lot deeper than it looked, because the knight sank right out of sight. We all forgot about the fast-growing tree and leapt forward. The Princess was faster than either Shiara or I. By the time I got to the pool, she had hold of the knight. She wasn't quite strong enough to pull him out, but she wasn't letting go, either.

Shiara got to the pool about the same time I did, and together the three of us managed to get the knight out of the water. He was unconscious, and he had a large dent in his armor where the dragon's tail had hit him. The Princess checked to make sure he was still alive, and then she burst into tears.

"Alas! See now how sad is my fate! For my love has been grievously injured and I am without protection in this awful place. Ah, woe is me!"

"Is he dead?" asked the dragon from right behind me. I jumped. It peered curiously over my shoulder at the knight.

"Monster!" said the Princess. "Your base attempt to slay my love has failed! No second chance shall you have to harm him while I can stand between you! For if my love be slain, I care not whether I live or die, and thus I now defy you." She threw herself across the knight's chest.

The knight coughed, moaned, and opened his eyes. "I say, Isabelle," he said weakly, "that really is a bit uncomfortable."

The Princess sat up and started weeping all over his face. It didn't seem to make him much more comfortable.

The dragon was still peering. "That was a very good fight," it said to the knight. "Except for the last part. My tail still stings. I think I may have sprained it. Is armor always that hard?"

The knight tried to answer and started coughing instead. The Princess cried harder, until Shiara said pointedly, "I don't think all that water is doing him much good." The Princess stopped crying and glared at Shiara for a minute, then turned back to the knight. Somehow, she looked a lot more unhappy now that she wasn't crying. I felt sorry for her.

Finally the knight managed to get his coughing under control. He looked up at the dragon and said, "I do believe I agree with you about the fight. That trick with the tail is quite good. I don't recall seeing it before. I really must remember it."

"Actually, it was something of an accident," the dragon said modestly. "But I think I could do it again if I tried. Did you really think it was good?"

"Oh, quite," the knight said. I got the feeling that he would have tried to bow if he hadn't been lying on his back. "I think perhaps you broke one or two of my ribs."

"I'm sorry," said the dragon. "Is that bad?"

"It is certainly a bit uncomfortable," the knight said. "I don't really blame—"

A coughing spasm interrupted him. The Princess looked alarmed, but she didn't start crying. I saw Shiara watching the Princess with a surprised look on her face, and right about then Nightwitch sprang up onto the knight's chest.

"What is this? Go hence, and leave my love in peace!" cried the Princess.

"You let my kitten alone," Shiara warned.

The Princess stopped in midreach and looked over at Shiara. "And shall I neglect aught that may bring comfort to my love in his hurt?" she said.

"Nightwitch isn't going to hurt—" Shiara started, then paused. "I guess it doesn't matter. Go ahead."

I stared at Shiara in surprise, but she was watching the Princess and Nightwitch. The Princess got scratched a couple of times before she finally managed to pick the kitten up and move her. By then, the knight wasn't coughing quite so hard anymore, but he still didn't seem up to talking. Shiara frowned at him. "You don't sound very good," she said.

The dragon stuck its head farther over my shoulder. "If you can't fix him, can I eat him?" it asked hopefully.

Nightwitch hissed. The knight looked alarmed and tried to say something, but all that came out was more coughing. The Princess said, "No!" loudly and looked as if she wanted to throw herself on top of the knight again.

"Of course not," Shiara said. "You promised."

"It wouldn't be polite," I added. "After all, that was why you had the tourney."

The dragon looked hurt. "I was just *asking*."

"Ah, what are we going to do about them?" I asked hastily, waving at the Princess and the knight. "They can't stay here, not when the knight's been injured like that."

"It's not so bad, really it isn't," the knight said, looking at the dragon nervously. He started coughing again right away, but it didn't sound as bad as it had before and he stopped fairly quickly.

"I suppose you could come with us," I said after a minute.

"That's frightfully kind of you," the knight said. He looked uncertainly at the dragon. "Very kind, to invite us to come with you. *All* of you?"

"I don't know," I said. "I haven't asked the dragon about its plans yet. But you're quite welcome to join us, if you want to."

"Yes," said Shiara. "I'm sure you'll be very useful when the wizard comes back."

"Wizard?" said the knight. He was so alarmed he almost started coughing again. "What wizard?"

"Well, actually, there are several of them," I said. "Every now and then one of them shows up and tries to do something to us. The last one left when the dragon showed up."

"I'm sure he'll be back in a little while," Shiara said. "Or one of the others will. They've been chasing us all over the Enchanted Forest."

"You know," the knight said, "I really don't believe it would be a good idea for me to join you. I should almost certainly be a bit of an inconvenience, you see. Wet armor rusts, and with that and the ribs I'm afraid I'd be a little slow. Thank you terribly, all the same."

"If you don't come with us, what will you do?" I asked.

"Mrow," said Nightwitch.

"Morwen!" Shiara said. "They can go to Morwen! She'll know what to do for them." Nightwitch started purring loudly, sort of like a pepper grinder with rocks in it.

I thought about it for a minute. "It sounds like a good idea, but will she want to?"

"Morwen seems to like helping people," Shiara said. "And I'm sure she can take care of both of them."

"You know Morwen?" said the dragon. "I like her. She gives me apples out of her garden."

I tried to imagine a dragon eating apples and failed. I could imagine Morwen giving them to a dragon, though.

"Who is this Morwen?" asked the Princess, clasping her hands in front of her. "Think you that she could help my love, indeed?"

"Morwen's sort of a friend of ours," I explained. "She lives back that way, with a lot of cats, and her house has kind of a strange door."

"I didn't have any trouble with it," Shiara said. "And she has nine cats. She told me while you were asleep."

"Nine cats?" said the Princess, looking puzzled. "But what has that to do with my love, who is so grievously hurt?"

"I said it wasn't that bad, Isabelle," said the knight uncomfortably. "Really, I wish you wouldn't make such a fuss. I shall be quite all right in a little, I'm sure."

"If this woman with the many cats can help you, then we shall go to her," the Princess declared with more spirit than she had shown about anything else. "For you are my love, and I will have you whole and well."

"Oh, but really, Isabelle—"

"I'm sure Morwen won't mind," Shiara put in. "She fixed Daystar up just fine. She's even good with wet swords."

The Princess looked thoroughly confused, but the knight brightened a little. "Are you quite sure? Because I'm frightfully wet, sword and armor and everything, and it would be very nice if I could keep it all from rusting. It's rather expensive, you see."

"I'm sure she could manage that," Shiara said. "Of course, you don't have to go. You could stay here and wait for the wizard to come back."

The knight didn't argue. I don't think he liked the idea of staying around the dragon, especially if a lot of wizards were going to show up any minute. As soon as he agreed, the Princess started telling him how wise and brave and wonderful he was. Shiara looked disgusted, but the knight seemed to like it. He sat up and even managed not to cough very much.

Shiara and I gave the knight directions back up the stream and through the woods to Morwen's house. He and the Princess said goodbye and started off.

"That's a relief!" Shiara said when they were out of earshot. "For a while I thought you were going to make us go with that stupid princess. It was bad enough having to listen to her here without following her around."

I blinked at her. "But I thought you changed your mind about her! You were being a lot nicer to her after the knight got hurt."

Shiara snorted. "So I feel sorry for her. She really cares about that klutz in the tin can. I could tell. That doesn't mean I like her! I still think she's dumber than you are, but I'm glad they're going to see Morwen."

I wasn't sure whether Morwen would object or not, but I didn't say anything else about it. By then, the knight and the Princess were completely out of sight anyway. I turned around to see where I'd put the bundle of food and things Morwen had given me. The dragon was staring at me.

"Why," it said, "do you have wizards chasing you?"

"It's long story," I said. "I'll be glad to explain, but you might want to make yourself comfortable first."

The dragon sighed. "Have you ever tried to be comfortable with a sprained tail?"

Shiara giggled. I ignored her. We waited while the dragon tried curling into a couple of different positions. One of them looked sort of like Suz when he was halfway through getting up on his tail. Finally, the dragon curled itself around the little tree that had sprouted up in the middle of the tourney. "That's better," it said. "Enchanted trees are always more comfortable than regular ones."

"Enchanted trees?" Shiara said.

"Of course," the dragon said. "What else do you expect to find in an enchanted forest? I'm going to have to remember to tell someone about this, though. There haven't been any new ones in a long time."

I looked at the tree a little more closely. It was nearly six feet tall now, and it seemed to have stopped growing. It didn't look very different from the other trees in the Enchanted Forest, except that it was a lot smaller than most of them. And, of course, none of the other trees had dragons wrapped around them.

"You were going to tell me about the wizards," said the dragon.

So I explained about Mother and Antorell, and the Sword of the Sleeping King, and everything. It took a long time. The dragon didn't say anything at all while I talked, but its tail twitched a couple of times. Whenever that happened, the dragon winced.

"That's very interesting," the dragon said when I stopped. "Where are you going now?"

"Morwen told us to follow the stream," Shiara said. "And Suz said we should go talk to someone named Kazul."

"It's the same thing," the dragon said.

"What do you mean?" I asked.

"The stream goes to the castle, and Kazul lives right outside it. I wonder why she wants to see you?"

"What castle?" Shiara said in an exasperated voice. "And who is this Kazul person, anyway?"

"It must have something to do with that sword," the dragon said, ignoring her questions completely. "Especially if it really does belong to the Sleeping King."

"You mean you know something about it?" Shiara said. "Well, then, tell us what the stupid thing does!"

The dragon looked sheepish. Dragons just weren't meant to look sheepish. "I don't know. I'm not old enough yet," it said.

"Not old enough?"

"That's why I wanted a princess," the dragon said. "Otherwise, Kazul won't tell me anything important until I'm two hundred. She says that before then dragons are irresponsible, unwise, and talk too much." It looked faintly indignant. "I don't talk too much."

"Who is Kazul?" I said. I was getting a little nervous about meeting her. I hadn't ever known anyone who could tell a dragon what to do, even a young one. Well, Mother might have been able to get away with it.

"Oh, I thought you knew," the dragon said. "Kazul is the King of the Dragons."

In Which They Take a Shortcut
and Run into an Obstacle

S hiara and I looked at each other. "Terrific,"
Shiara said. "And I thought wizards were
bad."

"Did I say something wrong?" the dragon
asked.

"No, not at all," I said hastily. "We were just a little
surprised, that's all."

"Hey!" Shiara said. "How can Kazul be King of the
Dragons if she's a she? That doesn't make sense."

"It does too!" the dragon said. "What else would
you call her?"

"How about Queen?" Shiara said sarcastically.

"Queen?" The little dragon wrinkled its nose. "Why
would you want to call her Queen? That's not the same
thing at all! You're the one who doesn't make sense."

"I do too make sense!" Shiara said. "Queens do the
same things Kings do."

"Not for dragons," I said hastily. I didn't want the
dragon to get offended again. "Dragons have a king,
period. The King of the Dragons is whichever dragon

can move Colin's Stone from the Vanishing Mountain to the Ford of the Whispering Snakes. It doesn't matter whether the dragon is male or female."

"It's silly to have two names for the same job," the dragon said complacently. "People get confused."

"Oh." Shiara looked skeptical, but at least she didn't object any more. I decided I was going to have to explain a few things to her soon, before she got us both in real trouble. For about a minute, no one said anything. Then Shiara looked over at me.

"Daystar," she said, "*why* are we looking for the King of the Dragons?"

I started to say something, then stopped because I wasn't really sure what to say. I mean, it would sound a little odd to say that I was looking for a dragon because a lizard told me to. Especially since the dragon was apparently King of the Dragons. I thought some more.

"I don't know," I said finally. "But I think we have to. At least, *I* have to."

Shiara sighed. "I was afraid you were going to say something like that."

The dragon looked puzzled. "What's the matter? It doesn't sound particularly unusual to me, but I suppose it'll be at least as interesting as running away to find a princess."

Shiara and I looked at the dragon, then at each other, then back at the dragon again. "You ran away?" Shiara said finally.

"It was the only way I could think of to get a princess." The dragon sighed. "It didn't work out the way I thought it would, though."

Shiara and I exchanged glances again. "You're sure you really want to come?" I said to the dragon. "I mean, there are wizards after us, and it might be a little inconvenient if they showed up again. And I doubt that we'll run into any more princesses."

The dragon looked thoughtful for a moment, then it shook its head. "I'm coming with you, wizards or no wizards," it said stubbornly. "Sneezing isn't so bad."

It was my turn to sigh. Dragons are awfully hard to talk out of things. "We'd better go, then," I said. "I'm sure Antorell will be back as soon as he thinks it's safe, and I'd sort of like to be gone by then."

Shiara grabbed Morwen's bundles and shoved one at me. "You're absolutely right. Here. Let's go."

I nodded and started toward the stream. "Not that way!" said the dragon. "It takes too long."

"How else are we going to find the stupid castle?" Shiara demanded. "We don't even know what it looks like!"

The dragon looked smug. "I do. And I'm very good at shortcuts."

"Morwen told us to follow the stream," I said doubtfully.

"Morwen didn't know you were going to meet me." The dragon looked at us for a minute. "I thought you were in a hurry."

"Come on, Daystar," Shiara said. "I don't care which way we go, but let's go!"

I decided not to argue. I still didn't like the idea of leaving the stream, but it didn't seem worth fighting over. Not with a dragon, anyway. Besides, if we didn't leave soon, the wizards would catch us. We started off, following the dragon.

Traveling with a dragon was rather nice, in a way. Nothing bothered us at all. When it started to get dark, we stopped and opened Morwen's bundles again. There was obviously something magic about them, because the leftovers from lunch had turned into a fresh packet of food, and there was plenty for everyone, even the dragon.

Nothing dangerous came near us all night, either. I stayed awake for a while, just to make sure, but evidently nightshades and wolves and things don't want to annoy a dragon any more than people do. Finally, I went to sleep, too.

WE STARTED OFF AGAIN as soon as we woke up next morning. The dragon went first because it knew the way, and we followed. After about an hour, I noticed that I didn't feel quite comfortable for some reason. I touched the hilt of the Sword of the Sleeping King a couple of times, but I didn't feel any new magic tingles, just the same familiar ones. I started watching the trees as we walked. Finally, Shiara noticed.

"What's the matter, Daystar?" she said.

"I don't know," I said. "But I feel as if I'm being watched."

"Watched?" Shiara looked at the trees quickly. "Who's watching us?"

"I don't know," I said. "I'm not even sure someone is. I just feel uncomfortable."

"You're being a little slow," the dragon called back over its shoulder, and Shiara and I stopped talking and ran to catch up. We didn't have a chance to discuss it again, but I noticed Shiara looking uneasily at the forest from time to time. Even Nightwitch seemed to notice something wrong; she stopped jumping at leaves and stayed close to Shiara. In fact, Shiara almost stepped on her once. After that, Shiara carried her.

In spite of all the worrying, nothing happened until late that morning. The dragon was moving on through the forest, ignoring all the little branches and things that happened to be in its way. Suddenly it gave a smothered yelp and stopped. Shiara and Nightwitch and I ran forward to see what was the matter.

The dragon was sitting back, rubbing its nose and glaring at a large open space in front of it. I looked around, but I didn't see anything else. "What happened?" I asked.

"I ran into something," the dragon said, glaring at me for a minute instead of the open space.

"But there isn't anything—Ow!" Shiara had started to wave toward the clearing, but her hand stopped about halfway through the wave, as if it had hit something. She rubbed her fingers, then put out her hand more cautiously. It stopped in midair, right where it had before. Nightwitch hissed and backed away.

I reached out, very carefully. It was a little strange to feel something where I couldn't see anything. It was cool and smooth, like stone, and it went up as far as I could reach. "It's an invisible wall," I said.

"No, it's an invisible castle," Shiara said. Then she

jerked her hand away and stared at the air in front of her as if she could make herself see something by trying hard. "Hey! How do I know that?"

"I don't know," I said. "When did you figure it out?"

"I didn't! I was just standing here, wanting to know what it was, and all of a sudden I did."

"That sounds like fire magic!" I said.

"I don't care what it is," the dragon said crossly. "I want to know where it came from. It wasn't here last time I came this way."

"No, I mean what Shiara did sounds like fire magic."

"Really?" The dragon looked at Shiara. "Then use your fire magic to find out what this invisible thing is doing in the middle of my shortcut."

Shiara looked doubtful, but she put her hand back on the castle. "It's an invisible castle, all right. Hey, I even know how to do it!"

"Do what?" asked the dragon. "Put your hand on a castle?"

"No, no, how to make things invisible," Shiara said.

"I don't want to know how to make things invisible," the dragon snapped. "What's it doing here?"

For once, I wasn't paying much attention to the dragon. I was staring at Shiara. Analyzing spells is *hard*. "You figured out how to turn a castle invisible just by touching it?"

"No, you have to do a lot of other things to it." Shiara's face changed, as if she had just remembered something she didn't like, and she stared at the open area for a minute. Then she swallowed so hard I could see it.

"Let's leave, Daystar. I don't think I want to meet anyone who would live in an invisible castle."

I looked at Shiara, then at the open space. I looked back at Shiara and opened my mouth to ask another question, but I stopped before I said anything. Shiara looked a little white, and a little sick, and a lot scared. I hadn't seen Shiara look like that before, not even when the wizard tried to catch us with his snaky water monster. Especially not then.

"All right," I said. "Let's go."

"But I want to know what it's doing in the middle of my shortcut," the dragon complained.

"We can talk about it somewhere else," I said.

Shiara was already backing into the trees, her eyes fixed on the open space where the castle would be if we could see it. I glanced back at the dragon. It shrugged. "Oh, all right. But I don't see what all the fuss is about."

Right then Shiara gave a half yell that stopped in the middle. I whirled around. There was a woman standing where Shiara had been. She was very tall, and she had long hair that was so red it was almost black. She was dressed in something green and shining and elegant that hung from a deep red jewel at her throat, and she was very beautiful. More beautiful than the Princess, even. I didn't care.

"Where's Shiara?" I said.

She smiled, the same way a very satisfied cat smiles, except that cats don't look evil. Well, most cats don't. "Shiara—is that your little friend's name? She's right here, my dear." She stepped aside, and I went cold. Behind her, where it had been hidden until she moved aside, was a gray stone statue that looked exactly like Shiara.

"That can't be Shiara!" I said. I was too upset to even think about being polite. "Shiara's a fire-witch, and fire-witches are immune to magic!"

The woman smiled another unpleasant smile. "Not to the magic of another fire-witch. I've been waiting a long time for someone like her to come by. I need her for something."

"How is turning her into a statue going to help?" I asked. I was hoping I could talk her into changing Shiara back. Then maybe I could do something to keep Shiara that way.

The fire-witch glanced at the statue. "It's an excellent way of storing people until you need them. I have quite a number in my garden. They're ornamental as well as useful."

"That doesn't sound nice," the dragon said.

The woman seemed to see it for the first time, which I thought was a little odd. After all, dragons aren't exactly easy to overlook. "I am not concerned with being nice," she said.

"Why not?" I asked.

The fire-witch turned and looked at me. Suddenly her eyes narrowed. "Who are you, boy?" she asked sharply.

"My name is Daystar," I said, "and I would appreciate it if you would change Shiara back."

"No," she said flatly. "Why should I?" She was still staring at me, as if she were trying to figure something out. "You're very interesting, Daystar," she said abruptly. "I think perhaps I'll let you go. I haven't done anything like that in a long time. It might be an interesting experience. I think you had better leave before I change my mind."

"I'm sorry, but I'm not leaving until you turn Shiara back," I said.

"Then I am afraid you will grow rather bored." The woman looked at me thoughtfully for a moment, then shook her head. "No, I don't have any use for you, and I can't be bothered storing things that aren't useful. Pity; you'd make a nice fountain." She lifted one hand and snapped her fingers.

I had just enough time to realize that I hadn't drawn my sword. I grabbed for it and pulled, knowing I wasn't going to make it. There was something like an explosion just in front of me, and a wave of heat, and then I was holding the Sword of the Sleeping King up in front of me and watching the fire-witch cursing and stamping at something. She didn't look at all elegant anymore.

Suddenly I realized why the fire-witch had missed. "Nightwitch!" I yelled. A small bundle of black fur darted out from under the witch's skirts and vanished under a bush. The fire-witch glared after the kitten, then turned back to me. "You'll suffer for—"

Right next to me there was a sound like someone blowing out several very large candles all at once, and a stream of fire shot out and enveloped the fire-witch. She laughed.

"Fire, to harm me? Even a dragon should know better! I'll see to you in a moment. Or do you think I am fool enough to grow a garden without dragonsbane?"

The dragon shuddered, and the fire-witch laughed again. Then she looked at me, and her eyes glittered. "I want you first, though. Now!" She pointed at me, and I raised the Sword of the Sleeping King a little higher, holding on to the hilt with both hands and hoping it could handle fire-witches as well as it handled wizards.

Something hit the sword, and pain ran through my whole body. It felt a little like the shock I'd gotten when Shiara and I had tried to pick up the sword at the same time, except it went on and on. The Sword of the Sleeping King began to get hot. I felt as if boiling lead were running down the sword and into my arms. I think I screamed; I know the fire-witch did, because I heard her.

The Sword of the Sleeping King glowed dull red in my hands. It wasn't behaving at all the way it had when it stopped Antorell's spell, and I got the distinct impression that this wasn't very good for it. It wasn't very good for me, either; the sensation of boiling lead was oozing farther up my arms.

I knew that if I didn't do something I was going to drop the sword. I shouted and *pushed.* At least, pushing is the only way I can describe what I did. I wasn't really thinking too clearly by then. I just wanted the lead to go back into the sword and quit hurting.

I heard a wail from the fire-witch that kind of died out, and the pain stopped very suddenly. I noticed that the sword wasn't glowing anymore, and then I fell over. It wasn't that I felt particularly tired or weak. I just couldn't stand up anymore. The last thing I remember thinking was that I had to hang on to the sword, no matter what.

I woke up because something small and warm and rough was rubbing my chin. I opened my eyes. Nightwitch was sitting on the ground in front of me, licking my face. I was lying face down on the moss. I could feel the Sword of the Sleeping King underneath me. It was very uncomfortable, but I didn't feel like moving. I closed my eyes again.

Nightwitch hissed and dug her claws into my shoulder. Kittens have surprisingly sharp claws, and I opened my eyes again very quickly. The dragon was staring at me from beside Nightwitch. At least, its head was beside Nightwitch. The rest of it wouldn't fit. It blinked at me.

"Are you dead?" it asked.

"No," I said. I thought about saying something else, but I didn't have the energy.

"Oh." The dragon sounded almost disappointed for a minute. Then it brightened. "I think that fire-witch is."

"That's nice." I had the feeling I should remember something, but I didn't want to think hard enough to figure out what.

Nightwitch hissed and dug her claws into me again.

"Stop that!" I said, and I rolled onto my back.

"What?" said the dragon.

"Nightwitch," I said. Rolling over had taken all the energy I had, and I didn't want to talk anymore. I didn't even want to think anymore. I wanted the dragon to just leave me alone, but I couldn't say so without being rude, so I closed my eyes and started drifting off to sleep instead. Then Nightwitch jumped onto my chest and dug her claws in hard.

I yelled and sat up. Nightwitch jumped down to the ground and ran off. I tried to see where she'd gone and saw Morwen's bundle instead. Suddenly I realized that I was very hungry. I started to reach for the bundle, then remembered that I was still holding the sword. I also remembered the boiling lead, and I was almost afraid to look at my hands. I was sure that this time I'd burned both of them worse than when I'd picked up the wizard's staff.

I looked down. There wasn't anything wrong with me—at least, not that I could see. I let go of the sword with one hand. It didn't hurt. I heaved a sigh of relief and put the sword back in its sheath, then got out some of Morwen's gingerbread and started eating. It was a good thing the food was right on top of the bundle, because I didn't have the strength to hunt for it.

The dragon watched me for a few minutes with a puzzled expression. "You're a very good magician," it said finally. "Where did you learn that spell?"

"Spell?" I was having a little trouble remembering the details of the fight. I wasn't sure whether it was because it had hurt so badly or because I was too busy eating.

"The one you shouted right before the witch went up in smoke," the dragon said, "You said,

'Power of water, wind, and earth,
Turn the spell back to its birth.'"

"Oh, that," I said, feeling a little silly. "It's just part

of a rhyme Mother taught me when I was little. I don't know why I said it."

"Your *mother* taught you? But that's a dragon spell! Your mother couldn't teach you dragon spells!"

"You don't know my mother," I said. I'd eaten most of the gingerbread, and I was feeling much better. "She taught me two more lines to the rhyme," I offered. "They go,

> *'Raise the fire to free the lord*
> *By the Power of wood and sword.'"*

The dragon looked at me suspiciously. "Where did your mother learn dragon spells?"

"She didn't tell me," I said. I finished the gingerbread and looked around. "Where did Shiara . . ." My voice died in midsentence as I remembered exactly where Shiara had been when I saw her last. I didn't want to look, but I had to. I took a deep breath and turned my head.

Sometimes, when witches or wizards die, all of their spells die with them. If the witch or wizard is skillful, sometimes the spells last.

The fire-witch had been skillful. Shiara was still a statue.

11

In Which a Lizard Suggests a Solution

I sat there for a minute, staring at the statue and wondering what to do. Finally I looked at the dragon. "Do you know anything about magic?"

"Of course I do!" the dragon said. "Everyone who lives near the Enchanted Forest knows something about magic."

I sighed. "I mean, do you know anything about turning statues that used to be people back into people again? Because I don't, and we have to figure out some way to fix Shiara."

"Oh." The dragon looked doubtfully at the statue of Shiara. "We could take her to the Living Spring and drop her in," it suggested. "That would bring her back to life."

"You *know* where the Living Spring is?" I said in surprise.

"No," said the dragon. "But I bet if we found it, it would work."

I shook my head. "I don't think we have time. There are wizards looking for us, remember?"

"Oh, that's right. I keep forgetting. I don't like to think about wizards." The dragon blinked. "What about your sword? You could say that spell again."

I nodded. I walked over to Shiara and pulled the Sword of the Sleeping King out of its sheath. I felt a little uncomfortable, partly because I hadn't thought of using the sword and partly because the dragon spell was still just one of Mother's nursery rhymes to me. The idea of standing in the middle of the Enchanted Forest holding a magic sword and reciting a nursery rhyme made me feel very silly. I looked at the statue of Shiara again and decided I'd try it anyway. Slowly, I lowered the point so that it touched the statue's shoulder, and I said,

> *"Power of water, wind, and earth,*
> *Turn the spell back to its birth.*
> *Raise the fire to free the lord*
> *By the power of wood and sword."*

For a minute I thought nothing had happened, but then three or four little tingles ran up my arm from the sword. I hadn't even realized they were missing until they started again. When I finally did notice, I was relieved. Mother wouldn't have been at all happy with me if I'd ruined the Sword of the Sleeping King.

Unfortunately, Shiara was still a statue. "I suppose we're going to have to look for the Living Spring," I said. "Unless you have some other ideas."

"No," the dragon said. "I've never been on an adventure before. How are we going to find the Spring?"

"I don't know," I said. Half of the heroes who

stopped at our cottage had been looking for the Living Spring, but I'd never heard of anyone finding it. I tried to think of someone who might know where the spring was. "Suz!" I said suddenly.

"What?" the dragon said.

"Suz is sort of a friend of mine," I explained. "He says he knows everything that goes on in the Enchanted Forest, so he ought to know where the Living Spring is. I wish he were here."

"You do?" said a squeaky voice by my right foot. "Yes, you really do! How intriguing. Why do you?"

"Suz!" I said. I looked around until I saw him, then carefully sat down on the ground. "I'm awfully glad to see you. Do you know where the Living Spring is?"

"The Living Spring?" Suz said. "Dear me! Why do you want to know?"

"What's that?" asked the dragon, who had finally managed to find the source of the squeaky voice. "It looks like a little dragon."

"Oh, I'm sorry. This is Suz. I was just telling you about him. He's not a dragon, he's a lizard."

"A lizard of extremely good family." Suz frowned at the dragon, but the dragon didn't seem to notice. Suz gave up and looked back at me. "Now, why do you want to know about the Living Spring?"

"Because Shiara got turned into a statue by the fire-witch who lived in the invisible castle," I said.

"She did?" The lizard peered around until he saw the statue, then scurried over. He cocked his head briefly and stared upward, then ran up the gray stone in a spiral until he was sitting on one of the statue's shoulders.

"She really did! How exceedingly distressing. What are you going to do about it?"

"We thought if we dropped the statue in the Living Spring, it would, well, fix Shiara," I said. "But we don't know where the spring is."

"You don't? No, of course you don't. It's a secret." Suz peered at me from Shiara's shoulder. "I suppose you want me to tell you where it is." He considered for a moment. "I couldn't possibly do that, so you needn't bother asking."

"But, Suz!" I said. "How else can we fix Shiara? I've tried the only other thing we could think of, and it didn't work."

"That is extremely obvious," the lizard said severely. He ran down the side of the statue and stopped right in front of me. "If it had worked, she wouldn't be a statue anymore, and you wouldn't be asking me silly questions." Suz did whatever the thing was that he did to balance on his tail. "People who are looking for things in the Enchanted Forest have to find them for themselves. You really ought to know that, you really ought."

"Well, what are we going to do about Shiara if you won't tell us where the spring is?"

"My goodness gracious, you certainly are persistent," Suz said. "Have you tried kissing her?"

"*Kissing* her?" I said incredulously.

"Kissing the statue," Suz explained condescendingly. "It's one of the standard cures for being made to sleep for years, or being turned into a frog or a statue or such. Have you tried it?"

I felt my face getting hot. "Um, well, no."

"Well, then," Suz said pointedly.

I thought about it for a minute or two. Shiara might not think much of my kissing her, but I didn't really object, especially if it would break the spell. In fact, I sort of liked the idea. At that point, I stood up very quickly because my face was getting even hotter and I could feel Suz staring at me.

I was right next to the statue, and as soon as I was all the way standing I leaned forward and kissed it. I didn't want to take time to look before I did it, because I didn't really want to think about it. First I felt cold stone, but it warmed up right away. A second later Shiara jerked away and said, "Hey! Daystar, what on earth do you think you're doing?"

"It worked!" I said. I was awfully relieved. If we hadn't been able to break the fire-witch's spell, we'd have had to bring the statue with us, and carrying a statue around would have been a lot of work. Besides, having Shiara back felt good, even if she *was* glaring at me.

"What worked?" Shiara demanded suspiciously. "And where did that witch go? She was here a minute ago."

"You were a statue," the dragon informed her. "The fire-witch did it, but Daystar got rid of her. I'm glad he did," it added thoughtfully. "I didn't like her. She wasn't polite at all, and she . . . and she . . ." The dragon leaned forward and said in a loud whisper, "And she grew dragonsbane!"

Shiara stared at the dragon, but before she could say anything there was a loud squeak from behind me, and Suz's voice started shouting. "Help! Murder! Wild beasts and dangerous lunatics! Oh dear oh my help help goodness gracious help oh!"

I turned around. Nightwitch had come out from wherever she'd been hiding and sneaked up on Suz while I was, well, kissing Shiara. Suz was rolled into a tight golden ball, and Nightwitch was batting him back and forth between her paws in wide-eyed fascination. I didn't think she'd ever played with a ball that yelled at her before.

I bent over to pick up Nightwitch, but before I actually got hold of her the lizard uncurled very quickly, slapped his tail sharply against the kitten's nose, and curled up tight again. He didn't stop yelling the whole time. The kitten jerked her head back so fast that she sat down hard on her tail, and I grabbed her.

"It's all right now, Suz," I said.

The lizard poked his nose out of the ball. "You're quite certain?" he said.

"Yes, of course," I said.

Suz uncurled a little more. "This sort of thing is quite unsettling," he said. "I do not approve at all. Dear me, no, not at all."

"I'm very sorry," I said. "I'm afraid I didn't know she was there."

"People who keep wild animals ought to know where they are so they don't go around eating other people," the lizard said. He uncurled the rest of the way and lay on the moss, peering reproachfully up at me.

I bent down, and Suz scooted back a couple of feet. "You keep that—that beast away from me!"

"Nightwitch isn't a wild animal, she's a kitten," Shiara said indignantly. "And I don't believe she meant to eat you. She just wanted to play."

"She's too young to know better," I said. Shiara glared at me, and I added hastily, "Nightwitch, I mean."

"She is?" The lizard squinted at Nightwitch from a safe distance. "Yes, I suppose she is," he said reluctantly. "How unfortunate. I really do think I had better leave. Dear me, yes, I really must."

Suz nodded and headed off into the woods.

"Suz, wait!" Shiara called.

The lizard stopped and looked back over his shoulder. "What is it?"

"I'm sorry Nightwitch scared you," Shiara said.

"You are?" Suz turned around and ran back to where Shiara was standing. He cocked his head at her, then did his tangled tail-balancing trick and stared up at her. "Why, you really *are!* How astonishing! How extraordinary! How extremely unexpected!"

I was a little surprised myself, but I decided I'd better change the subject before Shiara got offended. "Suz?"

The lizard turned his head and looked at me.

"What's the best way to get to the castle where Kazul lives?" I asked.

"Why, it's—" Suz paused. "Dear me, there seems to be an invisible castle in the way. How ridiculous. I'm afraid you'll just have to go around."

"That's what I thought," I said. "But thank you anyway."

"It's quite all right. And I really must be going now,

I really must. Goodbye." Suz bowed politely, then did a quick back flip and scurried off into the woods.

"And thank you for telling me how to change Shiara back!" I called.

Suz didn't answer. I turned back to find Shiara glaring at me again.

"All right, Daystar, explain. What's all this about statues and getting rid of witches?"

"I already told you all that," the dragon said in an injured tone. "Why do you want him to tell you again?"

"Because I didn't understand it when you told it," Shiara said. She sounded a lot like Mother. "And I want to know what's been going on." She sat down on the ground and looked at me. "So explain."

I explained. Shiara let me talk until I started to explain how we'd finally turned her from a statue back into Shiara, but then she interrupted. "You don't have to keep going," she said. She gave me an odd look. "I remember that part."

"Oh. I'm sorry," I offered. My face was getting hot again. "But no one could think of anything else, and it did work."

Shiara wasn't paying much attention. "Daystar, did your sword burn your hands when Antorell tried to throw that spell at you?" she asked suddenly.

"No," I said, relieved by the change of subject. "It didn't do anything at all."

"It did, too!" Shiara said. "It ate Antorell's spell. And it didn't do anything to you. Why didn't it work like that on the fire-witch's spell?"

"Who's Antorell?" asked the dragon.

"The wizard you were sneezing at when we met," I said. "He's not very pleasant."

"Wizards aren't," the dragon said.

"Daystar, this is important!" Shiara said. "Why didn't your sword work the same way on the fire-witch as it did on Antorell?"

"Fire-witches and wizards are different," I said. "It makes sense that the sword does different things to them. I wish it *would* get rid of Antorell, though. Then I could stop worrying about him."

Shiara said something else, but I missed it. All of a sudden I had the same itchy feeling I'd had earlier, as if someone were watching me. I looked over my shoulder, but there wasn't anyone there. Just trees.

"Daystar?" Shiara almost sounded worried.

"I'm all right," I said. "But can we get started and talk about this somewhere else? We still have to get to see Kazul, and there's an invisible castle in the way."

"Shouldn't we do something about the people she turned into statues for her garden?" Shiara said, looking nervously at the clearing where the castle ought to be.

"Why?" said the dragon in a puzzled tone.

"Because it wouldn't be right to just leave them there," I said.

No one seemed to like the idea of going into the castle. No one wanted to leave the fire-witch's statue people there, either. We spent a little while trying to figure out how to get into the castle. Shiara wanted to climb over the wall, but I didn't think that was a very good idea if we couldn't see the wall or what was on the other side. Finally, she agreed to help me look for a door or a gate or something.

We stretched our hands out in front of us and walked carefully toward the castle. It wasn't there. We went a little farther. It still wasn't there. We walked around the clearing for a few minutes while the dragon watched with interest. Eventually, we gave up.

"I don't understand," Shiara said as we came back to pick up Nightwitch and Morwen's bundles. "Where did it go?"

"Maybe the fire-witch moved it while she was talking to me," I said.

"A whole castle? That fast? Besides, didn't Suz say it was still in the way? It must have moved since he left." Shiara stopped, and her eyes widened. "Daystar, you don't think she could still be around, do you?"

"She isn't around anywhere," the dragon said positively. "She went up in smoke. I saw her."

"Good," Shiara said savagely. I must have looked awfully surprised, because Shiara glared at me and added, "She deserved it. You don't know what she had to do to make that castle invisible."

"What was it?" the dragon asked curiously.

Shiara glared at it, too. "I don't want to talk about it."

"Why not?" said the dragon.

"Because she tortured people to death!" Shiara shouted. "It was part of the spell, and I know how to do it, and I don't want to think about it!"

"I told you she wasn't a nice person," the dragon said.

Shiara snorted. She picked up Nightwitch and her bundle and walked straight across the clearing. After a couple of seconds, the dragon and I followed.

ONCE WE GOT ACROSS the clearing, the dragon took the lead again. Nobody said much for the rest of the morning, which was fine with me; I still felt as if someone was watching me, and I didn't like it. Finally even the dragon noticed.

"You look a little strange," it said. "Is something wrong?"

"I don't think so," I said. "I just feel like someone's watching me."

"You're imagining things," Shiara said. "I've been looking since you told me about it this morning, and I haven't seen anyone."

"Someone's following us?" the dragon said. It blinked at me, then turned in a slow circle, eyeing the trees. "You're right," it said finally. "Someone is following us. That's not polite."

Before Shiara or I could say anything, the dragon's head shot out toward one of the trees. I'd never seen anything move so fast. There was a loud yell from someone who wasn't the dragon. Then the dragon yelped and a bunch of leaves came drifting down to the ground. I heard a couple of crashing noises and another, louder yell, and then the dragon reappeared. Dangling by the seat of his pants from the dragon's mouth was an elf.

I stared for a minute, trying to decide whether this was the same elf we'd met before. He *looked* the same, but all elves look alike. Besides, he was yelling and kicking, and every now and then the dragon would shake its head, which made it hard to see the elf clearly.

I almost laughed; the dragon looked a lot like a very large cat with a very small mouse.

Nightwitch evidently thought so, too. She eyed the wriggling elf with some interest, then glanced up at me. "Mrrow?" she said.

"I'm afraid he's too big for you," I said.

"He certainly is!" yelled the elf. "Put me down! Let me down at once!"

"Mrof!" said the dragon through a mouthful of cloth.

"I don't think he wants to," I said to the elf. "Why were you following us?"

"Hey!" said Shiara. "Are you the elf we ran into before? Because if you are, I want to talk to you."

The elf stopped struggling and looked down at Shiara. Then he twisted around and looked at the dragon. "On the other hand, maybe I'm better off up here," he said.

"Mmnuf!" said the dragon, and shook its head violently.

"Yow!" said the elf. "Help! I surrender!"

"Really?" Shiara said skeptically.

"Really!" said the elf. "Absolutely! Completely and without question. Will you put me down?"

"Maybe you should," I said to the dragon. "I don't think he can get away from all of us, and it will be a lot easier for you to talk."

The dragon looked at me for a minute, then slowly lowered its head and dropped the elf in a heap in front of us. The elf lay there breathing hard while Shiara and the dragon and I closed in around him. As soon as we stopped moving, he bounced to his feet and spun rapidly in a circle, bowing to each of us. Then he sat down cross-legged and looked up at us with bright black eyes.

"Now," said the elf, "what can I do for you?"

In Which They Ask Many Questions

We looked at each other and then at the elf. "What you can do," said Shiara, "is answer some questions."

"My dear lady, I would be delighted," the elf said. "What do you want to know?"

"Why were you following us?" the dragon rumbled.

"I thought *she* was asking the questions," said the elf.

"We're *all* asking questions," Shiara told him. "So you can just stop dodging and answer that one."

"What one?" the elf said. The dragon growled and made a snapping motion at the elf, who jerked back hastily. "Yes, ah, of course," he said. "*That* question. I was, um, looking for information."

"Information? Ha!" said Shiara. "What kind of information?"

"Who you are, where you're going, and what you're going to do when you get there," the elf replied promptly. He was pointedly not looking at the dragon.

"That's all?" Shiara said sarcastically. "It sounds a lot like what we want to know about you."

"How nice," the elf said, beaming. "We have something in common."

"Excuse me," I broke in. "But who exactly are you?"

The elf looked at me with a pained expression. "I'm an elf."

"I can see that," I said politely. "But would you mind telling me your name? I mean, I'd sort of like to know to whom I'm speaking."

"My dear boy, I would be delighted." The elf rose and bowed with a flourish. "My name," he said, "is Janril." He sat down again and looked at me expectantly.

"Pleased to meet you, Janril," I said. "This is Shiara, that's Nightwitch . . ." I hesitated a moment. Dragons don't pick their names until they're old enough to pick what sex they're going to be, too, and I wasn't quite sure how to introduce one. I couldn't leave it out, though. "This is a dragon—"

"Somehow I guessed," the elf muttered.

"—and I'm Daystar," I finished.

Shiara was frowning at me, but before she could say anything the elf bounced to his feet and said, "Daystar! Not Cimorene's son? My dear boy, I can't tell you how glad I am you've finally come. It's about time things got straightened out a little."

"I don't trust elves," Shiara said. "And why should we listen to you, anyway?"

"My dear girl, if you expect me to answer questions, you're going to have to listen to me," said the elf. "Otherwise there's no point in it. Why don't you trust elves?"

Shiara didn't want to tell him anything, but I was beginning to like him. Also, I didn't see any good reason not to explain, so I told him about the first elf and the wizard's staff. When I finished, Janril nodded solemnly.

"That," he said, "makes your position entirely understandable. I'm afraid you ran into one of the Darkmorning Elves. They're a rather disreputable lot. They've been running wild since the King disappeared, so of course they'd cause you trouble."

"Why 'of course'?" said Shiara suspiciously. "And what king are you talking about?"

"The King of the Enchanted Forest," the elf said. "The Darkmorning Elves don't want him to come back. They like the way things have been run since he disappeared. Since you have his sword, of course they want to get rid of you. If they can," he added thoughtfully. "Personally, I don't think they really know what they're doing."

"How do you know about Daystar's sword?" Shiara asked suspiciously.

"My dear girl, everyone who lives in the Enchanted Forest knows something about the Vanished King's Sword," Janril said. "It—"

"Wait a minute!" I said. "I only have one sword, and I thought it was called the Sword of the Sleeping King."

"Sleeping, vanished, run away—what difference does it make?" Janril said. "He's *gone*."

"I don't care about the sword," the dragon said. "I want to know why you were following us."

The elf looked annoyed. "My dear ... ah ... dragon," he said, "I told you already, I wanted to find out more about you. I believe that's the usual reason for following people around."

"But that doesn't explain anything," the dragon complained.

Shiara's eyes narrowed suddenly. "All right, then, why did you want to know more about us?"

Janril considered for a moment, then grinned reluctantly. "Because I'm trying to find out what the Darkmorning Elves are up to."

"What does that have to do with us?" I asked.

"If I knew that, I wouldn't have to follow you," the elf said reasonably. "But the Darkmorning Elves have been very active in this part of the woods for the past few days, and we thought it might be you they were interested in. And of course, if they're interested, so are we."

"Who do you mean by 'we'?" I said.

"The Goldwing-Shadowmusic Elves," Janril said with a touch of pride. "*We* are on the side of the King, even if he is missing right now. We follow the sword."

"What does that mean?" Shiara demanded. "And how many kinds of elves are there?"

"Quite a few," said Janril. "But the only ones you have to watch out for are the Darkmorning Elves and the Silverstaff Elves. Fortunately, the Silverstaff Elves don't know the sword is back yet, but I doubt that your luck will hold much longer."

"How do you know these Silverstaff Elves don't know about Daystar's sword?" Shiara asked.

"My dear girl, if they did, you'd have wizards all over the place. The Silverstaff Elves are in league with them. Undiscriminating, that's all I can call it." Janril looked prim. A prim elf is almost as odd looking as a dignified lizard. I found myself wishing Suz were still around so I could compare them.

"How do we know you're telling the truth?" Shiara said.

"I suppose you don't," the elf said cheerfully. "But it doesn't really matter. We'll still be glad to help you."

Shiara snorted. "The last elf who said he was going to help us almost got Daystar killed."

"I'm sorry about that," Janril said politely. "But I simply can't take responsibility for the Darkmorning Elves. Now, I must be going; I have to let the rest of the Goldwing-Shadowmusic Elves know what's going on. We'll see you at the castle."

"Just a minute!" Shiara said. "What makes you think we're going to let you go?"

"Can you think of anything else we could do with him?" I said.

"I could eat him, I suppose," the dragon said dubiously. "I don't think I want to, though. Elves don't taste very good."

I decided not to ask how the dragon knew that. "You don't have to eat him," I said. "I think we should just let him go."

"But Daystar—" Shiara stopped and thought for a moment, biting her lip. "Oh, all right. If you want to let him go, let's do it."

"Are you sure?" I said, surprised. "I thought you didn't like the idea."

"I don't," Shiara said, glaring at me. "But we'll be here all day if we start arguing. Besides, it's *your* sword."

"All right," I said to Janril, "You can go, as long as you don't follow us around anymore."

"But of course!" The elf bounced to his feet again, bowed to each of us—including Nightwitch—and whisked off. Shiara scowled after him and opened her mouth, then apparently decided not to say anything.

"Well, let's go," I said after a minute. We picked up our bundles and started walking again. The dragon and I both watched the trees for a while, but Janril kept his promise.

Shiara walked just behind the dragon, looking thoughtful. "Do you really believe that elf?" she finally asked me.

"I'm not sure," I said. "I don't think it makes much difference, though. I'd still be going to see Kazul, no matter what he said. I want to find out about this sword and what it does and what's really going on around here."

I must have sounded annoyed, because Shiara frowned at me and asked, "What's the matter with you?"

"I'm getting sort of tired of people chasing my sword," I said. "I'd like to know why they want it so badly." I was also beginning to realize that I didn't know nearly as much about the Enchanted Forest as I thought I did, which made me very nervous. I wasn't going to mention that to Shiara just yet, though.

"Oh." Shiara looked thoughtful again. "Well, you could—"

The dragon looked backward over its shoulder.

"You're slowing down," it said. "Can't you two talk and walk at the same time?"

WE MADE FAIRLY GOOD TIME for the rest of the afternoon, and we were just beginning to think about finding a place to spend the night when we came to a clearing. The dragon stopped right at the edge of it, very abruptly. Fortunately, Shiara and I were back far enough to stop before we ran into it or stepped on its tail or something. Bumping into a dragon is not a particularly good way to end a day.

"What's the matter now?" asked Shiara.

"This looks just like that last clearing," the dragon said. "The one that had the castle in it."

"You mean we've been going in circles?" Shiara said.

"No," said the dragon. "I know my way around the Enchanted Forest better than that. I just don't like this."

"Why are you worried?" Shiara said. "*You're* not the one who got turned into a statue."

"Well, if you think banging into something you can't see is fun, you go first," said the dragon.

I put my hand on the hilt of my sword and felt a nice, strong rumble, like a cart full of bricks on a bumpy road. There was definitely a lot of magic in the clearing, or at least close by. I said so.

"If it's invisible, I don't want anything to do with it," Shiara said decidedly. "Can't we just go around?"

"No," said the dragon grumpily. "I want to know who's putting all these invisible things in my shortcut. If there's another one here, I'm going to find out about it." It stalked cautiously out into the clearing, heading straight through the middle.

Nothing happened. The dragon walked all the way across, then turned and looked at us. "Are you *sure* there's something here? I can't find anything."

I touched the sword again. "It feels like there is," I said. I looked at Shiara. She looked dubiously across the clearing. "Hurry up," said the dragon.

I sighed and started forward. I kept one hand on the hilt of my sword, just in case, and I walked across the same part of the clearing the dragon had. Shiara shook her head and started around the edge of the clearing.

I got about five steps. Then there was a *whooshing* noise and a wall of flames shot up around me, very hot and bright. I yelled, because I couldn't see where I was going, and I yanked at my sword. I think I had some vague idea that the sword might keep me from burning to death; I certainly couldn't see to fight anything.

Something hit me in the middle of my back just as the sword came out of its sheath. I felt a wave of anticipation from the sword followed very closely by a surge of disappointment. I was so surprised I nearly dropped it. Then I realized that it wouldn't matter if I *did* drop it, because I was lying on the ground. I was also much cooler than I had been a minute ago, and someone was pounding on me.

"Stop it!" I said.

The someone sat back, and I saw that it was Shiara. "Are you all right?" she asked.

"I think so," I said. "Why were you pounding on me?"

"Your clothes were on fire," Shiara said. "I was trying to put them out. If I'd known you were going to fuss about it, I'd have let them burn."

I apologized and thanked her, then looked around. Shiara and I were sitting on the ground, just inside a ring of fire. In the center of the ring was a short, round building with a pointed roof. It wasn't quite tall enough to call a tower, but it wasn't short enough to call a house, either. I moved away from the flames, which were uncomfortably warm, and looked at Shiara. "What happened?"

"How should I know? One second you were walking across the clearing, and the next second there was all this fire and you were yelling," Shiara said. "And when I tried to shove you out of it, we both got in here instead, and that thing was sitting there." She waved at the not-quite-tower.

"At least it isn't invisible," I offered. Shiara gave me a disgusted look, but she didn't say anything.

"Hello?" called the dragon's voice from the other side of the wall of fire. "Are you there?"

"We're here," I called back. "Both of us."

"How did you do that?" the dragon shouted.

"I don't know," I said. "And I don't want to stay here to find out." I picked myself up off the ground and put the sword back in its sheath. "I think maybe we'd better go," I said to Shiara. "Before something comes out of that house."

"It isn't a house," Shiara said. "But for once I agree with you."

"*Achoo!*" said the dragon from the other side of the fire.

"Just a minute, there!" a voice said behind me.

I turned around. A medium-sized man was standing about ten feet away, leaning on a staff that was about three feet taller than he was. He had black hair and three rings on each hand, and he was frowning irritably at Shiara and me.

"Oh, rats," said Shiara disgustedly. "Another wizard!"

"You," said the man, ignoring her statement completely, "are trespassing. I don't know how you got in here, but it was a great mistake for you to do so."

"We didn't exactly do it on purpose," I said. "We were just trying to get across the clearing."

"Young man, I surround my home with a wall of fire for a reason," the wizard said. "And the reason is that I do not like to be disturbed. I wish to know how you penetrated it, or I would not be wasting my time talking with you."

"I'm a fire-witch, that's how!" Shiara said. "And if you don't want to be disturbed, you ought to be more careful with your stupid wall. We would have gone right by if it hadn't jumped up all over Daystar when he tried to cross the clearing!"

"A fire-witch?" the man said. He gave Shiara an extremely odd look. "You haven't mislaid an invisible castle recently, have you?"

"No!" said Shiara. "It isn't mine!"

The wizard looked even angrier. "You know of it!"

"Well, sort of," I said. "It isn't ours, but we ran into it this morning."

"Did you," said the wizard. He sounded skeptical and very dangerous. I decided I didn't want to talk about the castle anymore.

"I think we ought to be going now," I said. "We're really very sorry to have bothered you."

"I'm not!" Shiara said.

"Shiara!"

"Well, I'm not," Shiara said. "He ought to apologize to us, not the other way around. And anyway, I'm not apologizing to any wizard, especially not one that messes around with invisible castles!"

The man with the staff frowned, but this time he looked more thoughtful than angry. "What is your complaint against wizards?"

"Ha!" said Shiara. "You should know."

"No," said the man, "I should not. I am not a wizard."

"ACHOO!" came the dragon's voice, and the wall of fire bulged inward on that side.

"Excuse me, but if you're not a wizard, why are you carrying a staff?" I asked. "And why is the dragon sneezing?"

The man looked startled. "Dragon? You travel with a dragon?"

"No, it travels with us," I said. "Does it make a difference?"

"Perhaps," the man said. He looked at the wall of fire and made a pass with his staff. The flames began to die, and a moment later we could see the clearing again.

13

*In Which They Learn the Difference
Between a Wizard and a Magician*

The dragon was still sneezing in medium-
sized puffs of flame. The man with the staff
examined it and shook his head. "That certainly is a dragon." He made another pass
with his staff.

The staff vanished, and the dragon stopped sneezing
abruptly. It sniffed a couple of times in an experimental
way, looking surprised, as if it expected to start sneezing
again any minute. I was surprised, too. I mean, wizards
never let go of their staffs — not willingly, anyway.

The man bowed politely to the dragon. "I apologize
for inconveniencing you," he said. "I offer you greetings
and welcome to my home, and I wish you good fortune
when you leave."

"What?" said the dragon.

The man looked a little startled and peered at the
dragon more closely. "Oh, I see," he said after a moment. "Well, you're welcome. Come and make yourself
comfortable."

Shiara scowled at him and bent to pick up Nightwitch, who had come running toward her as soon as the flames had died. The dragon looked suspiciously at the man.

"I don't like wizards," it said. "And I don't like people who put invisible things in the middle of my shortcut."

"I am not a wizard," the man said with a sigh. "And my tower has been here for years, and it isn't invisible. Now, come in and talk. There hasn't been a dragon by for a long time, and I'm a bit behind on the news."

"If you're not a wizard, what *are* you?" Shiara said, petting Nightwitch and glaring at the man.

"I'm a magician," the man said. "And my name is Telemain."

"Pleased to meet you," I said.

"Mrrow," said Nightwitch, and started purring loudly.

Telemain looked at the kitten, and suddenly he began to laugh. He had a nice laugh, sort of deep and friendly. I started thinking that I might be able to like him after all, even if his fire wall had nearly burned me to a cinder.

"I don't believe I have ever seen a group quite like this one," Telemain said when he finished laughing. "Please, tell me who you all are."

I introduced everyone, and Telemain nodded courteously to each of us. He gave me a sharp look when I told him my name. "I thought that was what your friend called you," he said. "Welcome to my home."

"Some welcome!" Shiara said. "You nearly got Daystar killed, and you started the dragon sneezing again.

And how come the dragon was allergic to you if you aren't a wizard?"

"Dragons aren't allergic to wizards," Telemain said, sounding surprised. "What gave you that idea?"

"I did!" the dragon said. It came forward and sat down emphatically, right next to me. "All dragons are allergic to wizards. I should know: I sneeze every time I get near one." It eyed Telemain belligerently.

"Oh, I don't doubt that at all," Telemain said. "But the hypersensitive reaction results from the indiscriminate absorption of magical energy through the enchantments fixed in their staffs."

"What?" said the dragon.

Telemain sighed. "It's not wizards you're allergic to, it's their staffs. You stopped sneezing as soon as I got rid of mine, didn't you?"

The dragon looked startled. "I did, didn't I?" it said after a minute.

"If you aren't a wizard, what are you doing with a wizard's staff?" Shiara asked.

Telemain raised his eyebrows. "Why do you ask?"

"We've been having some trouble with wizards," I said before Shiara could answer. I didn't want her to make him angry. We had enough people mad at us already.

"Really." Telemain looked as if he were going to laugh again. "All of you?"

"Well, mainly just Shiara and me," I said. "We've been sort of worried about them. Most of them are after Shiara," I added.

"What would the Society of Wizards want with a

fire-witch?" Telemain said. "I can see that I shall have to invite you in, if only to hear your tale."

"How do you know about the Society?" Shiara said angrily. "And why should we trust a wizard, anyway?"

"Anyone who knows much about magic can tell you're a fire-witch, and the only reason I can think of for a fire-witch to have several wizards after her is if she has done something to offend the Society of Wizards," Telemain said. He still sounded amused. "And for the third time, at least, I am a magician, not a wizard."

"What's the difference?" Shiara demanded.

"Magicians deal with many ways of magic," Telemain said. "Wizards with only one. Now, will you come in and sit down?"

Shiara was still looking at him doubtfully. Telemain smiled. "Will an oath content you? If you mean no harm, I am not your enemy, and I will do you no harm while you are my guests, save in self-defense. I swear by the sword."

I felt a kind of popping at my side, even though I wasn't touching the sword, and a ripple ran through the clearing, like a shimmer of light in the air. I thought it kept on going out into the forest, but I couldn't be certain. Shiara started and dropped Nightwitch, who landed on her feet with a yowl. The dragon stretched its neck, looking almost as if it were trying to purr.

Telemain suddenly looked very intense.

"That is the way of it, then?" he said when the ripple passed. "I don't think I blame you for your caution." He looked pointedly at my sword.

Shiara scowled again, but I thought she looked

a little more doubtful than the last time. "If you're so smart . . ." she began, and stopped. Nightwitch was rubbing against Telemain's leg and purring. *"Nightwitch?"* said Shiara.

"An intriguing name for a cat," Telemain said, bending over to pick up Nightwitch. "Even more interesting for a kitten. Where did you come by her?"

"She was a present," Shiara said grudgingly. "From a witch named—"

"Morwen?" said Telemain. Nightwitch purred louder. "I suspected as much. Now, will you come in? Or do you wish to continue this discussion where anyone may hear?"

We went in. The door of Telemain's home looked like an ordinary, normal-sized door, but it couldn't have been, because the dragon fit through it without any trouble. The room inside was made of stone and very bare. In the center of the floor, two iron staircases twisted around each other in a spiral and disappeared into the ceiling. The whole place seemed much taller from the inside. If I hadn't seen it before we came in, I would have been sure we were in a tower.

As the door closed behind the dragon, Telemain waved his hand. A table and three chairs materialized beside the stairs. "Sit down and tell me more about yourselves."

We sat down, except for the dragon, who sort of curled itself around the edges of the room. I started explaining about Mother and Antorell and everything that had happened in the Enchanted Forest. I even told him about the Sword of the Sleeping King, because I was pretty sure from the way he looked at it that he already knew something about it. The questions he asked made it pretty clear that I was right, although sometimes he got so technical that I had to ask him to repeat something. He sounded as if he knew exactly what answers he expected, too. When I told him about the voice that had said, "All hail the Bearer of the Sword," he nodded in satisfaction.

Then I explained how Shiara and I had met, and why the wizards were after her, and about the one who'd tried to get us at the stream. Shiara frowned at me, but she didn't interrupt. When I told him about meeting Morwen, Telemain seemed very interested.

"I haven't seen Morwen in a long time," he said. "How is she?"

"You know Morwen?" Shiara said.

"We grew up together," Telemain said. "Now, exactly what did she have you do to repair the damage to your hand?"

Telemain asked a lot of questions about the things the Sword of the Sleeping King had done, but he didn't seem particularly interested in the wizards. He wasn't interested in the Princess at all. Then I told him about the invisible castle and the fire-witch.

"So that's how you knew about it," Telemain said. "I wondered."

"That's how *we* knew," Shiara said. "How did *you* know?"

"The castle landed in my clearing sometime around noon," Telemain said dryly. "I was understandably curious as to why someone would go to all the trouble of making a castle invisible and then drop it on top of a magician who can't help noticing it."

"It's not there now," Shiara said.

"Of course not! What would I want with an invisible castle? When I found no one home, I cleaned the place up a bit and got rid of it."

"Cleaned it up?" I said, puzzled.

"The most recent owner had a number of unattractive habits," Telemain said even more dryly than before. "In addition to casual petrification of passersby, she indulged in seven varieties of involuntary metamorphosis, as well as necromancy and demonology. I don't believe you would be at all interested in the technical details."

"Oh." He was right; I didn't really want to know about it.

Telemain looked at Shiara again. "I owe you an apology," he said. "I knew that the castle was the property of a fire-witch, and I'm afraid that when you showed up, I thought you had some connection with it."

"Well, I don't, but I suppose I can see why you might have gotten mad." Shiara sounded a lot friendlier than she had before. I think she would have been friendly to anyone who didn't like that other fire-witch. Then she frowned. "How did the castle get into your clearing, anyway?"

Telemain shrugged. "As far as I can tell, the unit transportation spell operated on a set of totally random parameters, both in terms of time and location."

"What does *that* mean?" said the dragon.

"The castle was designed to move around the

Enchanted Forest more or less randomly. It's a rather unusual spell to put on a building, particularly an invisible one, because if you happen to be outside when it moves, you get left behind."

"Then why on earth would anyone put a stupid spell like that on a castle?"

"Presumably this fire-witch didn't expect to have any problems finding the castle again. I don't believe it occurred to her that someone else might find it first." He smiled. "I left a few surprises for her. I doubt that she'll be pleased."

"Oh, that's all right," the dragon said. "Daystar got rid of her."

Telemain looked at me. "Really. How did you manage that?"

"She threw some sort of spell at me, but Nightwitch scratched her, so she missed," I said. "And after that, I had the sword out."

"You used the Sword of the Sleeping King on a fire-witch?" Telemain said. He sounded somewhere between shocked and horrified.

"I couldn't think of anything else that might work," I said apologetically. "And it did work, sort of. I mean, it got rid of the fire-witch."

"She went up in smoke," the dragon said with considerable satisfaction. "I watched."

"She went up in smoke," Telemain repeated in tones of fascination. "And what were you doing while this was going on?"

"I was trying to hang on to the sword," I said. "It was glowing red, and my hands felt like they were burning or something, so it was sort of hard to do. But as soon as the fire-witch was gone, it stopped."

"You are extremely fortunate," Telemain said. "You might have gotten yourself killed and ruined everything. I don't recommend that you try that again. Stick to wizards. That's what the sword was meant for."

"It was?" said Shiara. "How do you know? What else does it do?"

Telemain looked at her. "Magicians know many kinds of magic." He turned back to me. "Please, continue."

I was curious about what the sword did, too, but Telemain obviously didn't want to talk about it, so I didn't ask. Instead, I explained about fixing Shiara and not finding the castle and meeting the second elf. Telemain listened carefully, then shook his head.

"So the war is beginning again," he said, half to himself. "I had best make my own preparations. I wonder why no one let me know?"

"War?" Shiara and I said together.

Telemain looked up, almost as if he had forgotten we were there. "The war between the dragons and the wizards," he said in the tones of someone trying to be patient.

The dragon, who had been falling asleep, suddenly came awake. "War with the wizards?"

"It is obvious," Telemain said a trifle crossly. "The elves are choosing sides, the dragons are restless, the wizards are coming into the Enchanted Forest in large numbers, and the Sword of the Sleeping King has returned. What more do you need to know?"

"What does the Sword of the Sleeping King have to do with a war between the dragons and the wizards?" I asked before the dragon could take offense.

"The sword is what started the war in the first place," Telemain said, and then he refused to say any more. "If Cimorene didn't see fit to explain, I certainly won't," he said. "When you meet Kazul, I am sure she will tell you whatever you need to know. I'm afraid I don't have time at the moment. I must see to things at once, if we are to win this war at last."

"Who do you mean, 'we'?" Shiara asked suspiciously.

"The dragons," Telemain said, "and the rest of us who follow the sword. Now, if you will excuse me?" He rose and started for the stairs.

"Wait a minute!" Shiara said. "What about us?"

"What? Oh, of course," Telemain said. He waved his hand again and muttered something, and suddenly the table was full of plates and bowls of food. I jumped. Telemain didn't seem to notice. "Help yourselves while I am gone," he said. "I don't expect to be long." He turned away and went up one of the iron staircases.

Shiara and I looked at each other. "Now what do we do?" Shiara said.

"*I'm* going to eat," I said. "Would you like something?"

Shiara snorted, but she reached for one of the bowls. There was plenty for all of us, including Nightwitch and the dragon. About the time we finished, Telemain came back.

"I was right," he said to no one in particular. Then

he looked at me. "You'd better stay here for the night. It will be much safer for everyone, and it will give me time to look into things a little more. You've been extremely lucky so far, but there's no reason to take any more chances until you must."

I started to nod, then looked at Shiara. Shiara looked at me, then at Nightwitch, who was curled into a small ball on Telemain's chair. She shrugged. "Let's stay."

"You will find rooms upstairs, on the second floor," Telemain said. "Just pick one and go in." He turned to the dragon. "I think you'll be more comfortable down here."

"I think you're right," said the dragon, eyeing the iron staircases a little dubiously.

"And thank you very much for your hospitality," I said.

Telemain nodded. Shiara and I started for the stairs. Shiara got there ahead of me and started climbing, but she didn't get anywhere. "What's the matter?" I asked.

"There's something wrong with this stupid staircase!" Shiara said. "I keep trying to climb up, but I don't go anywhere!"

Telemain, who had been talking quietly to the dragon, turned. "I'm sorry; I should have warned you. You'll have to take the other staircase. That one incorporates a unidirectional matrix focused groundward."

"Say that again, in English," Shiara said.

"That stairway just works going down."

"That's ridiculous!" said Shiara. "How can a staircase only work going in one direction?"

"He's a magician," I said.

We didn't have any trouble getting up the other stairway. Telemain's tower really was a lot taller than it looked from the outside; the stairs kept going after they got to the second floor. Shiara and I didn't climb any farther, though. We got off on the landing at the second floor and looked around.

We were standing on a narrow circle of wooden floor around the hole where the two staircases came through. Around the edge were six identical wooden doors.

"Well, he said to just go in," Shiara said.

Each of us picked a door and opened it. The rooms were all the same and very comfortable looking. They each had a bed, a table, a lighted lamp in a bracket on the wall, a padded chair, and a small set of drawers with a mirror above it. Shiara looked thoughtful. "I wonder if he keeps lights going in all these rooms?"

"He might," I said. "I mean, he *is* a magician. Does it matter?"

Shiara glared at me and went into the room she'd picked, slamming the door behind her. I stood there for a moment, wondering whether to knock on the door and apologize. In the end I decided to wait until morning to talk to her, since by then she probably wouldn't be mad anymore, and anyway I wasn't sure what I should apologize for.

I kept the Sword of the Sleeping King with me all night. It was a little uncomfortable sleeping that way, but I felt better knowing where it was. It wasn't that I didn't trust Telemain. I was just getting more and more worried about the sword. Everyone I met seemed to know about it, or want to know about it, or just want to get hold of it. I spent a lot of time thinking instead of sleeping.

TELEMAIN SERVED BREAKFAST the next morning on his magic table. He was very quiet while we were eating, but as soon as we finished he looked at me and said, "I have watched the Enchanted Forest all night, and there are some things you should know, but I do not wish to detain you against your will."

"What things?" Shiara demanded.

Telemain smiled slightly. "I fear you will have some difficulty in reaching the castle," he said. "I found no less than twelve wizards searching the area between it and you."

"Oh, great," Shiara said disgustedly. "Just what we need—more wizards!"

"I don't think it's very good," the dragon said. "Why do you?"

"I don't," Shiara said.

"Then why did you say so?"

"What can we do about them?" I asked Telemain.

"I think you can avoid them if you go through the Caves of Chance," Telemain replied.

14

In Which the Dragon Has an Allergy Attack

We all stared. "Ha!" Shiara said finally. "The Caves of Chance are even more dangerous than the wizards!"

"I don't think so," Telemain said. "I have been through them, and they're not as bad as most people think. Furthermore, there is an entrance to the caves within half a day's travel, and an exit that is very close to the castle. And once you are inside the caves, the wizards will not be able to find you."

"Why not?" Shiara asked.

"The Caves of Chance do not welcome wizards' magic."

"Can you give us directions?" I asked.

Telemain nodded and pulled a large map out of his sleeve. Most people don't even *try* making maps of the Enchanted Forest because things change so fast that an ordinary map is only good for a few days, so I'd never seen one before. This map must have been magical, because it seemed fairly accurate. At least, all the things Shiara and I had seen were in the right places.

Telemain showed us where his tower was and where the castle was, and he pointed out several places he'd found wizards. Then he showed us the entrance to the caves. It really did look a lot closer and safer than trying to get by all those wizards. Even Shiara looked less doubtful.

Then Telemain turned the map over, and on the back was a map of the Caves of Chance. He went over the routes from the entrance to the exit we wanted and what to do about some of the things we might run into inside. It was very interesting. I knew that trolls are allergic to milk, but I hadn't known that rock snakes like mirrors enough that they'll stop squeezing someone in order to look at their reflections. He also told us to hold anything we really didn't want to lose in one hand until we were out of the caves.

When Telemain was satisfied that we knew our way, he rolled the map up and put it back in his sleeve. We went outside to say goodbye.

"When you meet Kazul, tell her I will be coming for the battle," Telemain said. "I called her last night on the magic mirror to let her know that you're on your way, so she's expecting you."

"I'll remember," I said. "And thank you again for your help."

"Yes," said Shiara. I looked at her, a little surprised, but she was watching Telemain with an odd look on her face. "I think I ought to apologize to you," she said finally. "I wasn't very nice last night."

This time I really did stare, but she didn't seem to

notice. Telemain bowed. "Neither of us was blameless," he said. "I shall forget it, if you will."

Shiara nodded and turned to me. "Let's go, then."

I shut my mouth and picked up the bundle Morwen had given me. Shiara already had hers. We waved good-bye to Telemain and started off into the forest again.

NOTHING MUCH HAPPENED all morning. Shiara and I were both nervous anyway, thinking of all those wizards ahead of us. The dragon didn't seem bothered, though, and Nightwitch certainly wasn't. We found the first few landmarks Telemain had told us about, and we were fairly close to the entrance to the Caves of Chance when the dragon stopped and demanded lunch.

As soon as the dragon mentioned food, Shiara and I realized that we were hungry, too. We started looking for a good place to sit down and eat. Almost immediately, we found a huge tree lying on the ground in the middle of a small clearing.

The dragon wrapped itself around a medium-sized tree in front of us; it said it was much more comfortable that way. Nightwitch wandered around investigating the interesting holes and crannies around the fallen tree. Shiara and I sat down and passed out gingerbread and meat pies from Morwen's bundles.

"How much farther is it to the castle?" Shiara asked the dragon, handing it a slice of gingerbread.

"Oh, not very far," the dragon said. "About another day, if we weren't going through the caves. I've never been in the caves, so I don't know how long that will take."

"I thought you said this was a shortcut," Shiara said.

"It *is* a shortcut," the dragon said in a hurt tone. "How was I supposed to know a fire-witch was going to get in the way? Not to mention an elf and a magician."

"Do you think Kazul will tell us anything about the sword?" I asked. Nobody else seemed willing to explain, and I didn't see why Kazul should be any different.

"I'm sure she will," the dragon said reassuringly. "That is, if you're polite to her. Kazul is very particular about . . . about . . . *ahh* . . . *ach* . . ."

Shiara and I dropped our lunches and ducked hastily to either side.

"*Achoo!*" said the dragon. A large spurt of flame shot across the clearing, just missing us, and the dragon's tree shook. "*Achoo!* Oh, bother. *Achoo!*"

"Daystar!" Shiara shouted. "Over here!"

I ran around behind the dragon, who was now sneezing almost continuously. I pulled out my sword as I went. When my hand touched the hilt, I felt the same jangling that I'd gotten from Antorell earlier. Then I came around the tree, and even before Shiara pointed, I saw the wizards.

There were two of them right in front of Shiara, leaning on their staffs and looking from Shiara to the dragon and back.

"Hurry up," one of them said nervously. "We don't want this to get out of hand."

"I'm afraid you'll have to wait," another voice said from behind him. The first wizard jumped, and Antorell stepped out of the bushes. His beard and hair were several inches shorter than they had been, and his staff had a scorched streak near the top, but getting caught in the little dragon's fireball didn't seem to have done much to him otherwise. He smiled and went on, "You see, I want him, too."

"Um, can't we discuss this somewhere else?" said the nervous wizard, eyeing the dragon.

"Oh, you needn't worry about that," Antorell said, following his gaze. He smiled nastily. "I came prepared." He held up his free hand so that all of us could see the spray of spiky, saw-edged purple leaves he was holding. "Dragonsbane," he said unnecessarily.

The other wizards relaxed a little. "Such forethought," murmured the tall one. He exchanged glances with his companion, then bowed to Antorell. "Under the circumstances, we will be happy to split the reward with you."

"I am afraid that is out of the question," Antorell said over the dragon's sneezes. "The boy and his sword are mine."

"The boy!" said the nervous wizard. "But—" The tall one frowned at him, and he stopped.

The tall wizard turned back to Antorell. "As you say, the boy is yours. I trust you have no objection if we take the girl?"

Antorell frowned. He turned toward Shiara and stared at her for a minute, then shrugged. "She's no use to me. Of course I have no objection."

I started moving very, very slowly toward Shiara, so that when the wizards started throwing spells at us

I could try to stop them with the sword. The wizards didn't notice, and neither did Shiara. By the time the wizards finished deciding what to do with us, I was almost over to her.

"It's settled, then," Antorell said. "We help each other. The girl first?"

"Ah, why not start with the dragon?" the nervous wizard asked.

Antorell smiled condescendingly. "Very well." He stepped forward and started muttering over the dragonsbane. Right away the dragon started yelling.

"Yow!" it said. "*Achoo!* I hate wizards. Ouch! *Achoo!* Help!"

"You stop that!" Shiara said to Antorell. The wizards ignored her, and Antorell kept mumbling.

I started forward. If I could knock the dragonsbane out of Antorell's hand, the spell would stop. I wasn't sure whether it would be completely broken, but at least he wouldn't be able to hurt the dragon anymore. Unfortunately, I'd forgotten about the other wizards. I didn't even realize one of them had done something until my feet stuck to the ground and suddenly I couldn't walk forward anymore. If I hadn't been stuck, I'd have lost my balance. It was very disconcerting. Antorell was still out of reach.

I took a quick glance back over my shoulder. The dragon was sneezing much too hard now to say anything at all. I could see its coils going slack, and it was losing its hold on the tree. Here and there, its scales were turning pink around the edges. Even the tree looked wilted.

"Shiara!" I yelled. "Get the dragonsbane!" I didn't

think I could get loose in time, but the wizards wouldn't be able to stop a fire-witch.

I didn't wait to see what she did. I leaned forward a little and tried to lay part of the Sword of the Sleeping King across my feet. It hadn't helped Shiara when she was a statue, but this was a wizard's spell, not a fire-witch's spell, and Telemain had said the sword was meant to be used on wizards. Besides, I couldn't think of anything else.

It worked. I straightened up just in time to see a little tongue of flame shoot up from Antorell's hand. Antorell yelled and dropped the dragonsbane, which was burning brightly. Before it even hit the ground, there was nothing left of the plant except ashes.

I looked behind me. Shiara was standing with a surprised look on her face and one finger pointing at Antorell. The dragon was still sneezing, but the green was already starting to come back to its scales. I sighed in relief.

"This is the assistance you give us?" the tall wizard said to Antorell, who was brushing ashes off the front of his robe. "The dragon still lives!"

"Did I say anything about killing it?" Antorell said. I got the feeling he was trying to sound haughty, but he only managed to sound annoyed. "You need have no more fear of it. It will take some time to regain its strength, and by then we shall be finished. What next?"

"The girl, I think," said the tall wizard. "That is, if you're sure you can handle her?"

Antorell glared. "That is the least of my problems," he said grandly.

"Ha!" said Shiara loudly. I moved back over to her, holding the sword in front of me. The three wizards looked at us, then at each other. "Let us begin," said the tall one.

All three of them raised their staffs, but instead of pointing them directly at us, they brought them together, so that they made a kind of star about a foot from their ends. There was a bright flash as the three staffs touched, and I felt a shock from my sword. I jumped, and suddenly I realized that I could feel the forest. The magic of the forest, I mean; it was all around me, waiting. I felt almost as if the whole Enchanted Forest were watching me.

Right in front of me, I could feel the wizards' power growing and building. There was a kind of pattern in it that kept getting clearer and more complicated, and I knew I had to do something about it before the wizards finished. I stepped forward and swung the sword right through the middle of the pattern.

I felt a huge jolt of power from the sword, but it didn't hurt the way the fire-witch's spell had. In fact, it didn't hurt at all. The pattern collapsed in an invisible tangle. Antorell's eyes started to narrow; the other two wizards just looked stunned. And then something exploded.

I couldn't see anything. It wasn't that things had gone dark, and it wasn't that the light had blinded me. It was more as if the whole world had suddenly become invisible, so there was nothing left to see. There was a rushing noise all around me, and I felt as if I were floating. I heard a chorus of voices cry, "All hail the Wielder of the Sword!" and then the noise and the voices vanished, and I was standing in the clearing with the Sword of the Sleeping King shining in my hand and three very surprised wizards in front of me.

I stared at the wizards. The wizards stared at me. Antorell recovered first.

"Enough of this!" he cried, and raised his staff. As he did, the ground in front of him humped up a little bit. A second later, a tree shot up about twelve feet into the air. It reminded me of someone opening an umbrella very quickly. The branches shivered once as the leaves unrolled, and then it burst into bloom with a sound like a hundred little bells tinkling.

Antorell looked even more surprised than before, then he scowled angrily and pointed his staff at me again. The tall wizard next to him grabbed his arm. "Wait, fool! Don't you know what that sword *is?*"

"Of course I know, oaf." Antorell's eyes sparked. "It is mine! I will have it!"

"You will be dead, you mean," the tall wizard said, but he let go of Antorell's arm. "This is a matter for the whole Society of Wizards. There may still be time to stop him if we can bring them quickly enough."

"More wizards? *Achoo!* Oh, no you don't! *Achoo!* Oh, drat, *achoo!*" said the dragon. It dove out of its tree, unwinding itself like a spool of string, very quickly. Its head shot past me, and I got a fleeting glimpse of green scales and golden eyes and a very, very red tongue. One of the wizards yelled, and the dragon sneezed again. I jumped forward just in time to see all three of the wizards vanish hastily. Antorell looked a little white and he had one hand clutched around a dark, wet-looking spot on his other arm as he disappeared.

I looked at the dragon. It snapped its teeth together twice, swallowed something, and sat back, looking very pleased with itself. "Wizards," it announced, "taste *much* better than elves."

I swallowed hard and decided I didn't really want to finish my lunch. The dragon looked at Shiara. Shiara scowled.

"Don't you look at me like that!" she said. "I'm not a wizard, I'm a fire-witch."

The dragon looked thoroughly shocked. "But I wouldn't eat you! You're my friend. It wouldn't be polite at all!"

Shiara looked suspiciously at the dragon, then nodded. "I just wanted to make sure you remembered."

"I think we'd better get going," I said. "Those wizards sounded like they were going to come back with reinforcements."

"Oh, terrific," said Shiara. "Let's go, then. Where's Nightwitch?"

"Mrow," said a kitten voice from somewhere above me.

I looked up. Nightwitch was perched on a branch of the tree that had sprouted up in the middle of the fight. She was washing her paws. She stopped and looked down at me for a second, then went back to washing.

"Nightwitch, come down!" Shiara said. "Those wizards might come back any minute!"

Nightwitch ignored her. The dragon came over

and peered curiously at the tree. "Where did this come from?" it asked.

"It grew," I said. "I think you were sneezing when it happened."

"Kazul is going to be surprised about this!" the dragon said happily. "Two new trees in a couple of days!"

"What are you talking about?" Shiara said. "It's just a tree."

"No, it isn't," the dragon said. "It's a *new* tree. And it's the *second* new tree I've seen in two days, so it's important. The other one hit me on the nose," it added in an aggrieved tone.

"You mean it's been a long time since there were any new trees?" I asked.

The dragon nodded. "Kazul mentioned it once. She sounded worried. *I* think they're a nuisance, popping up like that."

"But where do they come from?" Shiara asked. "And why do they show up when we—" She stopped short, and we looked at each other.

"Daystar," said Shiara finally. "It's the wizards."

"It can't be," I said. "What about the first one?"

The dragon tilted its head to one side and looked at us. "What are you talking about?"

"The trees," Shiara said. "Both of them grew in places where a wizard threw a spell at us . . . But there wasn't any tree when the first wizard tried to drown us, so it can't be wizards."

I looked down, trying to think, and saw the Sword of the Sleeping King in my hand. "It's the sword!" I said. "It stopped Antorell's spell the first time, and a little while later a tree sprouted. This time it stopped a bigger spell, and we got a bigger tree. It didn't stop any spells when the first wizard made that water monster, so no new trees grew. It *has* to be the sword."

"You didn't get a tree when you fought the fire-witch," Shiara objected, but she sounded half-convinced.

"Well, Telemain told us the sword was meant for wizards. It probably only does that for wizards' spells."

"Your sword grows trees?" the dragon said skeptically.

"It does sound a little silly," I said.

"Mmmrrrow!"

We all looked up. Nightwitch launched herself at Shiara, who just barely managed to catch her.

"Good," said Shiara. "Now, if you're all done fussing about trees and swords, how about leaving? Before the wizards come back."

The dragon and I looked at each other and nodded. We picked up our things and started off.

In Which They Take a Chance

The entrance to the Caves of Chance wasn't very difficult to find. That worried me a little, partly because Antorell and the other wizards would probably figure out where we had gone, and partly because it isn't usually that easy to find something in the Enchanted Forest. Especially if you're looking for it.

Not that the way into the Caves of Chance looked as if it would move around easily. It was a large, smooth, circular hole in the ground with moss growing right up to the edge of it, and it was very dark. The dragon and Shiara and I stood around the edge, staring down into it.

"How are we going to get down there?" Shiara asked finally. "I can't even tell how deep it is."

"We'll have to use the blankets Morwen gave us," I said. "We can tie them together."

"What about me?" said the dragon. "*I* can't climb down blankets."

"I don't know," I said. "Maybe we'll think of something once we know how far it is."

"What if you can't think of anything?"

"Hey!" Shiara had opened her bundle to get the blankets out, and now she was staring at it as if she'd never seen it before. "Daystar, look at this!"

The dragon looked a little put out. It usually isn't a good idea to interrupt someone's conversation with a dragon, but for once I decided not to say anything, because I was glad Shiara had yelled. I didn't *know* what was going to happen if I couldn't think of a way to get the dragon into the Caves of Chance, and I didn't really want to say so.

I said, "Excuse me," to the dragon and went over to Shiara. "What is it?"

"This," said Shiara. She pulled a coil of rope out of the top of the bundle. "It wasn't here before."

"Are you sure?" I asked.

"Of course I'm sure!" Shiara said. "Look in your pack. Maybe you have one, too."

Shiara was right: There was another coil of rope in my bundle, along with a little silver lamp and a set of flints, and I didn't remember seeing any of them before. We tied the ropes together, then looped one end around the tree closest to the hole. The dragon watched, grumbling the whole time.

When we finished, Shiara and I argued about who was going to get to climb down first. We wound up tossing a coin, and I won.

I stuck the flints and the lamp into my belt, right next to the Sword of the Sleeping King, where I could find them easily. Then I lowered myself over the edge of the hole and started to climb down the rope. It wasn't easy. The rope kept twisting around, which made me dizzy, and I kept bumping into the side of the hole. I'd gotten about three feet from the top of the hole when the lights went out.

I stopped climbing for a minute and just hung there. I couldn't see anything except a circle of sky right above me, and that looked much farther away than it should have. Then I realized that I had to start climbing one way or another because my arms were going to get tired very quickly if I didn't move. I looked up at the sky. I knew I'd only come down a couple of feet, and it shouldn't have been difficult to climb back up. On the other hand, I knew it could be extremely dangerous to start things and not finish them in the Enchanted Forest. I started down again.

Climbing in the dark is not pleasant. I couldn't see where I was going; I couldn't even see the rope. It seemed like years before my feet finally touched something flat below me. I felt around to make sure what I'd found wasn't just a narrow ledge, then I let go of the rope and called to Shiara that I was at the bottom.

The next thing I did was to get out the lamp and light it. I had a little trouble, since I was doing everything by feel, but I finally got it going. At first all I could see was the tiny yellow flame. Then the lamp made a popping noise and suddenly I could see the cave.

Actually, it was more like a tunnel. Where I was standing, the walls were a smooth, speckled stone, but as soon as the tunnel got out from under the hole the walls looked rough. It was cool and dry and dusty, as if no one had been there in a long, long time.

"That's not so bad," said a voice above me. I looked up. The dragon was peering over the edge of the hole. "I can jump that far."

"I think you should wait until Shiara climbs down," I said. "Then you can untie the rope and bring it with you."

Shiara's head appeared beside the dragon's. "You're right; it's not nearly so bad when you can see the bottom."

"If you drop the bundles Morwen gave us, I can catch them," I said. "Then you can climb down and we can get started."

"All right." Shiara's head vanished for a few seconds, then reappeared, along with a pair of hands and a bundle. "Ready? Catch."

Nightwitch was more of a problem than the bundles. I got a few scratches catching her. As soon as I had everything, Shiara climbed down. We picked up our things and moved into the tunnel while the dragon took care of the rope, and then the dragon jumped down.

"That was easy!" it said.

I thought about sliding down the rope in the dark and didn't say anything.

Shiara looked from me to the dragon and back. "Well? Are you going to stand there until the wizards show up again?"

"We have to decide what we're going to hold on to first," I said.

"Daystar, we have to carry everything ourselves anyway," Shiara said. "What difference does it make?"

"I don't think that's what Telemain meant," I said.

"There are all sorts of ways to lose things in the Caves of Chance if you aren't paying attention, but if you have something in your hand all the time and never set it down, it's less likely to disappear."

"If you really believe that, you'd better carry the sword," Shiara said. "The only thing I don't want to lose is Nightwitch, and she can take care of herself."

"You're right," I said doubtfully. I didn't really want to march through the Caves of Chance with the Sword of the Sleeping King in my hand, but I certainly didn't want to lose it. Finally I decided to take the sheath off my belt and carry the sword and sheath together. I had some trouble doing it, though, and Shiara had to help.

"Are you sure this is necessary?" she asked. "Why can't you just wear it?"

"Magic things are particularly easy to lose here," I said. "And Mother told me to take care of this sword." I tucked the sheathed sword under my arm and picked up the silver lamp and the bundle Morwen had given me. "Let's go."

THE TUNNEL SLANTED DOWN for a long way, then leveled. Every now and then we came to a dark opening in the wall that led to a side passage, but we ignored all of them. Telemain had been very specific about that. Not that they were particularly tempting. The silver lamp had no difficulty lighting up our part of the tunnel, but it didn't penetrate into the side passages at all.

After a while, the tunnel we were following jogged sharply left, then right again, and suddenly it opened out into an enormous cave. The walls were crystal, and they seemed to have hundreds of different-colored lights shifting behind them. I stopped abruptly, staring, and the dragon bumped into me from behind.

"Excuse me," I said automatically.

"You shouldn't stop so fast," the dragon complained. It craned its neck to see around me. "Hey! This is nice!" It stretched upward, and a minute later it was clinging to the crystal wall several feet above us.

I backed away hastily. I didn't want to be underneath if the dragon slipped.

"Where are we supposed to go from here?" asked Shiara, ignoring the dragon.

"This must be the Cave of Crystal Lights," I said. "Telemain said to walk straight across. There ought to be three passageways on the other side, and we want to take the left one."

"I see them," the dragon said. It squinted across the cave, then climbed down and sat beside us. "They aren't straight across. They're over that way a little." It waved toward the right.

I looked at the dragon. "I think we should follow Telemain's directions. The Caves of Chance are even trickier than the Enchanted Forest. I don't want to risk getting in trouble if we don't have to." I didn't mention that the last time we had taken the dragon's advice we'd run into the fire-witch and Shiara had gotten turned into a statue, but I was thinking it. Shiara nodded in agreement.

"All right," the dragon said sullenly. "But I think you're being silly."

We started walking again, trying to go straight across the cave. The walls curved in and out, and the floor humped up in low mounds and ridges. Between that and the shifting colored lights, it was hard to be sure we were going straight. Shiara and I backtracked a couple of times, just to check, and every time we did the dragon grumbled.

Finally we got to the other side and saw the three openings. The dragon stared at them, then looked around suspiciously. "Where did these come from? These aren't the ones I saw!"

"Well, then, it's a good thing we followed Telemain's directions," Shiara said. "Otherwise, we'd be lost. Come on, let's go." She scowled and headed for the left-hand passageway.

I started after her, and right away I tripped and fell.

"Ow!" I said. Shiara looked around, then came back to help me up.

"What happened now?" she asked.

"I tripped," I said. "I've still got the sword, but I dropped the lamp. Where is it?"

"I don't see it." Shiara sounded a little worried. She had reason to be. Without the lamp, we wouldn't be able to see anything once we got out of the Cave of Crystal Lights.

"It can't be very far away," I said, and we started hunting. Shiara went one way and I went the other. About half a minute later, I saw something glittering. "There it is!"

"No, it's over here," said Shiara. She bent over and

picked something up from behind a rock. "It's still burning," she said, sounding surprised.

"It lights up more space than it ought to, too," I said over my shoulder. "Morwen probably put a spell on it."

"Where are you going?" Shiara said.

"I saw something over here, and I want to know what it is," I said. "Especially since it obviously isn't the lamp."

Shiara started to object, but right then I saw the glittering thing again and I bent to pick it up. "Here it is," I said. "See?" My fingers touched metal, and a fountain of sparks shot up from the floor of the cave where my fingers were.

I yelled and fell backward. The fountain hissed and sizzled angrily, getting bigger and brighter and hotter every minute. I scrambled back toward the others. Blue and white and purple sparks started falling around us, and all of us ran for the left-hand tunnel. Nightwitch yowled as one of the sparks hit her, and Shiara scooped her up and kept on running.

We made it to the tunnel, but no one stopped until we were well inside, not even the dragon. When we finally got out of reach of the falling sparks, we stopped and panted for a while. Fortunately, Shiara had hung on to the lamp as well as to Nightwitch. When she set Nightwitch down, the kitten glared back toward the mouth of the tunnel, then began determinedly washing a spot on her back where the fur was a little singed.

"What was that?" Shiara asked as soon as she had her breath back.

"I don't know," I said. "I was just trying to—" I stopped. I was holding something in my right hand. I didn't even remember grabbing it. "It went off when I picked this up," I said, and I opened my fingers.

I had three pebbles of various sizes, a little sandy dirt, and a small gold key. A tingle ran down my back as I looked at the key, and I jumped. "Now what?" said Shiara.

"I felt something," I said. "Sort of like the sword when it's finding magic, but not the same."

"Is it magic?" the dragon asked.

"I don't know."

"Well, find out!" Shiara said impatiently. "I thought that was what the stupid sword was for."

I sighed a little and shifted all the things I was carrying until I could put my left hand on the hilt of the Sword of the Sleeping King. I didn't feel any tingles, but the key started to glow.

We all stared at the key for a minute.

"I knew it was magic!" the dragon said happily.

"I don't feel anything from the sword, though," I said. I took my hand off the hilt, and the key stopped glowing.

"So? The sword makes it glow, doesn't it?" Shiara said. "It *has* to be magic. What are you going to do with it?"

"I'm going to keep it, at least until we talk to Kazul," I said. "She may know what it's for, or who it belongs to."

"It b-b-belongs in the c-c-cave," something said in a bubbly voice behind us.

I jumped and turned around. There wasn't anyone there. Shiara and the dragon and I all peered into the darkness. Nightwitch looked up from washing her back long enough to hiss, then continued washing.

"Who said that?" Shiara demanded.

"M-m-me. You b-better put that k-k-key back right away," said the same voice.

I still didn't see anyone.

"Why?" I asked.

"B-because it b-belongs there!" the voice said. It sounded like water hitting a hot frying pan. "Gug-give it to me, and I'll put it back."

"If you want it, you'll have to come out here where we can see you," Shiara said firmly.

There was an unhappy bubbling noise from the dark part of the tunnel, then a series of unpleasant squishing sounds. A moment later something wobbled into the light from the silver lamp. It was about four feet tall, and it looked like a slightly sloppy pillar of very dark blackberry jelly.

"There!" it said. "Now, gug-give me that key!"

I was so busy trying to figure out how it could talk when it didn't have a mouth that I didn't answer. I was still trying when Shiara asked, "How do we know it's your key?"

"It isn't my key. I just take care of it. Gug-give it to me!" The jelly was shaking angrily and bobbing up and down like the lid on a teakettle. Every time it bobbed up, the pillar of jelly stretched thin; and when it bobbed down, the jelly made a sort of flattened lump; and every time it moved at all, it wobbled.

The dragon, who had been standing behind Shiara, poked its head over her shoulder to see better. "That stuff reminds me of something," the dragon said. "I can't think what, though. What is it?"

"*I*," huffed the jelly, "am a quozzel." It leaned forward as if it were trying to peer at us and asked haughtily, "What are *you*?"

"It's a dragon," Shiara said, a little nastily. "Can't you tell?"

The pillar froze in midwobble. "There are n-n-no dragons under-gug-ground," it said. "None!" It leaned cautiously in Shiara's direction for a minute, then started bobbing again. "You aren't a dragon. I want that k-k-key! It belongs in the cave, and it's g-going to stay there!"

"Of course she's not a dragon!" the dragon said. "*I'm* a dragon. And I've never heard of a quozzel before."

The quozzel bent a little, then froze again. "Glurb," it said.

The dragon tilted its head to one side. "I don't think you're very polite," it said.

The jelly burbled unhappily to itself. It looked as if it were boiling. The little dragon kept staring at it, and suddenly the dragon's eyes started to glow. "I know what this reminds me of!" it said triumphantly. "Dessert!"

The quozzel shrieked and collapsed backward into the darkness just as the dragon's head shot toward it. The dragon kept going, knocking Shiara and me out of the way as it went past. We heard several squishing noises, then an angry snort from the dragon, followed closely by a small puff of flame that lit up the dark end of the tunnel. I got a brief glimpse of the dragon before the light died, but I didn't see the quozzel anywhere. There was a disgusted-sounding growl, and a moment later the dragon stalked back into the light from the silver lamp. "It got away."

"Well, I'm glad it's gone," Shiara said. She frowned. "You shouldn't go around trying to eat things all the time, especially if you don't know what they are. I wouldn't be surprised if quozzels were poisonous or something."

"Dragonsbane is the only thing that poisons dragons, and that quozzel wasn't polite, and I'm *hungry*," the dragon said. It shook its head sadly. "Wizards taste good, but they aren't very filling."

I put the key in my pocket and rummaged in Morwen's bundle. I was sure I still had some meat pies, and I didn't like the idea of traveling with a hungry dragon. I found the food and offered it to the dragon, who brightened up a little and accepted.

"We ought to keep going," Shiara said as the dragon sat back against the wall of the tunnel and started eating. "Suppose that quozzel thing comes back?"

"I don't think it could really do much to us," I said. "It didn't look very dangerous."

"You can't always tell by looking," Shiara said darkly. "And if that marmalade mess wants the stupid key badly enough, it'll think of something."

"Marmalade is orange," I said. "The quozzel looked more like blackberry jelly to me. And I still don't think it's going to come back. Not while the dragon is around."

"Well, you'd better carry that key in your hand," Shiara said. "I think it's important, and it might fall out of your pocket or something."

"All right, but you'll have to keep the lamp. I don't think I can manage the sword *and* the things Morwen gave us *and* the lamp, *and* still hold the key." I dug the key out of my pocket again. Maybe it did belong to the quozzel, but the more I thought about it, the less likely that seemed. And if the key had something to do with the sword, I wanted to hang on to it.

"You won't have to juggle things until we start walking again," Shiara said, but she kept the lamp.

Just then the dragon looked up. "I'm done," it said. "Where do we go now?"

16

In Which Things Get Very Dark for a While

We started walking again. I don't know how far we went or how long it took us. The tunnel forked and we turned right, then it forked again and we went left. We walked through a large cave with walls like black mirrors, and a damp one that dripped water onto our heads, and an unpleasant slimy one with gray moss on the walls. I was very glad that Telemain had told us which way to go. We would have gotten lost very quickly without his directions.

A few times I thought I heard squishing noises behind us, but I wasn't sure enough to say anything. I was a lot more worried about remembering all the things Telemain had told us than I was about the quozzel.

Just when I was beginning to think we had taken a wrong turn somewhere, we came to another cavern.

This one was long and narrow, full of orange light and very hot. The tunnel came out halfway up one wall, about a hundred feet above the floor of the cave. A narrow path ran along one wall from where we stood to a dark opening on the opposite side of the cave.

"Are you sure we're going the right way?" Shiara asked, eyeing the path dubiously.

"I am now," I said. "This was the last cave Telemain mentioned. Once we're on the other side, it shouldn't take long to get to the castle."

"We have to get to the other side first," Shiara pointed out. "That doesn't look very safe."

"The Caves of Chance aren't supposed to be safe," I said. "I'm surprised we haven't run into something a lot more dangerous than the quozzel."

"I suppose—Nightwitch!" Shiara shouted, a minute too late; the kitten was already halfway across the narrow path. Shiara sighed. "Well, now we *have* to go across."

Shiara insisted on going first, because Nightwitch was her cat. I didn't argue much. I went next, and the dragon came last. I had to hug the wall to keep from losing my balance and falling, which was hard to do with the key in one hand, Morwen's bundle in the other, and the sword under one arm. The dragon didn't have nearly as much difficulty as I did, even though it was a little too large for the ledge. It just dug its claws into the rock and kept coming.

When we finally made it to the other side, Shiara and I were covered with black rock dust. We took turns brushing each other off while Nightwitch sat far enough back to avoid getting any of it on her and the dragon looked superior. Evidently rock dust doesn't cling to dragon scales, which was very nice for the dragon but didn't do much to improve Shiara's temper.

"How much farther is it?" Shiara asked as we started off.

"I don't know," I said. "But it shouldn't take much longer."

"I hope not," said the dragon. "I don't like this tunnel."

"Why not?" Shiara asked.

"It isn't finished," the dragon said.

I looked around. The tunnel was a lot rougher than the others we'd come through, and there were rocks sticking out at odd angles from the walls and the roof and even the floor. Every now and then it narrowed into a crooked little passage. If the dragon had been much bigger, it wouldn't have been able to fit through sometimes. We still saw side passages once in a while, but they seemed smaller and farther apart than they had in the first part of the tunnel.

"It does look sort of incomplete," I said. "I think somebody—"

"Daystar, look out!" Shiara yelled. A large rock fell out of the ceiling, just missing my head. Along with the rock came a shower of pebbles that didn't miss.

I heard a creaking noise and felt more pebbles.

"Get back!" I shouted. I dropped Morwen's bundle and shoved Shiara. "Run!"

Shiara stumbled backward. Nightwitch yowled and made a tremendous leap right onto the dragon's nose. The dragon jerked in surprise, and Nightwitch made another jump and vanished into the darkness behind it. I heard more rumblings, and I shoved Shiara again, just as the roof came down on top of us.

When I woke up, it was very dark and I was lying face down on the tunnel floor. Somehow I'd managed to keep hold of the sword and the key. I could feel them, one halfway under me and the other digging into my left palm. I ached all over. I tried to move, but my legs were pinned under something heavy, and I couldn't drag them free. I pushed myself up a little and stared into the darkness. "Shiara? Nightwitch? Dragon?"

No one answered. They couldn't all have gotten caught in the cave-in. I'd been closest to the falling rocks, and only my legs were pinned. I started wishing I had the lamp, and then I remembered that the key glowed when I touched the Sword of the Sleeping King. I pushed up farther and felt around under me for the hilt, and something very moist and heavy hit me in the middle of my back.

I slammed back into the floor and almost lost consciousness again. The thing on my back bubbled, "The k-k-key! Let go, drop it, gug-give it to me!" Instinctively, I shoved my right hand farther under my chest, groping for the sword.

My fingers touched the hilt, and the key started to glow. It wasn't quite as good as the lamp, but at least I could see. I heard a muffled shriek, and the weight left my back very suddenly. An instant later, I saw the quozzel bending over my hand, and I tightened my grip on the key.

The quozzel bounced angrily. "You're still alive! I don't want you alive. I want that k-k-key. That's why I fixed the rocks."

I shook my head to clear it. "*You* made the tunnel cave in? Just to get a *key?*"

"Of c-c-c-course!" the quozzel spluttered. "I'm supposed to take c-care of it. I'll get it, too. All I need is m-m-more rocks."

The quozzel wobbled backward, toward the caved-in part of the tunnel. I rolled onto one elbow and looked back over my shoulder, trying to see what it was doing.

A medium-sized rock came crashing down beside me. The quozzel made an angry whistling noise. "H-hold still!"

"So you can drop rocks on me?" Out of the corner of my eye, I saw a long pile of something that seemed to end in a tangle of red hair. Shiara hadn't been buried under the rocks, then. Unfortunately, she didn't look like she would be able to help me with the quozzel anytime soon, and I still didn't know where Nightwitch or the dragon was. I twisted sideways, moving off the sword as much as I could with my legs pinned, and started working the Sword of the Sleeping King out of its sheath. It's not easy to draw a sword when you're lying on top of it, but I thought I might need it if the quozzel came any closer.

There was a sizzling noise from somewhere behind me, and a dozen or so rocks of assorted sizes came rolling down on top of me. Some of them hit places that had already been battered by the cave-in, and I yelled. The quozzel bubbled happily, and a few more rocks went by on one side. I shoved myself up on my hands as far as I could and yanked the sword the rest of the way out of the sheath and out from under me at the same time. I twisted around, just as two more large rocks came rolling down.

Awkwardly, I swung at the rocks with the flat of the sword, trying to deflect them a little. There was a bright flash as the sword hit them, and the rocks went flying toward the far wall of the tunnel. I heard a low humming sound that changed suddenly into a rumble, and the light in the cave went out. For some reason, I thought of the clearing where I'd said the spell at the Sword of the Sleeping King, when everything had gone dark and the voice had called me the Bearer of the Sword.

This time I didn't hear any voice, but the rumbling got louder and louder, and suddenly I realized that my legs were free. I curled them up under me, so I wouldn't be trapped again if the quozzel started another cave-in or something. The rumbling began to die down, and I heard faint shouts mixed in with it, and the bubbling noise that the quozzel made, and someone groaning. Then the rumbling stopped, and I could see again.

Carefully, because my legs felt kind of rubbery, I stood up and looked around. I could still hear the shouting; it sounded faint and far away, and after a moment it faded completely. Shiara was the person who had groaned. As I looked at her, she moved a little, and suddenly I felt a lot better about things generally. Then I heard squishing noises from in back of me, and I whirled.

Behind me, the tunnel was completely blocked by a sloping pile of rocks and dirt. At the base of the pile, where I had been trapped, was an empty space that looked as if something had sliced cleanly through the rocks and lifted them out of the way. Midway up the slope was the quozzel. It was wobbling hastily toward the tunnel floor. I pointed the Sword of the Sleeping King at it, and it stopped abruptly.

"Just a minute, you!" I said. "You have some questions to answer."

"I d-d-d-didn't know," said the quozzel. "I still don't. K-k-keep the k-key. Nice to m-m-meet you. Glug-gug-goodbye."

"Oh, no, you don't." I stepped in front of it, so that if it wobbled forward any more it would get stuck on my sword.

"I'm gug-gug-gug-going," said the quozzel. It seemed to be stammering a lot more than it had before. I found myself hoping it was even more nervous than it looked.

"You aren't going anywhere until you explain why you want this key so badly," I said. "And maybe not then. I don't think I ought to leave something as sneaky and treacherous as you running around loose." I tried to sound intimidating, even though I had no idea what I was going to do with the quozzel. I didn't think I could just kill it, and I certainly didn't want to bring it along with me, but I wasn't about to tell the quozzel any of that. After what it had tried to do, I thought it deserved to worry a little.

"Daystar?" Shiara's voice distracted me from the quozzel, which was bubbling and popping worriedly to itself. "Daystar, what happened?"

"The quozzel made the tunnel cave in," I said. "It was trying to kill me so it could get the key. Are you all right?"

"Of course I'm—yow!" said Shiara. I looked quickly around and saw her sitting up very carefully. She looked a little pale. "I think I broke my arm," she said.

"Can I do anything to help?" I asked.

"You can keep that stupid quozzel away from me!" Shiara said. "I'll be fine as long as I don't move much."

I didn't believe her, but I couldn't have done much to help anyway. I didn't know anything about setting broken arms, except that you can make things a lot worse if you don't know what you're doing. And if Shiara wanted me to keep watching the quozzel instead of trying to help her, she would probably get mad if I didn't. I doubted that that would be good for her arm, either. Besides, I didn't want the quozzel to get away and try dropping the roof on us again.

"Where's Nightwitch?" Shiara asked after a while. "And the dragon?"

"I don't know," I told her. "I haven't seen them since the tunnel fell in."

"You miserable little blob!"

I looked around in surprise and was very relieved to see Shiara glaring at the quozzel and not at me.

"If anything's happened to Nightwitch because of your stupid cave-in, I'll—I'll melt you into a puddle!" she went on.

"You'd better not try," the quozzel said, starting to bounce. "The w-w-wizard will gug-get you if you do!"

"What wizard?" I said.

The quozzel bubbled unhappily. "I can't tell you."

"Oh no?" Shiara said. She stood up slowly and came over beside me, holding her right arm carefully in her left one. "I guess I'd better just melt you, then, and save some time."

"No-n-*no!*" said the quozzel. Little ripples ran over it, and it seemed to shrink.

"Then you'd better tell us what wizard you're talking about," I said.

"The one who gug-gave me the key," the quozzel said unwillingly. "He told me to take care of it until he came back for it."

"How long ago was that?" I asked, ignoring Shiara, who was rubbing her bruises and muttering to herself.

"A long time," the quozzel said. "He never came back, so it's still m-m-my responsib-b-bility."

"Not if I melt you, it isn't," Shiara said, and the quozzel subsided very suddenly.

"What is it the key to?" I said. "And why did the wizard leave it here?"

"D-d-don't know," the quozzel said sullenly. "He said people would come look for it and try to take it. That's why he wanted m-m-me to look after it. You aren't supposed to take it. No one's supposed to take it b-b-but the wizard!"

"What did this wizard look like?" I asked, although I had an unpleasant feeling that I knew already.

The quozzel's description sounded a little like Antorell, but he was definitely older and he'd been wearing blue-and-gray robes instead of blue and brown. I was extremely relieved. Shiara didn't recognize the description, either, but she wasn't as relieved as I was.

"How do we know this stupid thing isn't lying?" she said. "I think we should—what's that?"

I could hear something far down the tunnel, but it echoed too much for me to be able to tell what it was. It seemed to be getting louder.

"I think something's coming," I said to Shiara; then, "You stay where you are!" to the quozzel, who had been trying to wobble a little closer to the bottom of the rock pile.

The quozzel froze again, and Shiara gave me a disgusted look. "I know *something's* coming, but what is it?"

I didn't answer. The noise came closer, and I saw a flickering light partway down the tunnel. I shifted position so I could watch the quozzel and still see some of the rest of the tunnel. The light got brighter, and a moment later a bunch of people came through one of the side passages. They were all short and sort of squashed looking, bigger than the elves we'd met, but considerably shorter than a normal person. Most of them were carrying picks or shovels or long, pointed iron poles, and a couple of them had torches. They seemed to be following something, but they were too far away and the light was too bad for me to be sure.

"Dwarves!" I said. They must have heard the echo, because two of them looked up and saw us. One of them shouted something, but I couldn't make out the words.

"Terrific!" Shiara muttered as they started in our direction. "What'd you have to do that for?"

"They'd have seen us anyway," I said. "I mean, we'd be sort of difficult to miss, with the key lighting up the tunnel like this. And maybe they'll help us. Dwarves do, sometimes; Mother had me study a whole lot of examples two years ago, after the prince came through looking for the glass coffin."

"I thought princes looked for glass *shoes*, not coffins," Shiara said. She squinted into the dark part of the tunnel between us and the dwarves. "They're coming this way. What's that in front of them?"

I didn't have to answer, because a second later Nightwitch came bounding out of the darkness with her tail held very high. She looked extremely proud of herself. She went straight to Shiara and started rubbing against her legs and purring.

"I'm glad to see you, too," Shiara said. She started to bend over and winced. "Sorry, kitten; you'll have to wait to get petted until somebody does something about this stupid arm."

Nightwitch stopped rubbing and looked up. "Mmrew?"

"Well, I said I was sorry," Shiara said. "I didn't *ask* to break it."

The dwarves had reached the edge of the key's glow, and the whole tunnel was lit up by their torches. It made things a lot more cheerful, as well as letting me get a good look at the dwarves. There were seven of them, five males and two females, all carrying shovels and picks. I could see the dragon in back of the dwarves, looking almost as smug as Nightwitch had.

"Look!" it said when it got close enough to talk without shouting. "I found a whole lot of dwarves!"

"I see that," I said. I bowed to the dwarves as well as I could while trying to watch the quozzel at the same time. "My name is Daystar, and that's Shiara. We're very pleased to meet you."

"They're going to dig through the part of the tunnel that came down," the dragon said.

"Hold on just a minute!" one of the dwarves said. "I didn't say I'd help. Not exactly. I said I'd look at this cave-in of yours."

"Me too," said another. "Proper mess it looks."

"Not natural," said a female dwarf. She looked at Shiara and me suspiciously.

"How do you know?" Shiara said belligerently.

"We made this tunnel," still another dwarf said. "And dwarf-made tunnels don't just fall in."

"Not ever," agreed the first one.

"Of course not," I said. "The quozzel made the tunnel cave in. It was trying to stop us from getting out of the Caves of Chance."

"The quozzel?" the dragon said, looking interested. "That dessert thing is back again?"

"You can't eat it until we find out if it knows anything else," I said. "Besides, you had plenty of lunch."

The dragon sighed. "I suppose so. All right, I'll wait."

I looked at the dwarves. "We'd be very much obliged to you if you would help us get through this, or show us a way around it, or something," I said.

"Now, why should we do that?" one of them said.

"I don't see any reason," said another.

"Lot of work for nothing," added a third.

"And I don't like dragons!" said a voice from the middle of the group. The dragon glared, but it couldn't pick out the dwarf who'd spoken.

"Could you at least set Shiara's arm?" I asked.

One of the female dwarves started to reply, but she was cut off by a yell from Shiara. "Daystar! Behind you!"

I raised the sword and spun around just as the quozzel bunched itself together and jumped at me. It came flying through the air, and I ducked. Something dark and purple shot out of it toward me, and I slashed at it with the sword. I got most of the purple stuff and part of the quozzel as well. I heard it shriek, and then it had landed and launched itself again, straight for the wall of the tunnel.

"I'll kill all of you!" it whistled angrily. "Key stealers! Cannibals! I'll kill you d-d-dead!"

I lunged for it, but I was too late. The quozzel hit the tunnel wall, and instead of bouncing, it vanished into the rock like water being absorbed by a sponge, only faster. An instant later a shower of rocks fell out of the roof of the tunnel, and I heard the walls creaking ominously.

"Run!" I yelled. I started to follow my own advice but saw a large rock shifting in the wall of the tunnel just above Shiara's head. I shouted again and swung the sword at it, hoping it would be deflected like the other rocks the quozzel had tried to drop on me.

The flat of the sword hit the rock, and everything seemed to slow down suddenly. There was a lot of creaking, and the top of the tunnel started to sag, as if it were trying to fall in again but couldn't quite manage it. The sword got very heavy, and then there was an angry-sounding rumble and the whole tunnel shook. The rock that had been heading for Shiara went bouncing off the opposite wall of the tunnel, and all the creaking and rumbling stopped very abruptly.

I didn't move for several seconds at least. I didn't think the quozzel would give up this easily. Then I saw a thin trickle of dark purple stuff dripping down the wall of the tunnel where the quozzel had disappeared. I watched it for a minute or two and decided that we probably didn't have to worry about the quozzel anymore. I looked at Shiara.

"Are you all right?"

"That's a stupid question," Shiara said. "My arm is broken!"

"I mean, you didn't get any more hurt than you were already, did you?"

"No," she said. She looked at me. "Thanks."

I was so surprised that I couldn't think of anything to say for at least a minute.

"Um, you're welcome," I said finally. I realized suddenly that my sword still had some wet purple stuff on it from hitting the quozzel, and I started digging in my pocket for my handkerchief so I could wipe off the sword.

I couldn't find it. I sighed. It had probably fallen out of my pocket somewhere on the trip through the caves. I didn't really mind losing it, except that now I didn't have anything to get the purple goo off my sword with. I turned to the dwarves. "Excuse me, but do any of you—"

I stopped. The dwarves were standing in a tight group, and all seven of them were staring at the sword.

"Now, why didn't you think to mention you had that?" one of them said.

*In Which They Get out of the Caves and into
Even More Trouble*

Shiara and I looked at the dwarves. "He's been
holding it since before you got here!" Shiara
said finally. "Why should he have mentioned
it?"

"It would have saved a lot of bother," one of the female dwarves said in an aggrieved tone.

"Time, too," said another.

"Inconsiderate, I call it."

"Well, not inconsiderate, exactly," said one of the
male dwarves, eyeing the dragon. "A little thoughtless,
maybe."

"Thoughtless?" The dragon looked puzzled.
"Why? What difference does it make if Daystar has a
sword?"

"*A* sword is one thing. *That* sword is something else
again."

"Someone should have told us."

"Someone should *definitely* have told us."

"After all, we aren't elves."

"Of course you're not elves," the dragon said.

"Anyone can see that! What does that have to do with Daystar's sword?"

"It's not his sword!" one of the dwarves objected. "It's the King's!"

"And elves can recognize it just by *looking* at it," a female dwarf said in a resentful tone.

"So can some other people," said another darkly.

"But not dwarves."

"Unless we get a good look at it, of course. Which we couldn't, because of the light, not to mention the fact that you were standing there talking and distracting our attention."

"Which is why you should have mentioned it," a dwarf in the back finished triumphantly.

"I didn't mention it because there seem to be a lot of people who want it," I said. "One of them is a wizard."

About six of the dwarves started talking so fast it was hard to tell whether they were all speaking at the same time or whether they went one after another.

"Of course there are a lot of people who want it!"

"*Particularly* wizards."

"It *is* the King's sword, isn't it?"

"Maybe it isn't; he hasn't said."

"It has to be the King's sword, silly. There aren't any other swords that the earth obeys."

"What about Delvan's blade?"

"That's not a sword, it's an ax."

"And the earth doesn't *obey* it, it just shakes a lot."

"So this has to be the King's sword."

"Wait a minute!" I said. "What do you know about my sword?"

"It's the *King's* sword," one of the dwarves said indignantly. Another dwarf shushed him, and a dwarf near the front of the crowd stepped forward and bowed.

"We follow the sword," she said, as if it explained everything.

The other dwarves all smiled and nodded. I sighed and gave up. Either none of them really knew anything else, or they knew and weren't going to tell me, and I didn't think it mattered much which it was. "If you aren't going to tell me about my sword, could one of you do something about Shiara's arm?" I asked. "And after that, we'll be going."

"Going where?" the dragon said.

Some of the dwarves jumped. Evidently they'd forgotten the dragon was behind them. I was surprised; if a dragon were standing behind me, I certainly wouldn't forget it was there.

"We have to find another way out of the Caves of Chance," I told the dragon. "I don't really think we can dig through this one."

"That will not be necessary," said the dwarf closest to me. "Had we known you were the Bearer of the Sword, we would not have objected to your request."

"Not at all," said the dwarf next to him. She turned and waved at the others. "Lord Daystar requires this tunnel cleared. Begin!"

I stood and stared while the dwarves all grabbed their picks and shovels and things and started toward the rocks that were blocking the tunnel. In a few minutes they were all digging furiously—except for one, who came over to Shiara and bowed.

"I am Darlbrin," he announced.

"That's nice," Shiara said sarcastically. I sighed, but I didn't say anything. You can't really expect a fire-witch with a broken arm to be particularly polite.

Darlbrin didn't seem to notice. "I have some skill at mending things," he said, and bowed again. "If you will permit it, I would like to examine your arm." He looked at Shiara a shade anxiously and added, "To see if I can mend it."

Shiara rolled her eyes, but she walked over to the edge of the tunnel and sat down so the dwarf could see better. Nightwitch followed, alternately purring reassuringly and meowing anxiously.

I watched for a minute or two, then turned away. I couldn't do anything to help, and I wanted to think.

I didn't get the chance. As soon as I turned, the dragon stuck its head over a couple of dwarves and said, "I didn't know you were a lord. Why didn't you tell me?"

"Because I'm not a lord!" I said. I think I sounded a little desperate, and I know I felt desperate. I didn't have the slightest idea what was going on, except that it had something to do with my sword. *Everything* seemed to have something to do with my sword. I was getting tired of it, and more than a little worried.

"Well, if you aren't a lord, why did they call you one?"

"Because he has the King's sword," said a dwarf who was walking under the dragon's chin with a boulder more than half as big as he was. The dragon pulled its head back far enough to eye the dwarf, who ignored it and kept walking.

"I really wish you'd explain a little more," I yelled after the dwarf, and then I thought of something. "Why did you call me the Bearer of the Sword?"

"I didn't call you anything," the dwarf said without stopping. "That was Cottlestone." He set the boulder down and headed back toward the pile of rocks, which was beginning to look smaller already.

"Excuse me," I said loudly, in the general direction of the crowd of dwarves, "but would one of you tell me which of you is Cottlestone? I'd like to talk to him, please."

"Cottlestone!" shouted half a dozen voices.

For a minute I thought the roof was going to cave in again, but all that actually happened was that one of the dwarves stepped out of the crowd and bowed to me. He looked as if he really meant it, not as if he were just being polite.

"Don't do that," I said.

"As you wish," the dwarf said, bowing again. "What do you want to know from me?"

"Why did you call me the Bearer of the Sword?"

Cottlestone looked surprised. "It's obvious. When the Bearer of the Sword holds the King's sword, the earth obeys it. So when you held up the sword and the earth obeyed, we knew you were the Bearer of the Sword."

"Oh." I thought for a moment. "Have you ever heard of the Holder of the Sword? Or the Wielder of the Sword?"

"Who?"

"Never mind," I said. "How does someone get to be the Bearer of the Sword?"

"No one knows," Cottlestone said, looking at me curiously.

"Oh," I said again. I was trying to think of something else to ask when there was a shout from the top of the caved-in section of the tunnel. Cottlestone bowed again. "If you will excuse me, I think they've gotten through to the other side. I ought to go help. It's my job."

"All right," I said uncomfortably. Cottlestone turned away, and I watched him melt into the crowd of dwarves. I wasn't sure what I'd found out, except that I didn't like people bowing to me. I found myself hoping that the rest of the dwarves wouldn't imitate Cottlestone.

"Did he say they're almost finished?" asked Shiara from behind me. "Wonderful! I can't wait to get out of here."

I turned. Shiara was standing, holding Nightwitch in the crook of her left arm. Her right arm was covered from her fingers almost to her shoulder in something smooth and gray and shiny. She looked a little white, but that might have been the torch light. "Well, what are you staring at?" she demanded.

"I wasn't staring," I said. "I was just checking to see if you were all right."

Darlbrin stepped up beside Shiara and bowed. "Not quite all right. But not bad, not bad at all."

"I wouldn't call a broken arm 'not bad,'" Shiara said sourly.

"Oh, I didn't mean that!" Darlbrin said hastily. "I was referring to the mending."

"I'm sure you did a very good job," I told him. "And I really appreciate it."

"I suppose I do, too," Shiara mumbled. "Thanks."

"It isn't really mended yet, you know," Darlbrin said with a touch of anxiety. "People aren't as easy to fix as ax handles. It'll be a month before you can take the sheath off."

"Yes, I know. I've had a broken arm before." Shiara scowled at the sheath.

"Then you're very welcome!" The dwarf beamed. "Happy to be of service!"

Shiara snorted, but quietly. Darlbrin didn't notice. He bowed to each of us and went off to help the rest of the dwarves finish clearing the tunnel. I looked at Shiara. "I didn't know you'd broken your arm before."

"That's because I didn't tell you about it," Shiara said. She looked at me for a minute, then sighed. "I was stealing apples from the Prince's gardens and fell out of the tree, all right?"

"Oh. What prince, and why were you taking his apples?"

"The Prince of the Ruby Throne," Shiara said after a minute. "He had a house and garden just outside town, and he never picked any of the apples. He just left them to rot. And I was hungry. So I sneaked over the wall and climbed the tree, but there was a big snake in it, with wings. So I fell out of the tree and broke my arm, and the snake went away."

"Shiara," I said, and stopped. She obviously had no idea what she had almost done. I sighed and changed what I was going to say. "Shiara, the Prince of the Ruby Throne raises magic apples. All kinds of people have been trying to steal them for years and years, but he's a very powerful sorcerer, and there are hundreds of spells protecting his gardens."

"That must be why he was so upset," Shiara said in a tone of sudden enlightenment. "I'm pretty sure he was the one who told the Society of Wizards about me. I *thought* it was a lot of fuss to make about a few apples."

I looked at her for a minute. "I don't want to be nosy or anything, but I'd really appreciate knowing if there's anyone *else* who's mad at you."

"I don't think so," Shiara said, frowning.

"Good. I don't think I want any more people chasing us. Particularly people with powerful magic. It wouldn't be so bad if you could use your fire magic."

"She can!" said the dragon, and Shiara and I both jumped and turned around. "She burned the dragonsbane, and she can make her hair burn."

"When did *you* see Shiara's hair burning?" I asked. The only time I'd ever seen Shiara's hair on fire was when she'd gotten mad at me right after we'd met, and the dragon hadn't been there then.

"Just a few minutes ago," the dragon said. "You were fighting that dessert thing, so you might not have noticed."

I looked at Shiara, and she blushed. "I was trying to do something to the quozzel. I thought it would work because it worked on the dragonsbane."

"It worked on the dragonsbane," I repeated slowly. "And that first wizard, the one who made a water monster out of the stream—you did something to that monster, too. That's at least twice that you've made your fire magic work properly. Can you think of any others? Maybe we can figure out why it happens."

"She used it at the invisible castle," the dragon offered. "The one where that *other* fire-witch lived."

"I did not!" Shiara said. "I didn't have time. We ran into the castle, and she came out, and *bang!* I was a statue."

The dragon sat back, looking smug. "You said you wanted to know what the castle was, and then you did. That's fire magic, isn't it?"

"I suppose it is," Shiara said slowly.

"Then that's three," I said. "Can you think of any more? Before you came to the Enchanted Forest, for instance?"

Shiara frowned and was silent. "No," she said finally in a very positive tone. "Those are the only times I've ever gotten my magic to do what I wanted it to, ever."

"So it's only been happening since you came to the Enchanted Forest," I said.

"And met you and got bitten by that stupid sword," Shiara added, and stopped. We looked at each other for a minute.

"Not again!" I said. I thought for a minute. "It can't be the sword alone, or you would have been able to do something to the quozzel. There has to be something else, too."

"Like what?"

"I don't know. Did you do anything differently when it worked?"

"No."

"Well, then did you do anything differently right

before it worked?" I said. "There has to be some—" I stopped, remembering. "Oh," I said.

"What is it?"

"I think I know what makes your magic work." I didn't think Shiara was going to like it much, but I couldn't just keep quiet about it. "I think you have to be polite to people."

"That's *stupid!*"

"It makes sense," I said. "You apologized to me after we got out of the hedge, and then when the first wizard came along your magic worked against the snake thing. You were nice to the Princess because you felt sorry for her, and right after that you knew about the invisible castle. And you said thanks to Suz and apologized to Telemain, and then you made the dragonsbane burn."

"But that other fire-witch wasn't polite!" Shiara objected.

"I didn't say *all* fire-witches have to be polite to people before their magic will work," I said. "I only said *your* magic works that way. And I'm not positive. I mean, it could be something else."

"Well, I'm not going to go around being nice to people just so I can do magic!"

"I don't think it would work, anyway," I said unhappily. "I mean, I don't think you can just say things. I think you have to really mean them. You meant it when you apologized to me, and when you were nice to the Princess, and when you were talking to Telemain."

"Oh, great," Shiara said disgustedly. "I bet this is all that stupid sword's fault." She glared at me for an instant, then turned her back.

I sighed.

"Excuse me, Lord Daystar," said a voice by my elbow. I looked down, and the dwarf bowed.

"Don't *do* that," I said.

"Certainly, my lord," she said, and started to bow again, then stopped and looked confused. "The tunnel is clear. You may continue your journey whenever you wish."

I looked around. The pile of rocks that had been blocking the tunnel was nearly gone. A few boulders were left along the sides, but there was plenty of room to walk through, even for the dragon. "Thank you very much," I said. "But I really ought to tell you: I'm not a lord."

The dwarf smiled tolerantly. "Of course not, my lord. Is there anything else we can do for you?"

"I'd appreciate it if we could borrow one of your torches," I said. "Our lamp got lost in the cave-in."

"We would be pleased to offer you a torch," the dwarf said. "You can leave it by the exit, and someone will get it later. The exit isn't far."

We gathered up what we could find of Morwen's bundles, and the dwarves did some more bowing. One of them handed Shiara a torch. She grumbled a little because she had to put Nightwitch down in order to take it, but she was the only one of us who could carry it. I had the sword in one hand and the key in the other, and the dragon couldn't hold a torch. Fortunately, Nightwitch didn't seem to mind walking. We thanked the dwarves and said goodbye, and they all bowed again, and finally we started off.

The tunnel started slanting upward almost as soon as we were past the cave-in, and shortly after that we stopped seeing side passages. Eventually we came to a wide flight of stairs that curled around and around until all of us were dizzy. Just when I didn't think I could climb anymore, the stairs ended against a hard, rocky surface, like a trapdoor made of stone.

I shoved against it, but it didn't budge. "It's too heavy."

"Really?" said the dragon. "It doesn't look so bad."

I looked down at the dragon, who was last on the stairs because neither Shiara nor I had wanted to be behind it if it slipped. "It probably isn't too heavy for you. Why don't you try it?"

The dragon agreed, and Shiara and I squashed ourselves against the side of the stairs so it could climb past us. There were a couple of minutes' worth of grunts, and the dragon's tail whipped back and forth, which made Shiara and me retreat farther down the stairs. Finally there was a loud noise like extremely rusty hinges, and the dragon started moving upward. A moment later, it stopped. "Uh-oh," it said.

"What's the matter?" Shiara called.

The dragon didn't answer, but it moved out of the way so we could climb up. Shiara and I got to the head of the stairs at almost the same time and looked around.

We were standing at the top of a small rise. The sun was starting to set, but there was still enough light to see the castle clearly. It was quite close, not more than a few minutes' walk from where I was, and it fascinated me. At first, I thought it was made of something shimmery, like mother-of-pearl; then I realized that it wasn't the castle that was shimmering, it was something around the castle, like a giant soap bubble. I was still trying to figure out what it was when Shiara poked me, and I looked down.

There were approximately two hundred dragons sitting on the ground around the little hill we were standing on. Watching us.

18

*In Which the King of the Dragons Does Some
Explaining*

I swallowed hard, and for a moment I wished I
were wearing my sword instead of carrying it
under my arm. Every dragon from inside the
Enchanted Forest had to be there, and quite a
few from the Mountains of Morning as well. They were
spread out in all directions, so I couldn't even see the
ground. The forest encircled the castle at a distance, and
there seemed to be something *wrong* about the trees. I
couldn't tell what, though, and besides, I had other
things to worry about right then. Two hundred dragons,
for instance.

I stepped forward and bowed carefully in all directions. One of the first things Mother taught me about
dragons was that they expect a new arrival to make the
first move. They always allow you one chance to convince them that you're too polite or too important to
eat. I didn't think I could convince two hundred dragons that I was particularly important, especially since I
didn't believe it myself, so I was going to have to rely on
being polite. I took a deep breath.

"Sirs and madams, I apologize most profoundly for intruding upon you in this fashion, and I hope we have not inconvenienced you in any way," I said, trying not to shout while still talking loudly enough for all the dragons to hear. "Nevertheless, I offer you greetings in the name of myself and my companions, and I wish you good fortune in whatever endeavors are most important to you."

The dragons stirred briefly, then settled back again. After a moment, an old gray-green male slid forward. "We greet you and wish you well," he said. "May we know your names?"

I bowed again, the half bow of respect for a dragon of great age and uncertain status. "I thank you for your greeting," I said. "I am called Daystar, and my companions are Shiara and Nightwitch. This young dragon has graciously accompanied us for part of our journey." Since some of them presumably knew the little dragon already, I didn't have to introduce it.

I didn't ask for the dragons' names. It's perfectly acceptable not to, and I didn't feel like standing there through two hundred introductions, especially since the dragons would expect me to remember them all.

"Well met, Daystar," the old dragon rumbled. "We've been expecting you since early this afternoon."

"I'm sorry if I kept you waiting," I said. "We had problems with some wizards, and a cave-in, and a quozzel, and I didn't really know you were all here."

"Of course not. Telemain only told Kazul yesterday that you were coming. Silly way to do things, making everyone gather in such a hurry." He looked at me for a minute, then nodded approvingly. "Well, come along; no sense wasting any more time. You might as well bring the girl and the cat, too. This way."

Our dragon lifted its head. "What about me?" It looked much smaller next to the full-grown dragons all around us, and it sounded considerably younger as well.

"*You* had better keep quiet," the older dragon said indulgently. "You're in quite a bit of trouble already. I wouldn't make it worse if I were you."

"I don't have to keep quiet!" our dragon said. "I found a princess, even if I did decide not to keep her, and I fought a knight and bit a wizard. I can talk if I want to!"

The crowd of dragons shifted again, very slightly. Shiara shivered and held Nightwitch closer. I thought about wiping my hands on my tunic, but I didn't want to look too nervous. The older dragon just stood and stared at our dragon, which finally shook its head and settled back, watching the crowd below us with a sulky expression.

The old dragon smiled slightly. "What do you think?" he asked the crowd of dragons behind him.

All of the dragons roared at once. I couldn't tell what they were saying, or even if they were saying anything, but the old dragon nodded again and looked at the little dragon. "You'll get your wish, then. Well, don't just stand there."

I nodded and stepped forward as the old dragon turned. Shiara followed behind me, very closely, and our dragon came behind her.

"Where are we going?" Shiara whispered to me.

The old dragon looked back over his shoulder, and his eyes glinted with amusement. "You're going to see Kazul."

"Oh," Shiara said. We stepped down from the little hill, and there was a loud clattering and rumbling as the dragons moved out of our way. I stopped short in shock.

The ground around the hill was dry and brown and bare. It looked even worse to me than it would have normally because I'd spent several days looking at the rich green moss in the Enchanted Forest and the contrast was striking. Then I remembered that we were still *in* the Enchanted Forest, and I started being worried as well as shocked. I knew from experience how fast the moss grew and how hard it was to clear off even a small strip of ground. I didn't like to think about what had stripped the moss from the area around the castle.

Shiara poked me, and I moved forward again. Fortunately, the dragon ahead of us hadn't noticed my pause. A few of the ones at the edge of the crowd had, but they seemed more amused than anything. I walked a little faster, trying to ignore the large shapes on either side of me. With two hundred dragons around, I could waste a lot of time worrying if I wasn't careful.

The old dragon led us toward the castle. As we got closer, I could see that there were two shimmerings in the air around the castle, one a few feet inside the other. The outer one looked like a shifting green-and-silver veil, very thin and transparent. The inner one seemed to be a pale golden glow, but I couldn't be sure because the one on the outside kept shifting around, interfering with my seeing the inner one clearly. After a few minutes, I gave up on trying to look *at* the shimmerings and tried looking *through* them instead.

The shimmerings didn't get in the way at all, so I could see quite a bit of the castle. There was no wall around it, only the shimmerings and a water-filled moat just inside them. The castle itself was a wonderful, rambling-looking place, with six towers of various sizes, large square windows, and four balconies. I could see several stairways running up to oddly shaped doors or around the outsides of towers, and a lot of walls that seemed to be there just to confuse people. I was so busy studying the castle and the shimmerings that I almost didn't notice when the old dragon stopped. I was lucky not to step on his tail.

We were about halfway around the castle, and there seemed to be fewer dragons around. I was trying to guess which one was Kazul when the old dragon who had been leading us stepped a little to one side and bobbed his head respectfully.

"King Kazul, these are the travelers who wish to see you. That one's Daystar, the other one's Shiara, and the cat is Nightwitch."

Right away I bowed very deeply, and so did Shiara. I was relieved. I hadn't been completely sure Shiara would do any of the things I'd suggested. As I straightened up, I got my first look at Kazul.

Even lying on the ground, she looked large for a dragon. Her scales were just beginning to turn gray around the edges, which surprised me; I'd expected someone older. Her eyes were hypnotic, green-gold ovals. She was the most dangerous-looking dragon I'd ever seen.

Kazul smiled broadly. Dragons have a *lot* of teeth.

"So," she said, "you are the people Telemain sent through the Caves of Chance, and you have the Sword of the Sleeping King."

"Yes, Your Majesty," I said. I took the sword out from under my arm and held it up so she could see it better. "Mother gave it to me a few days ago, and I was told you would want to know about it."

"Ahhhhhh." As she looked at the sword, Kazul's eyes glowed. Literally. The light from them was a little like firelight, except it didn't flicker. After a minute, she transferred her gaze to me. "And you got it here safely. Well done, Cimorene's son."

"Thank you, Your Majesty," I said. "You know my mother?"

Kazul smiled again. "Cimorene was the best princess I ever had."

Shiara choked, and my jaw dropped.

The little dragon said, "So *that's* how she knew dragon magic!" in a pleased tone.

I closed my mouth, swallowed hard, and bowed to Kazul. "Excuse me, Your Majesty. I was, um, startled. Mother is a princess?"

"She certainly was once," Kazul said. She looked at the sword again. "I'm glad she managed to keep it safe. We didn't have a lot of choice at the time, but it's still worrying to have to take a risk like that."

I wasn't certain what to say. Kazul didn't seem to be

talking to me, but it isn't a good idea to ignore a dragon. So, just to be safe, I bowed again.

Kazul looked up from the sword. "You needn't be quite so formal. I have a lot tell you, and the conversation will go faster if you're not so stiff."

Before I could reply, Kazul turned toward the old dragon, who was still standing beside me. "It will be tomorrow morning. Let everyone know."

The old dragon nodded and left. Kazul looked back at us. "Come with me." She started to rise.

"What about me?" the little dragon demanded.

Kazul sighed. "Yes, you may come, too." She stood, which made her look twice as big as she had before, and started walking. Shiara and I looked at each other, then followed.

By this time the sun was completely down, but there was still enough light in the sky to see where we were going. Kazul led us a little farther around the castle, then turned away from it. As we walked along, the other dragons slid out of the way for Kazul and bowed their heads respectfully. Then Shiara and I walked by and bowed respectfully to the dragons. It kept us too busy to see much of where we were going.

Kazul led us to what looked like a jumbled pile of rocks a little way from the castle. There was a dark opening at one side of the pile, and Kazul went right in. Shiara and the little dragon and Nightwitch and I followed.

It was very dark inside, almost as black as the Caves of Chance. I stopped immediately, since I didn't want to step on Kazul's tail in the dark or run into her accidentally. Shiara bumped into me, squeezing Nightwitch between us. Nightwitch said, "Mrowww!" in a complaining tone, and Kazul's voice came out of the darkness.

"I suppose you human people need some light."

"Only if it won't be inconvenient," I said.

"Not at all," Kazul replied, and added about five hissing words.

Silvery light sprang up all around us. I squinted, and then I blinked. The inside of the pile of rocks looked a lot like a cave. I looked for the source of the light and realized that the light was coming from the rocks.

That shook me. Dragons don't usually do magic casually. In particular, the King of the Dragons wouldn't normally work a spell just for a visitor's convenience. I looked at Kazul, wondering exactly what was going on.

"Sit down," said Kazul, nodding toward a row of rocks. We did. The little dragon sat down by the entrance, looking half-sulky and half-defiant. Kazul ignored it.

"I think you had better tell me your story first," she said, looking at me intently. "Start at the beginning, when Cimorene gave you the sword."

"I'm sorry," I said. "I'll start with the sword if you want me to, but I think the beginning is the wizard."

"Wizard?"

"His name's Antorell, and he came to our cottage the day before Mother gave me the sword. Mother melted him."

"Oh, him." Kazul shook her head. "Sounds like he

hasn't learned anything since the last time he tangled with Cimorene. Yes, start with him, by all means."

So I told Kazul everything that had happened to me since Antorell had walked up to our cottage and knocked the door in. It took a long time—especially the part after Shiara and I met the little dragon, because then the dragon kept adding things. Finally, Kazul told it to either be quiet or go away. It looked terribly offended, but it quit talking.

Kazul didn't ask any questions at all. Once, when I mentioned finding the key in the Caves of Chance, she made a noise that sounded like an astonished snort, but she apologized for interrupting and told me to go on. I did, once I got over the shock of having the King of the Dragons apologize to me.

When I finished, there was silence for a minute or two. Then Kazul stirred. "So. You have accomplished a great deal in a short time, Daystar."

"It doesn't seem like much to me," I said.

"A great deal," Kazul repeated. She sounded as if she were talking to herself.

Shiara shifted restlessly. "Are you going to explain about Daystar's sword?"

"Shiara!" I said, horrified. *Nobody* talks to the King of the Dragons in that tone of voice.

Except Shiara. "No," said Kazul. "Or at least, I'm not going to tell you as much as you want to know. The Society of Wizards has more than a hundred spells hunting for that sword right now, and all of them depend on finding someone who knows what he's carrying.

Fortunately, wizards' magic can't detect the sword itself. If Daystar finds out too much about that sword, we'll be up to our wings in wizards in no time. I don't want that to happen yet."

"I don't like wizards," the little dragon said suddenly. "They make me sneeze."

Kazul's head turned and she eyed the little dragon for a minute. "I think it is time you made yourself useful," she said at last. "Go find Marchak and tell him to bring us dinner. Then go back to your teacher and apologize for running off, and after that you can start getting ready for tomorrow."

"What happens tomorrow?" the little dragon said suspiciously.

"We have a war," Kazul said. "Which you *might* live through, if you're ready for it. So go!"

"Yes, ma'am!" The little dragon disappeared out the door of the cave.

Kazul looked after it for a minute, then shook her head. "That is undoubtedly the most irritating grandchild I have."

"Who are you going to be—'*Grandchild?*'" said Shiara.

"Yes, of course." Kazul looked mildly surprised. "It's an annoying youngster, but precocious children frequently are. I'm hoping it will grow out of it."

"Oh." Shiara stared out the entrance thoughtfully.

"I enjoyed its company, most of the time," I said honestly.

"I'm glad," Kazul said.

After another minute, I went on, "Um, if you

wouldn't mind telling us, I'm sort of curious about whom you expect to be fighting tomorrow." I was also wondering whether Kazul thought Shiara and I were going to be included in this. I wasn't particularly anxious to get involved in a war between dragons.

Kazul smiled; I got the feeling she knew what I was thinking. "Wizards," she said. "There will be a few elves, of course, and maybe some ogres and trolls, but mostly we'll be fighting wizards."

"Oh. Of course." I was even less interested in getting involved in a war between dragons and wizards. Dragons alone might overlook Shiara and Nightwitch and me, but wizards certainly wouldn't.

"I'm afraid you already are involved," Kazul said.

"Because of the sword?" Shiara asked while I tried to remember whether I'd said anything out loud about not wanting to get involved.

"Yes," said Kazul. "The sword and other things. It's a long story. I hope you're comfortable."

We both nodded, and Kazul smiled again. "Well, then. There are two types of magic in the world: the kind you're born with, and the kind you get from something else. Dragons"—Kazul looked smug—"elves, unicorns, and fire-witches are born with magic. Ordinary witches and magicians get their magic from objects or from rituals involving things that have magic, which works quite well and doesn't upset things.

"Wizards, on the other hand, get their magic from everything around them that happens to have magic. Those staffs of theirs absorb little bits of it constantly, and the suction gets worse every time a wizard stores a new spell in his staff. That, by the way, is why dragons are allergic to wizards. Whenever those staffs get near us, they start trying to soak up some of our magic and we start sneezing."

"Telemain said something like that," I said.

Kazul nodded. "Wizards' staffs create other problems, too."

"You mean those stupid wizards have been grabbing my magic every time they come near me?" Shiara said indignantly.

"Not yours," Kazul said. "Wizards can't use firewitches' magic; it's too different. Their staffs explode if they try."

"Good!" Shiara's face grew thoughtful. "I wonder if I could learn to do that on purpose?"

Kazul looked as if she agreed with Shiara. "Wizards get most of their magic from the Enchanted Forest, but if they absorb too much magic in any one place, things die."

"The moss!" I said. "That's why it turns brown when a wizard's staff touches it."

"Yes," said Kazul. "The King of the Enchanted Forest had a way of reversing the process, taking magic out of a wizard's staff and putting it back in the forest, so wizards weren't too much of a problem until about seventeen years ago. The fellow who was Head Wizard then decided he was tired of stealing magic in bits, so he stole the tool that the King used to keep wizards from swiping magic in large chunks."

"The sword?" I said. "Telemain said it was supposed to be used on wizards."

"Telemain talks too much," Kazul said a little sourly. "Almost as soon as they had the sword, the wizards attacked the castle. They thought that without the sword the King would be easy to take care of. They forgot that the King of the Enchanted Forest has friends." She smiled fiercely. I felt almost sorry for the wizards.

"They wound up in a full-fledged battle, and while we were all fighting, the sword got stolen again. A few wizards managed to get inside the castle, but without the sword they couldn't actually kill the King. So they found some way of keeping him out of action while they hunted for the sword."

"They put the King to sleep?" I said doubtfully. It sounded a bit unlikely. Sleeping spells are very effective on guards and princesses, and even a kingdom now and then, but they can't usually do much against a good magician. And whatever else he was, the King of the Enchanted Forest had to be a master magician.

"We don't know exactly what they did," Kazul admitted. "We know the King isn't dead, because the Enchanted Forest reacts very strongly when a King dies. We know they did something, though, because the seal they have around the castle wouldn't hold the King in by itself."

"You mean those shimmerings around the castle?" I said.

"The outer one is ours," Kazul said with a grim smile. "The wizards put up a spell to keep everyone but themselves out of the castle, so we put up one to keep the wizards out. Without the sword, there wasn't anything more we could do."

"Then how did Daystar's mother get hold of the sword?" Shiara asked.

Kazul smiled again. "Cimorene was the one who stole it back from the wizards in the first place. They've been trying to get hold of it again ever since. They'll show up as soon as we break through their barrier tomorrow, but by then we should be ready for them."

"Uh, you expect Shiara and me to help you fight wizards?" I said.

"Of course not," Kazul replied. "Shiara may help us if she wishes, but you, Daystar, will be going into the castle to break whatever spell the wizards put on the King seventeen years ago."

In Which the Battle Begins

That took some explanation. What Kazul meant was, the dragons would lower the barrier they had put up around the castle. Then I would draw the Sword of the Sleeping King and put it into the wizards' barrier, which, according to Kazul, would bring it down. The wizards would know immediately that something was happening, and they would start trying to get to the castle. The dragons and their various allies would hold off the wizards and whoever they brought to help them while I ran into the castle, found the King, and broke the spell.

I didn't like the sound of it at all, but I couldn't say much. After all, Mother had given me the sword, and I was pretty sure this was what she'd wanted me to do with it. Besides, Kazul seemed to think I was the only one who could use the sword to break the spell. And how do you tell the King of the Dragons that you won't do something she wants you to do?

Shiara, on the other hand, had a lot to say. She

thought it would be stupid for me to go into the castle by myself. Kazul asked if she was volunteering, and Shiara said that she wasn't going to be left out just when things were getting interesting. Kazul pointed out that Shiara's arm was broken, and Shiara told her that being inside the castle with me sounded safer than being outside with a lot of wizards and dragons fighting.

Finally Kazul said Shiara could go with me if she wanted to. Shiara said, Good, and were the dragons going to be able to keep all of the wizards out of the castle, or were some of them going to sneak in after us? They kept on like that for quite a while. I was very glad when a middle-sized dragon arrived with dinner and interrupted. I couldn't see why Kazul was being so patient with Shiara, and I was getting worried that her patience wouldn't last much longer.

DINNER WAS EXCELLENT. Kazul spent most of the meal lying on the floor and watching us inscrutably. Dragons are very good at being inscrutable. I found it a bit unsettling, but it didn't seem to bother Shiara. Or Nightwitch.

After dinner we talked some more. Kazul told us about the castle and what the floor plan was. She also told us about a lot of things to watch out for. Most of them were magical items that would be dangerous only if we accidentally did something to them, but there were a few traps, too.

"This castle sounds awfully big," Shiara said after a while. "How are we supposed to find this King, anyway?"

"You look for him," Kazul said. "I'm afraid I can't tell you exactly where. The only people who knew where the King was were the wizards who went in and put the spell on him, and as far as I know they're all dead."

"As far as you know?" I asked.

"Some of them didn't come out of the castle."

"But you're sure that the ones who *did* come out are dead?"

"Positive." Kazul smiled reminiscently and licked her lips.

"So what?" said Shiara. Kazul and I looked at her. "I don't care about the wizards who came *out*," she went on defensively. "I'm worried about the ones who might still be *in* there."

"They have to be either dead or enchanted," Kazul said. "Even a wizard can't live seventeen years without food."

Shiara relaxed a little. "I suppose not. All right, then, what does this King look like?"

"You'll know him when you see him. Besides, he's the only other person in there."

"Oh, great." Shiara wrinkled her nose disgustedly. "We have to hunt through an empty castle for someone we don't even know while a bunch of wizards try to get in and stop us."

"It shouldn't be that bad," Kazul said. "The sword and the key should both help considerably."

"The key?" I said.

"Of course, the key!" Kazul said impatiently. "It can open any door in the castle; that's what it was made for.

225

You could have managed with the sword alone, but it will be much faster with the key as well."

"Are you saying I just picked up the key to the castle by *accident?*"

"Accidents like that happen all the time in the Caves of Chance," Kazul said dryly. "Where do you think they got their name?"

"How do you know it's the right key?" Shiara demanded. "The quozzel said some wizard put it there."

Kazul shrugged. "That's what makes it likely that it's the Key to the Castle. We caught one of the wizards coming out of the caves near the end of the battle, and he'd been inside the castle more than long enough to take the key. But if it will make you more comfortable, I can look at it."

I dug the key out of my pocket and held it out to Kazul. Kazul glanced at it and started to nod, then stopped suddenly and stared at the key very intently.

"It's the Key to the Castle, all right, but that wizard's *done* something to it." She sounded outraged.

"Wonderful," said Shiara disgustedly. "All we need is another wizard to get mixed up in this."

"He isn't *another* wizard," Kazul said. "He's the same one who stole the sword in the first place. And he's dead."

"You're sure he's not one of the wizards who didn't come out of the castle?" Shiara asked.

"I ate him myself."

"Oh." Shiara frowned. "Can you tell what he did?"

Kazul didn't answer. She stared at the key instead, and her eyes started glowing. The key began getting warmer and warmer in my hands. Just before it got too hot for me to hold, the key jerked in the direction of the castle outside. A second later, I dropped it. I stood shaking my fingers, while Kazul and Shiara stared down at the key, and Nightwitch walked over and sniffed at it.

"Nightwitch!" said Shiara. "Stop that. You'll get enchanted or something." She bent over and grabbed awkwardly for Nightwitch with her left hand. The kitten jumped away, and Shiara's fingers brushed the key. A look of surprise came over her face, and she picked the key up. "It feels like fire," she said.

"I know," I said. "It burned my fingers."

"No, I don't mean it's hot," Shiara said. "It just feels like fire."

"It shouldn't," Kazul said, sounding interested. "Bring it over here."

Shiara took the key to Kazul, who looked at it for a few minutes and handed it back. "I thought so. It's part of what that wizard did."

"But what's it for?" Shiara said.

"I don't know," Kazul admitted. "The fire spell is connected to something inside the castle, but I can't tell what with the barriers around the outside. He may have set a trap with it."

"May I have my key back, please?" I said. Kazul and Shiara both looked at me, and Shiara handed me the key. "Thank you," I said, and put it in my pocket. I wasn't quite sure why I wanted it; I only knew that keeping it felt right, somehow.

"Is there anything else we need to know?" I asked. "I mean, we've walked a long way today and we've been in a cave-in, and Shiara has a broken arm, and if we're going to do all these things tomorrow, I would sort of like to get some rest."

"Mrrrroww!" said Nightwitch emphatically.

Kazul chuckled. "It seems you aren't the only one who would like rest. Very well. Marchak!"

The middle-sized dragon who had brought us dinner appeared, and Kazul had him show us to our rooms. They turned out to be normal, human-sized rooms and quite comfortable. I was surprised until it occurred to me that the King of the Dragons would probably have occasional human visitors who would need a place to stay. Then I wondered how many human magicians kept special places for visiting dragons in their castles and towers and things, and right in the middle of wondering, I fell asleep.

A LOUD POUNDING NOISE woke me. Someone, probably a dragon, was knocking on the door of my room. "Just a minute, please," I called, and the pounding stopped.

I got out of the bed, which I couldn't remember having gotten into, and picked up my sword belt. I checked my pockets to make sure I had the key, started for the door, and stopped suddenly in the middle of the room. If the dragons expected me to do things with the Sword of the Sleeping King, I wasn't going to carry it under my arm like a bag of laundry. I put the sword belt on and opened the door.

"It's about time," said the little dragon in the hall. Shiara and Nightwitch were already there.

"I'm sorry," I said. "I didn't know you were in a hurry."

The dragon snorted and started off down the hall. We went after it. It didn't seem to be in a particularly good mood. Shiara explained that it wanted to come into the castle with us, but Kazul wouldn't let it. I couldn't see why it wanted to come. There weren't supposed to be any wizards inside the castle, and I thought the little dragon wanted to fight wizards. I didn't say anything, though. Arguing with a grouchy dragon isn't safe, even if it's only a small dragon.

The dragon brought us back to the cave where we'd talked to Kazul the previous night. Kazul wasn't there, but breakfast was, and we sat down right away. We were just finishing when Kazul arrived to take us out to the castle.

Kazul led us out of the caves and across the hard brown ground. All around us, dragons were polishing their teeth and sharpening their claws, and some of them were muttering spells under their breath. A couple of times, I saw elves hurrying through the crowd, and once I saw a group of intense-looking, red-haired people who had to be fire-witches. Everyone was very serious and grim.

None of us said anything until we got to the castle. Kazul led us around the outside of the shimmerings until we were at the front of the castle. If I concentrated on looking through the barriers, I could see a flat wooden bridge across the moat and a large door with steps leading up to it.

Kazul stopped and turned to the little dragon. "You'd better go find your place now," she said.

"But I want to—"

"Go!"

The little dragon went. Shiara and I looked at each other, and then at Kazul. Kazul smiled. "Are you ready?"

I nodded jerkily. Shiara bent and picked up Nightwitch. Kazul's smile widened. "When I say 'Now,' draw your sword and run for the castle. Don't look back, and don't stop for anything."

I nodded again because I didn't trust my voice just then. Kazul turned to the crowd of dragons, and suddenly everything was completely silent. A shiver ran down my back, and I put my hand on the hilt of the Sword of the Sleeping King.

I felt the bee-in-the-jar buzz that was Shiara's magic, and a strong humming from all the dragons, but the strongest feeling of all was the purring I'd felt from the first time the sword made my arm tingle. It came from the castle. Not from the shimmerings around the castle; they just got in the way. What I was feeling was the magic of the castle itself.

I took a tighter grip on the hilt of the sword. The tingling from the dragons got stronger and more positive, and abruptly Kazul turned and shouted, "Now!" As she spoke, the silver-and-green shimmering around the castle vanished.

I yanked the Sword of the Sleeping King out of its sheath and swung it at the golden glow that was still left between me and the castle. I felt an enormous shock as the sword hit, and then the shimmering vanished in an explosion of golden light.

I shook my head and heard Kazul shout, "Run!"

I took two steps and almost lost my balance. The ground wasn't hard and bare anymore; it was covered with slippery green fuzz. Shiara grabbed my arm just as I heard a series of explosions from behind us.

We ran. I could feel the jangling from the sword that meant there were wizards around somewhere, but I didn't stop to look for them. I was too busy trying to keep up with Shiara, hang on to the sword, and dig the key out of my pocket, all at the same time.

Shiara was standing in front of the door, panting, when I got up to it with the key. I didn't see a keyhole, but as soon as my foot touched the top step of the stairs, the door swung open.

"Daystar," Shiara said, "are you sure—"

Something hit the stone of the castle next to the door and exploded, showering us with little chips of rock. Shiara and I dove through the door and landed on the floor inside with Nightwitch on top of us. I sat up just as the door closed silently behind us.

"Hey!" Shiara said. "Watch what you're doing with that sword!"

"I'm sorry." I stood up, stuck the key in my pocket again, and held out a hand to help Shiara up. "Is your arm all right?"

"I think so," she said absently. "At least, it doesn't hurt any more than it did already. Now, which way do we go?"

"I don't know." The door shook as something hit it, and a moment later there was a muffled explosion. "I think we should get out of here, though."

"Aren't you going to put that stupid sword away first?"

"No," I said. "I'd rather have it in my hand, in case some of the wizards do get into the castle."

Shiara scowled, but she didn't object again, and we started hunting.

The castle was even more confusing on the inside than it was on the outside. Rooms opened into more rooms and then suddenly into a hallway or a flight of stairs. All of them were full of chairs and tables and books and suits of armor, and everything was dusty. The wizards' spell had kept spiderwebs and cobwebs out of the castle, but it hadn't done anything at all about the dust. Nightwitch didn't like it at all. She kept sneezing, until finally Shiara picked her up and carried her.

It took a lot longer to figure out where we were going than I'd expected. I could feel the sword pulling me toward the center of the castle, but it was very hard to just go in that direction. In spite of Kazul's instructions, Shiara and I kept getting into hallways that curved the wrong way and chains of rooms that ended with nowhere else to go. It was very discouraging.

Finally, we came to a pleasant room with a big window and a desk in one corner. "This doesn't look right, either," Shiara said. "Do you think—"

"Doesn't look right?" growled a voice up near the ceiling. "Of course it doesn't look right! It's been seventeen years since anybody has dusted in here. *And* I haven't had any visitors except the mice."

I looked up and saw a wooden gargoyle in one corner. It made a face at me and went on, "Who are you, and what are you doing in here?"

"I'm Daystar, and I'm looking for the King of the Enchanted Forest," I said.

"Oh yeah? What for?" the gargoyle demanded suspiciously.

"I think I'm supposed to return his sword."

"His—Oh, I see. Well, he isn't here. Hasn't been for seventeen years, and boy, am I going to give him an earful when *he* gets back."

"Come *on*, Daystar, we're wasting time," said Shiara.

"Try the great hall, down the corridor to your left," the gargoyle yelled after us as we left the room. "And send somebody to wipe the dust out of my ears! The things I put up with—"

Since nothing else had worked, we followed the gargoyle's directions and found ourselves in front of a large door at the end of a long hall. It was three times as wide as a normal door, and much taller, and it was made of gold with designs in relief. There was a staff lying on the floor in front of it, and I could tell from the jangling of the sword that it was a wizard's staff. When I stopped to look at it, the sword jerked impatiently toward the door.

"I think this is the place we've been looking for," I said.

Shiara tried the door. "It's locked. Where's the key?"

"Just a minute." I dug for it. As soon as I touched it, I

felt the key pulling at me, the same way the sword was. "Hey!"

"What is it?" Shiara said. "Come on, hurry up!"

"It's this key," I said as I unlocked the door. "It feels almost like the sword, except—"

I stopped as the door swung open. The room inside was very large and very high, full of light and not dusty at all. In the center of the floor stood something like a shallow iron brazier, about three feet tall and nearly five feet across, full of glowing coals. On the other side of the brazier was a couch, and lying on the couch was a man.

He was dressed in expensive-looking clothes, but there were tears in them, as if he had been in a fight. He didn't look old, even though his beard was long and gray. His head was bare, and at his side was a jeweled scabbard, empty. He was asleep.

Shiara took a deep breath. "That must be him. Come on, Daystar, let's get this over with."

I stepped into the room and walked slowly toward the couch. *This is too easy*, I thought. As I came around the brazier, I saw that there was another wizard's staff lying beside the couch. Something felt wrong, and I slowed down even more. I stopped, standing next to the couch with the key in one hand and the sword in the other.

"Well, now that we're here, how do we break the spell?" Shiara asked, coming up on one side of me.

"Something's wrong," I said, and as I spoke I realized what it was. The key was still pulling at me, but as soon as I had stepped into the room, the pulling from the sword had stopped. All I could feel from the sword was the jangling of the magic in the wizards' staffs.

"Maybe if you lay the sword on him it'll work," Shiara said, ignoring me. "You have to try something or we'll be here all day."

"I wouldn't try anything at all, if I were you," said a voice behind us.

Shiara and I spun around. The doorway was full of wizards.

In Which Daystar Uses His Sword

I stared at the wizards for an instant, then turned and jumped for the couch, hoping I could break the spell before the wizards did anything. I didn't make it. As I brought the flat of the sword down, the sleeping man vanished. The sword clanged softly against the couch, and I spun back to face the wizards.

Something hit me as I turned, and suddenly I couldn't move my body at all. I could turn my head far enough to see Shiara, but that was all. Shiara looked as if she were concentrating on something, so I turned my head back to the wizards. They were standing around the sleeping man, who was now lying on the floor in front of the doorway.

"Well done," said one of the wizards to another.

"Thank you," the second wizard said. "It was a mere trifle."

There was a stir at the back of the group of wizards, and a moment later Antorell pushed forward to the front. He had a bandage around one arm, probably where the dragon had bitten him. "I want the boy!" he said. "Now!"

The wizard in front, who seemed to be the leader of the group, looked at Antorell coldly. "We permitted you to join us in order to give you an opportunity to repair some of the damage you did seventeen years ago. Not to further your private ambitions."

"But you said I could have the boy!"

"Antorell, you're a fool," the leader said. "You may have the boy, but *after* we have possession of the sword, not before."

"I'll give you the sword, then!" Antorell said angrily. He strode around the edge of the brazier and reached for the hilt of the sword, just above my hand. I wanted to jerk away, but I still couldn't move.

As Antorell touched the sword, there was a flash of blue-and-gold light that flung him backward onto the floor. If he'd fallen a few inches to the other side, he'd have gone into the brazier. I found myself wishing he had, then found myself staring at the brazier. Something about it nibbled at my mind, but I couldn't make it come clear. I didn't have time to think about it, because the wizards started talking again.

Antorell was picking himself up off the floor, and the leader of the wizards smiled at him nastily. "You see?"

"You knew this would happen!" Antorell said furiously.

"Of *course* I knew," the leader said. "Had you spent your time hunting that sword instead of trying to get some sort of ridiculous revenge on Cimorene, you, too, would know."

"Then demonstrate the proper method for me," Antorell said sarcastically. "If you know so much, you take the sword."

"I am not so foolish," the other wizard replied. "No one save the King of the Enchanted Forest can take that sword from a bearer who is not willing to give it up, especially not inside this castle."

"Then how do you expect to get it?" Antorell said even more sarcastically than before.

"We kill the King," the wizard said, gesturing at the sleeping figure on the floor in front of him. "When the line of the Kings of the Enchanted Forest is ended, one of us can take up the rule of the castle."

"What good will that do?" Antorell said. "The boy will still have the sword. And, as you have reminded me so many times in the past two days, he seems to be able to use it."

The leader shrugged. "If your tale is true, I shall admit to some surprise. I thought no one but the King could use the sword. Which is why one of us must become King."

"You accuse me of lying?"

"Why should I bother?"

Antorell scowled and started to raise his staff, then seemed to change his mind. "When the boy blows your own spells back at you, perhaps you will see what I mean."

"Nonsense!" the leader of the wizards replied. "You obviously know little of what you speak."

"No, of course not. I have only seen the boy in action," Antorell said with awful sarcasm.

The leader shrugged again. "What the boy has learned matters little. The power of the sword passes to the ruler of the castle, and there is nothing he can do about it. He will be easy enough to take care of then."

Out of the corner of my eye, I saw a flicker of movement. Shiara was edging toward me. I had to force myself not to turn my head. The wizards seemed to have forgotten both of us, and I didn't want to remind them. I hoped they wouldn't remember until after Shiara had done whatever she was planning to do. I also hoped Shiara was planning to do something. I certainly couldn't, and I didn't think Nightwitch would be much help against all those wizards.

"Stop talking and let's get on with it," one of the wizards in the back said.

"An excellent suggestion. That is, if you are quite satisfied, Antorell?" said the leader.

Antorell glared and stalked over to the rest of the wizards. The leader looked around and nodded. "Begin."

Under other circumstances, the spell casting would have been very interesting to watch. The wizards spent quite a bit of time arguing about where each of them should stand, and exactly what the correct angle was for each staff, and in what order the spells should be said. The leader seemed particularly concerned that things be done right. Evidently there was something about the castle that would cause problems if everything wasn't perfect. Finally, they agreed on what they were going to do, and they got started.

As the wizards started chanting, something touched

my arm. If I could have moved, I'd have jumped. It was Shiara. "Do something before they finish!" I whispered.

"I've been trying!" Shiara whispered back. "But it isn't working."

"Oh no." I was so upset that I spoke the words in a normal tone of voice. Fortunately, the wizards were too busy chanting to notice. "You haven't been polite to anyone since you apologized to Telemain, and you used that up on the last bunch of wizards."

Shiara looked stricken. "Daystar, I'm *sorry!*"

"There isn't anything we can do about it now," I said. "If you—"

I stopped because the wizards had stopped chanting. Shiara and I both looked at them, but the wizards didn't seem to be finished with what they were doing. They looked more like they'd been interrupted in the middle of things. The leader bent over the man on the floor, who was still sleeping. A moment later the wizard straightened with an exclamation and stretched his staff out over the man's body.

The figure dissolved into sparkles, leaving a little blob of mud on the floor, and the other wizards stirred in surprise. "A simulacrum!" said someone.

I let out my breath in relief. Simulacra are very hard to make. You have to mix earth, air, fire, and water in exactly the right proportions in order to get a good one, and that's fairly tricky. A really good magician can make a simulacrum that looks exactly like someone but doesn't have any connection to the actual person at all. As a result, a simulacrum can't be used against someone the way other types of magic can. What they're mainly good for is confusing people.

This one seemed to have done an excellent job. The wizards were glaring at each other accusingly. "If that was a simulacrum," one of them said finally, "where's the King? Who put it there, anyway?"

"Old Zemenar, probably," an older-looking wizard said. "The simulacrum looked like him, and setting up a decoy is just the sort of thing he would do."

"That doesn't make sense! He started this whole affair in the first place. Why would he put a false king in the castle to distract us?"

"Zemenar never trusted anybody. He probably wanted to do this himself, so he made it as hard as he could for anyone else to finish the job. Or maybe he was just being ornery." The older wizard shrugged. "Either way, I doubt that he expected to get eaten by a dragon."

"We have wasted enough time here," the leader of the wizards said with sudden decision. "Silvarex, take three others and begin searching for the King at once. We cannot allow him to escape again."

He went on giving instructions, but I stopped paying attention. He wasn't talking to me, and I had other things to worry about. I was still holding the key in my left hand, and as soon as the simulacrum disappeared, the key had stopped tugging me and started getting warm. My other arm, the one with the sword, was tingling under the jangling of the wizards, and my head felt very light. I had a sudden, strong feeling that there was something important I ought to remember, but the jangling of the wizards' magic kept distracting me before I could figure out what it was.

"Daystar!" Shiara hissed, practically in my ear.

I jumped a little and realized that the wizard's spell holding me was beginning to weaken.

I couldn't move very much or very fast, though, and if the wizards noticed, they'd just throw the spell at me again. I decided not to move at all until I was sure I could move the sword fast enough to block another spell, then whispered to Shiara, "Don't *do* that. They might notice."

Shiara snorted. "If you don't want them to notice, you'd better try to notice sooner. That was the third time I called you."

"I'm sorry," I said.

"So am I. What are we going to do?"

"If you could — Nightwitch!" I broke off in midsentence as a small black streak darted toward the group of wizards. One of them raised his staff; Shiara cried out and Nightwitch dodged. The spell hit the marble floor in a ball of light, and a moment later the kitten was among the wizards' feet. I couldn't see what was happening, but I could hear the wizards shouting.

"There it goes!"

"Stop it!"

"It got away."

"Find it," the leader of the wizards commanded. "You, Grineran, go after it. It may lead you to the one we seek."

One of the wizards nodded and left, and I blinked. There were only three wizards left now: a short, round one, the one who was giving orders, and Antorell.

Antorell was staring at Shiara and me. "What about them?" he said suddenly. "They may know something."

The leader of the wizards looked thoughtful. "For once, Antorell, you may have made a useful suggestion. Persuading them to explain what they know may be difficult, however."

Antorell grinned nastily. "I think I can manage it."

"Really." The leader sounded skeptical. "The girl is a fire-witch, and the boy has the sword, remember."

"Sword or no, he cannot be immune to spells or Silvarex would never have been able to bind him," Antorell said.

"What did you have in mind?"

"Something like this."

Antorell waved his staff casually in my direction as he spoke. Even if I'd been able to move, I wouldn't have been able to twist the sword into a position to block the spell before it hit me, especially since I didn't realize what he was doing until the pain struck. It felt as if I were fighting the fire-witch again, only this time the pain was all through my body instead of just in my arms. It was worse than anything I'd ever felt. I think I screamed, but I'm not sure.

Beside me, Shiara shouted, and a long ribbon of fire shot through the air in front of me, straight at Antorell. Antorell caught fire almost at once. As he slapped at his clothes and his staff, trying to put out the flames, the pain stopped abruptly and the key in my left hand got even hotter. Neither of the other wizards even tried to help Antorell. They just stood and stared at Shiara and me.

The ribbon of fire still hung in the air above the brazier, making a curtain of flames between us and the wizards. Slowly, reluctantly, it began to fade, and as it died, the heat from the key in my left hand faded along with it. *Fire,* I thought. Fire in the brazier, fire in the key; Kazul had said the key could open any door in the castle, and Shiara had said something about the key and fire . . .

I lifted my left hand, fighting the remnant of the wizard's spell, and threw the key forward into the brazier.

There was a *whoosh* of flame that leapt all the way to the ceiling, then died. I thought I saw something in it, but it vanished before I could be sure. The brazier began to glow, and the whole room was suddenly thick and heavy with magic, like the air just before a summer thunderstorm. I could feel the magic growing stronger, as if it was getting ready for something, but nothing else happened. I was sure there was something else I should do, but I couldn't think what.

"Stop them!" the leader of the wizards shouted.

"Move, Daystar!" Shiara cried, and ducked down behind the brazier.

I tried to follow her, but I couldn't move fast enough because of the remains of the binding spell and because I was worrying about what else I was supposed to do in order to finish the spell I'd started with the key. I saw Antorell and the other wizards bring their staffs up, and I tried desperately to move the sword far enough to block whatever they were throwing at me.

I made it, but only just.

The sword flashed as the wizards' spell hit it, and

a tingle ran through me. The spell that had been binding me vanished. I could feel what was left of it flowing through the sword, along with the rest of the magic the wizards had thrown. It felt a lot like the jolt of power I'd gotten in the forest, when I'd used the sword on the spell the wizards had aimed at Shiara, except that this time I could tell where the power was going. It was flowing through me, into the magic of the Enchanted Forest itself. Back where it had come from in the first place, if Kazul was right about where wizards got most of their magic. Back to . . .

I felt my eyes widening and almost missed blocking the next spell. Then four more wizards appeared behind the three in the doorway. If I didn't do something soon, I wouldn't have time for anything except blocking spells. There was no way to find out whether I was right except to try.

I stepped up to the edge of the brazier, took a deep breath, and said loudly,

> *"Power of water, wind, and earth,*
> *Turn the spell back to its birth.*
> *Raise the fire to free the lord*
> *By the power of wood and sword."*

As I spoke the last word, I thrust the Sword of the Sleeping King into the middle of the coals in the brazier.

As the sword touched the coals, all the waiting magic around me surged forward, and suddenly I knew where it had come from. It was the magic of the castle and the Enchanted Forest itself, alive and growing, running like a net through the ground and the trees and the air. Fire shot up to the ceiling, the same way it had when I threw the key into the brazier, but this time the flames didn't fade. They got brighter and brighter until all I could see was fire. I heard a rumbling sound like the roof of the Caves of Chance falling in, and the floor shook under me.

A voice said loudly, "All hail the Waker of the Sword!" and voices all around me shouted, "Hail!"

Echoes from the shout rolled around the room, like thunder rolling back and forth across the sky. I couldn't see anything except fire, I couldn't hear anything except echoes, and I couldn't feel anything at all. Then something in my head seemed to snap into place, and the noise stopped abruptly.

I let go of the sword and stepped back a pace. The light in my eyes started to dwindle into flames again, but now I could see pictures in them, outlined in fire: dragons fighting wizards outside the castle, and dwarves fighting elves, and elves fighting wizards and other elves. I couldn't tell who was winning. Sometimes it seemed to be one set of fiery little shapes, and sometimes it seemed to be the other.

As I stared at the fire, I realized that I could feel the jangling from all the wizards' staffs and the deep rumbling of the magic of the Enchanted Forest and the purring of the castle itself, even though I wasn't holding the sword anymore. I could even feel the shape of the wizards' spells inside and outside the castle, including the one around and over the brazier. I could feel the magic of the sword, too, weaving a bright pattern through all the other types of magic. I followed the pattern until I saw how it worked, and then I reached out toward all the different kinds of magic and *twisted*.

The jangling of the wizards' staffs stopped abruptly as the power of the Enchanted Forest swallowed up the power of the staffs. Immediately, the flames in front of me swirled and pulled together, so that the pictures I'd been watching disappeared, and I found myself staring at a crowd of very angry ex-wizards through a shifting curtain of fire.

At least two of the wizards were wearing swords, and they were reaching for them. The leader started to point in my direction, and I ducked instinctively. Almost every wizard who's any good carries a spell or two outside his staff, just in case the staff gets stolen. The wizards at the castle didn't have any magic in their staffs anymore, but they could still make trouble with their spare spells.

I dove behind the brazier just in time to avoid something like a large lightning bolt. I swallowed, hoping these wizards didn't have very many more spells like that. I heard shouts, and I peered around the edge of the brazier, expecting to see the wizards with the swords coming after me.

Wizards were running in several directions, but none of them seemed to be heading for me. For a moment, I was puzzled, but then I saw Morwen, Telemain, and a couple of elves charging into the room from the hallway. I didn't stop to worry about how they had gotten there. I turned back to the brazier, to pull the Sword of the Sleeping King out of it so I could join the fight—and stopped.

The flames were still swirling in the air above the brazier, but they were denser somehow, and brighter. All I could see was a mass of white-and-yellow light, shot with power. Then something flashed so brightly that I had to cover my eyes. When I could see again, there was a door in the center of the brazier, right on top of the place where I had thrown the key, and facing the point of the sword. The door hung between two pillars that looked as if they were made of solid light, and I couldn't see anything around it except light and flames.

I stared at the door for a moment as it grew even more solid. I wasn't sure I wanted to find out what was on the other side. Doors like that are even worse than the one in Morwen's house; they can go *anywhere*. I reached for the Sword of the Sleeping King, but before my hand touched it, the door opened and a man stepped through.

He didn't look at all like the simulacrum. He was taller, with black hair and tired-looking gray eyes, and he didn't have a beard. He was dressed in plain clothes, but there was a feeling of strength about him, and power. Even without the thin gold circlet he wore I would have guessed who he was. I took a deep breath of relief as he stepped down from the brazier and onto the marble floor in front of me.

As he did, the doorway behind him melted back into leaping flames, which faded quickly until there was nothing there except the brazier and the glowing coals. The room was utterly silent. I looked up at the

King of the Enchanted Forest for a moment, then turned to the brazier and reached for the hilt of the Sword of the Sleeping King.

The sword wasn't even warm from the fire, but the blade shone even more brightly than it had the day Mother brought it out of the Enchanted Forest and gave it to me. I looked at it for a minute, then turned back to the King and held it out.

"I've come to return your sword, Father," I said.

In Which the Battle Ends and Antorell
Makes Trouble Again

For a long moment the King of the Enchanted Forest looked at me over the hilt of the sword. Then he reached out and took it. He held it up for a moment, then turned and brought it down hard on the edge of the brazier.

The brazier split and fell apart, scattering embers. As soon as it hit the floor, it started to melt and vanish, and in a few seconds there was nothing left of it except the key. The King bent and picked it up, then turned back to me and smiled. "Thank you."

"You're welcome," I said automatically. Then I noticed Shiara sitting on the floor, where she had dived when the wizards started throwing spells around. She was looking from me to the King and back, as if she couldn't believe what she was seeing. "Oh, I'm sorry," I said. "Shiara, this is the King of the Enchanted Forest. Father, this is my friend Shiara. She's a fire-witch."

Father bowed. Shiara looked at him and cleared her throat, then cleared it again and said, "Hey, um, are you really Daystar's father?"

The King smiled slightly and nodded. "Of course. Only the Kings of the Enchanted Forest can use the sword." He raised it so that the light flashing from the blade filled the room, then in one fluid motion he sheathed it in the empty scabbard at his side. He looked at me and smiled again.

Shiara blinked, then turned her head and glared at me. "Why didn't you tell me the King of the Enchanted Forest was your father?" she demanded.

"I'm sorry, but I didn't know it myself until just now," I said.

"Ha!" said Shiara. "Why—"

Before she could finish her sentence, Nightwitch pounced on her.

"Nightwitch!" Shiara sounded relieved. "Where did you come from?"

"I believe she came with them," Father said, nodding toward the doorway.

Shiara and I turned. A dozen wizards were sprawled on the floor in a tangled pile. Some of them were wrapped in vines, some of them seemed to be frozen, and some of them had elves and cats sitting on them. As soon as we turned to look at them, the elves all got up and bowed, then sat down again quickly before the wizards could get up and do anything. The cats just sat and blinked at us.

"I don't think you need to be quite so careful," the King said to the elves. "If you'll let them up one at a time, I'll decide what to do with them."

The elves nodded, and one of them stood up and bowed politely to the King. Father walked over to the wizard the elf had been sitting on and started asking him questions. The wizard didn't answer. Finally, Father shrugged and waved a hand. The wizard disappeared, and Father went on to the next one.

As soon as they got off the wizards, the elves started gathering up the staffs into a big bundle. Most of the cats just sat down and washed their paws. None of the wizards would say anything to Father, and he didn't waste much time on any of them. In a few minutes, there were only three wizards left. I was watching them when Shiara poked me.

"Daystar, where's Morwen?" she asked when I turned around. "Those are her cats; she has to be around somewhere."

"I don't know," I said. "I remember seeing her right before Father showed up, and Telemain was with her." I looked toward the door, where the last few wizards were, and blinked. "Shiara, where's Antorell?"

"Didn't he disappear already?"

"No, he didn't. I was watching," I said. Shiara and I looked at each other for an instant, then headed for the doorway.

No one tried to stop us. One of the elves gave us an odd look, but another elf grabbed his arm and whispered something to him, and he only bowed deeply as we passed. It made me feel almost as uncomfortable as I felt when the dwarves bowed to me.

Outside in the hallway we found Morwen kneeling on the floor beside Telemain and wrapping long strips of black cloth around his right shoulder. Pieces of odd-looking plants littered the floor, and a little way down the hall was a puddle of something dark and slimy. The puddle had a wizard's staff lying across it, and a wizard's robe was sort of crumpled up under the staff.

"Morwen!" Shiara said. "What happened? Can I help?"

"What happened was a battle," Morwen said. "I should think that would be obvious enough."

"But how did—" Shiara stopped because Telemain was stirring. A moment later he opened his eyes and looked up at all of us.

"What was that?" he asked rather hazily.

"That," said Morwen, "was a sword. They are long, pointed, and very sharp. You're lucky it didn't take your head off."

Telemain started to shake his head, then winced. "A plain sword. No wonder I couldn't block it. I thought it was a spell."

Morwen snorted. "You may be one of the greatest magical theoreticians in the world, but you don't have a particle of common sense," she said acidly. "Why, in heaven's name, didn't you duck?"

"I *did* duck!" Telemain said, looking startled and indignant. "He was aiming for my chest, not my shoulder. And if you think I'm going to put up with you and your —"

"You," Morwen said firmly, "are going to put up with me until that shoulder is healed. Which, may I remind you, means that I will have to put up with you for the same period of time. Fortunately, it shouldn't take very long—a few days, at most."

"A few days!" Telemain said. "Are you mad? It'll take at least a week!"

"Not if I change the herbs twice a day," Morwen said in an irritated tone. "I should know. It's my field."

"Well, it's *my* shoulder!"

"I'm so glad you noticed," Morwen said. "Stop fussing, or you'll make things worse and I *will* have to put up with you for a week."

"If I have to continue lying on this floor—which is cold, hard, and extremely uncomfortable—you'll have to put up with me a lot longer than that!"

Morwen got a peculiar look on her face. "I'll consider the idea carefully. Meanwhile"—she looked past Shiara and me—"Mendanbar, can you provide a room for this stubborn . . . magician?"

"Easily," said the King of the Enchanted Forest, from the doorway behind us. "Which room do you want?"

"The brown one," Morwen said before Telemain could answer. "He'll need a firm bed to support that shoulder."

Father laughed. "Of course." He started to lift his hand, and I cleared my throat.

"I would like to ask them something before they go," I said when Father turned toward me. He nodded, and I looked at Morwen. "Did you notice what happened to the wizard who was halfway around the brazier when you came in? I didn't see him afterward."

"You mean Antorell? Yes, I thought I saw him," Morwen said. "I'm afraid I don't recall. He wasn't the one I melted, if that's what you're asking."

"Could he have gotten away?" Shiara asked.

Morwen glanced at the King. "If you will allow me, I can find out fairly quickly." Father nodded, and Morwen made a chuckling sort of sound. Two of the cats poked their heads around the corner of the door frame.

"Daystar wants to know what's become of one of the wizards," Morwen said to the cats. "The one named Antorell."

The cats looked at each other, and one of them twitched its tail. The other one looked back at Morwen and said, "Rroowww!" and they both pulled their heads back out of sight.

"He got away," Morwen said, turning back to the King. "Scorn says he ducked down the hall while Telemain and I were busy with the rest of them."

Father frowned. "I'd better find him before he causes any more trouble." He looked back at Morwen. "The brown room, I think you said?"

Morwen nodded, and Father waved his hand. Morwen and Telemain disappeared. Father raised his hand to make another gesture, then paused and looked at Shiara and me. "I suppose you want to come, too?"

"Yes, we do. That is, if it isn't going to cause problems," I said.

I hadn't quite finished my sentence when the castle dissolved into mist around us. The mist cleared immediately, and we were standing on springy green moss with the trees of the Enchanted Forest all around us. At first I thought Father had taken us to a place a long way from the castle, but then I saw dragons and elves among the trees. I looked back over my shoulder, and there was the castle right behind us.

Shiara looked around. "Hey, where did all the trees come from?"

"They came from the wizards' magic," Father said. "When Daystar released the magic they had stored in their staffs, it went back into the forest, and things got back to normal in a hurry."

"When Daystar did *what?*"

"It was part of the sword and the fire and the brazier," I said hastily. "I think you were busy ducking."

"Oh," said Shiara.

By that time the dragons and elves had seen us, and everyone started cheering and bowing. In the middle of the cheering, one of the elves came over and bowed deeply. "It is good to see Your Majesty again," he said.

"It is good to be here again, Willin," the King replied. "How goes the battle?"

"I believe the dragons are the proper persons to provide that information," the elf said, sounding more and more pompous with every word. "If Your Majesty will wait here, I will arrange—"

"Mendanbar!" shouted one of the dragons. "So it worked!" As she made her way through the crowd toward us, the elf frowned ferociously.

"Your Majesty," he said in a low tone, "if you would prefer a more formal audience—"

"I haven't time for that, Willin," said the King. "Besides, I need you inside the castle, not out here. Someone has to look the place over, and arrange dinner for all these people, and see about getting some of the housekeeping staff back."

"Yes, yes, of course! At once, Your Majesty!" Willin

bustled away, looking much happier now that he had a suitable job.

"How's the battle?" the King asked again as the dragon reached us.

"Quite finished," the dragon said. "There are a few still out herding prisoners together, but that's about all."

"Excellent!" the King said, but he was watching the trees out of the corners of his eyes, and there was a tiny crease between his eyebrows. "If King Kazul is about, I would like to speak with her."

The dragon smiled, and her eyes glittered as if she were enjoying a private joke. "Kazul will be here in a moment."

Father nodded, managing to look impatient and polite at the same time. Suddenly the cheering got much louder, and then the dragons drew apart and Kazul came through the trees toward us. She was smiling, and she looked very large and green and shining. She was so magnificent that none of us saw the figure with her until they were both quite close to us.

I was the first to notice that Kazul had someone with her. When I saw who it was, I blinked and swallowed hard. *Mother?*

"Cimorene!" shouted Father. He took three strides forward and took her in his arms. Kazul smiled and sat back, looking smug.

Mother was laughing and crying at the same time; I'd never seen her do that before. Not ever. I was still staring when Shiara poked me.

"Don't stare," she whispered when I turned. "It's not polite."

I looked at Shiara for a minute, and my face got hot. I couldn't really say anything, though, because she was right. I felt very peculiar, but fortunately Mother and the King stopped hugging each other just then and started paying attention to the rest of us.

Father went to talk to Kazul, and Mother came over to us. She gave me a quick hug and said, "Well done, Daystar."

"Thank you, Mother," I said. Shiara shifted uncomfortably, and I remembered that I still hadn't introduced her. "Oh, and this is my friend Shiara. She's a fire-witch."

"I can tell that by looking at her." Mother smiled at Shiara. "You'll stay with us for a few days, won't you?"

Shiara nodded.

"Good," Mother said. "Now, if you will excuse me, there are still a few things I have to attend to."

"Mother," I said, and she turned. "That wizard, Antorell. He was in the castle, but he got away. I thought you should know."

"He did not get away!" said a familiar voice behind me. "I caught him myself. Do you want him for anything, or can I eat him?"

We all turned. The little dragon was sitting on the other side of the bridge, holding on to one of Antorell's arms. Antorell's robe was dirty and he didn't have his staff anymore. He looked tattered and very unhappy, and the dragon looked extremely pleased with itself. "Well?" it said. "Can I eat him?"

I looked at Mother, and she shook her head.

"I don't think you should eat him," I said to the

dragon. "The King talked to all the other wizards, and he'll probably want to talk to this one, too."

"Well, I want him back when the King gets finished with him," the little dragon said. "I caught him, and I'm going to eat him."

"He'll probably give you a stomachache," Shiara said.

I stopped listening to the conversation, because Antorell had straightened and was glaring past me, at Mother. He looked more powerful, somehow, but no one else seemed to have noticed anything unusual. I glanced uneasily over my shoulder and saw Father still talking to Kazul. I looked back, wondering whether I really had anything to worry about. Without his staff, all Antorell had were his extra spells, and he'd probably used them up in the battle. At least, I hoped he had.

Shiara and the dragon were still arguing. Suddenly, Antorell twisted and made a throwing motion with his left hand. The dragon shrieked in pain and let go of him, and he ran toward the bridge, waving his hands and shouting. I felt a sudden, intense surge of magic around him, and an instant later a demon appeared.

It materialized right in front of us, all purple scales and orange claws and silver-green teeth. Antorell shouted again, in a language I didn't understand, and pointed at Mother. The demon nodded, and one arm darted out.

I grabbed something I couldn't see out of the air in front of me and pulled. The demon vanished, and Antorell cried out in surprise. I yanked at the something again and sent Antorell along with the demon. After what he'd been trying to do, I didn't care whether the King wanted to talk to him or not. Then I saw that the little dragon was turning pink around the edges again. I let go of whatever it was, grabbed a different one, and twisted. The dragon gave a surprised-sounding squeak and turned green again, all at once.

I dropped the piece of nothing I'd been holding and turned. Mother was shaking her head. "That was a bit extreme, Daystar," she said, but her expression was proud.

"Daystar, what on earth did you . . . I mean, how did you . . ." Shiara gave up and just stared at me.

"I don't know," I said. I was at least as surprised as she was. "I'm not even sure what I did."

"What happened?" the little dragon asked. It looked around suspiciously. "Is that wizard dead?"

"No, but he probably wishes he were," Mother said. "Demons do not like surprise visitors."

"Oh, is *that* what Daystar did with him?" said Father's voice from behind me. "I wondered."

I jumped and turned around to see the King and Kazul standing there. The King was looking at Mother; Kazul was looking at the little dragon.

"Where have you been?" Kazul asked in a resigned voice.

"I've been catching wizards!" the little dragon said proudly. "Well, one of them, anyway. He threw dragonsbane at me again and called a demon and Daystar got rid of both of them. I didn't even get to eat him," the dragon finished sadly.

"I see," Kazul said, shaking her head. "I think you'd

better spend the rest of the day with me. It may, just possibly, keep you out of trouble."

"I don't understand!" Shiara burst out. "How could Antorell do any magic without his staff? And how could Daystar do any magic at all? And what did Antorell have to do with the sword and everything?"

The King smiled at Mother, then looked at Shiara and me. "As long as things seem to be quiet out here, why don't we go inside? That way, we can be comfortable while I explain."

Shiara and I nodded. Father waved his hand, and the Enchanted Forest dissolved into mist around us.

Which Contains an Engagement,
a Feast, and a Happy Ending

We appeared in one of the rooms inside the castle, a small, cozy-looking place with lots of bookshelves. It was just as dusty as all the other rooms Shiara and I had been through, but when Father waved, all the dust vanished. Mother muttered something about instant cleaning being no excuse for letting things get into such a state, and we all sat down. The King looked at us.

"I believe this should begin with you, Cimorene," he said. Mother looked thoughtful for a moment, then nodded and began.

Apparently, Mother really *was* a princess. She was the youngest daughter of the ruler of a very large kingdom on the other side of the Mountains of Morning, and she'd thought it was boring. So she ran away and became Kazul's princess.

Kazul wasn't King of the Dragons then. She and Mother got along very well, and after a while, Kazul started teaching her dragon magic. And then the wizards helped someone poison the old King of the Dragons, and all the dragons went to the Ford of Whispering Snakes to try and move Colin's Stone, and Kazul was the one who did.

Practically the first thing Kazul did after she became King was to kick the wizards out of the Mountains of Morning, which made the wizards plenty mad. So they decided to start a war by getting the dragons to attack the Enchanted Forest.

That was how Mother met my father. He came to see Kazul about some burned parts of the forest, and he found Mother instead. Then the two of them went searching for Kazul, who'd been kidnapped by the wizards, and by the time they got her free, they had decided to get married. Kazul was mother's matron-of-honor.

The wizards didn't make any more trouble for almost a year, but when they finally did, they made up for the wait. They stole Father's sword right out of the castle armory.

"They'd figured out that the sword was the main thing keeping them from absorbing magic in the Enchanted Forest," Father said, "and they thought that if they got rid of it, they could soak up the whole forest and use all that extra magic to wipe out the dragons. They didn't realize, at first, that even without the sword I could use the magic of the forest against them."

"Well, then what good was the stupid sword, anyway?" Shiara asked. "If you didn't need it to stop the wizards—"

"I *did* need it," Father said. "I can deal with one or two wizards at a time, but not the whole Society of

Wizards at once. And I can't be everywhere. The sword is connected directly to the magic of the Enchanted Forest, so it protects the whole forest and not just the area where it happens to be. If you want the technical details, ask Telemain. He helped me set it up."

With the sword gone, Father had to stay in the Enchanted Forest to keep the wizards out. Kazul and Morwen and Telemain all volunteered to go steal the sword back, but there was a problem. When the sword is outside the Enchanted Forest, only the King of the Enchanted Forest or a member of his family can stand to hold it for more than a few seconds. And Mother was the only other member of Father's family then.

Father wasn't too pleased about this, because Mother was going to have a baby—me—but they didn't really have any other choice. So Mother and the rest left to find the sword, and Father stayed in the Enchanted Forest to fight off the wizards. They didn't expect the whole Society of Wizards to attack the castle the day after they left, but that's what happened. Fortunately, Mother had a feeling something was wrong, and she sent Kazul back to check. When Kazul saw all the wizards attacking the castle, she flew back to the Mountains of Morning and ordered all the dragons to come help.

Meanwhile, Mother and the others found the sword, with Antorell guarding it. He was the son of Zemenar, the Head Wizard of the Society of Wizards, and Mother didn't like him much. So when he tried to keep them from taking the sword back, Mother melted him.

Unfortunately, by the time they got back to the castle, the battle was over and the wizards had put their shield up. Kazul sent some dragons out to look for wizards who had gotten away, and then she and Mother and Morwen and Telemain had a long talk about what to do next.

All of them were sure that the wizards had put a spell on the King, and they were just as sure that the sword could break the spell. Unfortunately, the sword could only be used by one of the Kings of the Enchanted Forest or his children, and then only when the earth, air, and water of the Enchanted Forest and the fire of the sword itself had recognized the person holding it as a rightful heir. And the only way to be recognized was to go out in the Enchanted Forest and hope you would do the right things at the right times.

So the dragons put their own shield up around the castle, to keep the wizards from sneaking inside, and after a while Mother had me. About that time Antorell found her. He blamed her for his father's death, because she'd taken the sword, and he tried to kill her. Mother had to melt him again.

After that, Mother decided that she'd better find somewhere to hide until I was old enough to use the sword. As long as it stayed inside the Enchanted Forest, the sword was invisible to wizards' magic. Mother, however, wasn't. If she stayed in the Enchanted Forest, one of the wizards' spells would find her. On the other hand, she couldn't take the sword out of the forest and still keep it hidden, any more than the wizards could.

So Mother hid the sword inside the forest, then left and never went back until the day she gave the sword to me. She put up some good spells to keep Antorell from finding us, then waited. She taught me all the right spells and manners and history and things, without ever telling me anything about the sword or the King of the Enchanted Forest or the war with the wizards. That way, I would have a chance of being recognized by the sword and reaching the castle without getting caught by one of the wizards' spells.

"I'm afraid it was rather hard on you, Daystar," she said. "But we couldn't think of anything else that had a chance of working."

"Well, I think we were lucky," Shiara said.

The King smiled at me. "Kings of the Enchanted Forest are supposed to be lucky."

Shiara blinked. "You weren't very lucky, were you? What did those wizards do to you, anyway?"

The King shook his head. "Zemenar and about ten others broke into the castle during the battle. I got a couple of them, but without the sword I was outnumbered a little too badly. They wanted to kill me, but they couldn't do it inside the castle without the sword, and they couldn't take me outside the castle because of the dragons. So Zemenar decided to put me in storage, in a manner of speaking, while he went back for the sword. The simulacrum was a decoy, in case someone managed to get into the castle while he was gone."

"But where were you for seventeen years?" Shiara said.

"There are . . . places that can be reached through the proper doors, places that can't be gotten into or out of except through such a door. Some of them are very large; some aren't. Zemenar found one that suited him and put me in it, then hid the door. Without the sword or the key, I couldn't get out until someone put the door back up." His smile was a little crooked. "I'm lucky that one doesn't need to eat in those places, or I wouldn't have lasted seventeen years."

"But I still don't understand about Antorell. He acted as if he wanted to do something to Daystar a lot more than he wanted the sword."

"Antorell never knew what the sword was," Mother said. "Zemenar, the Head Wizard, was the only one who knew the whole story, and after the way Antorell failed to guard the sword, the new Head Wizard wouldn't tell him anything"

"Ha!" said Shiara. "Served him right. But what did Daystar do to Antorell, anyway? And how? He never did anything like it before."

"He couldn't do it before," Father said. "The Kings of the Enchanted Forest can use the magic of the forest directly, but only after the sword has acknowledged them. Daystar wasn't acknowledged until he put the sword into the fire."

"Oh." Shiara sat back, looking thoughtful.

There was a moment's silence, then I thought of something else I wanted to ask about. "Mother, do you know anything about fire-witches' magic?"

"Yes, of course," she said. "Why do you want to know?"

"Could you teach Shiara how to do things?" I said. "That's why she came to the Enchanted Forest in the first place. She helped me a lot, and I think she ought to have some sort of reward."

"I didn't do very much," Shiara objected. "You kept me from staying a statue, and I think you saved my life when the roof of the Caves of Chance fell in. You're the one who deserves a reward."

"I think," Mother broke in before I could answer Shiara, "that it is time you told us what you have been doing these past few days. I have a general idea, but I would like a few more details, and Mendanbar hasn't heard anything about it yet."

I looked at Father, and he nodded, so Shiara and I went through our story again. I did most of the talking, with Shiara putting in a comment now and then when she thought I was leaving something out. I finished by explaining about Shiara's magic. Both Mother and the King looked rather startled, and then the King began to smile.

"A polite fire-witch," he said thoughtfully. "Very unusual."

"I don't want to have to be polite to people!" Shiara said angrily.

"Why not?" I asked. "You're getting much better at it."

"*Especially* not to *you!*" Shiara said.

"I can understand that," Father said. "It's his fault, after all."

"What?" Shiara and I said together.

"It's Daystar's fault that you have to be polite," Father repeated. "His and the sword's. One of the things the sword does besides control wizards is unlock people's talents, particularly magical talents. When you met

Daystar, both of you touched the sword at the same time. You wanted to use your magic and Daystar wanted you to be more polite. I think the sword did the best it could, under the circumstances."

"I knew it!" Shiara glared at me. "I *said* it was that stupid sword's fault!"

"I'm sorry," I said. "I didn't know. But at least you can use your magic now, sometimes. Isn't that better than not being able to use it at all?"

"*No!*" said Shiara. "It's worse! I have to go home and be *nice* to people, and it probably won't work most of the time, because I have to mean it, and how can I mean it if I'm always thinking about being able to do magic? And it's *boring* at home, and people will still keep expecting me to do things I can't do. I don't even know anyone who could teach me about magic even if I could get it to work all the time. I'll never learn anything!"

Little flickers of flame started running down Shiara's cheeks. It took me a minute to realize that she was crying fire, and when I did, I didn't know what to do about it.

"That is *quite* enough of that," Mother said while I was still thinking.

Shiara looked up. "You don't know what it's like! It's horrible."

"On the contrary, I know quite well what it's like," Mother said. "And the solution is obvious. In fact, it's the same one I used."

"What?" Shiara blinked, and the flame tears stopped running down her face. "What do you mean?"

"You can become Kazul's princess," Mother said. "She doesn't have one at the moment. It would have a great many advantages on both sides. You will learn considerably more about magic, dragons, and the Enchanted Forest than you would anywhere else, and Kazul will get a princess who can't be accidentally roasted if one of the other dragons gets out of hand. And you'll be living nearby, which will give Daystar and Mendanbar a chance to figure out how to reverse that ridiculous politeness spell."

"But I'm not a princess!" Shiara said.

"If Kazul says you are a princess, then you are a princess," Mother said firmly. "No one is going to argue with the King of the Dragons. Besides, it will be excellent experience for you later."

I opened my mouth to ask what Mother meant by that, but Shiara asked, "But are you sure Kazul would be willing to do it?"

"Kazul will have no objection whatsoever to training the next Queen of the Enchanted Forest," Mother said calmly. "You don't need to worry about that."

I closed my mouth very quickly and looked at the floor, feeling my face getting hot. I heard Shiara say, "Oh," in a small voice, and then the King laughed.

"Cimorene, you're going a little fast," he said, still chuckling. "If Shiara wants to go live with Kazul, I'm sure we can make the arrangements, but there's no reason to hurry. She can stay here until she decides. There's plenty of room. Now, if you don't mind, I'd like to go back outside. Kazul was going to talk to Willin about a feast, and I haven't had a good meal in seventeen years. As a matter of fact, I haven't had *any* meals in seventeen years."

Mother didn't object, so the King moved us all to the feast with another wave. Everyone was there: dwarves and dragons and elves and cats, and even a few wizards who had been on the King's side. Morwen was there, too, but she spent quite a bit of time popping back to the castle to make sure Telemain wasn't doing anything she disapproved of.

Mother and the King sat at one end of a long table, and Kazul sat at the other. The elf Willin scurried up and down making sure everyone had enough to eat and plainly having a wonderful time. Shiara and I sat at the middle of the table, and the people sitting next to us kept changing. All of them wanted to hear about how Mother had stolen the sword back, and how Shiara and I had gotten into the castle and broken the spell.

"I'm getting tired of this," Shiara whispered to me while some of the people next to us were changing seats. "Let's go someplace else for a while, and let them tell each other about the stupid wizards."

"I'm tired of it, too, but I don't think we should leave," I said.

"You don't? No, of course you don't. How very irksome," said a squeaky voice from the ground by my left foot.

"Suz!" I said, looking down. "Where did you come from?"

"The forest, of course." The lizard ran up the leg of

the table in a thin gold streak, then stopped and looked around nervously. "Is that—that *kitten* anywhere close by?"

"No, she's inside," said Shiara. "I don't think she likes the crowd. Why?"

The lizard looked at her. "If you'd ever been jumped on by something four times as big as you are, and been rolled around until you were dizzy, not to mention bruised, you wouldn't have to ask." He balanced on his tail and peered over the edge of a bowl of nuts.

"Would you like something to eat?" I said.

"I believe I would," Suz said. He made a very fast bouncing motion, and a moment later he was holding one of the nuts. "What are you going to do now that the wizards are gone?"

"They aren't all gone," I said. "I think a few of them were on our side, and some of the others actually got away."

"They did?" Suz considered for a moment. "I suppose they did. How very annoying. But what are you going to do?" He looked from me to Shiara and back.

"I'm going to be Kazul's princess," Shiara said before I could answer.

Suz fell over backward, just missing a silver bowl full of cranberry jelly. "Oh my gracious goodness my oh!" he squeaked. "However did that happen?"

"Mother suggested it," I said. I looked at Shiara. "But I thought you hadn't made up your mind yet."

"I just decided," Shiara said. "Home is boring, and this way I can learn things and maybe even stop having to be polite to get my magic to work."

I suspected Shiara was more interested in not having to be polite than she was in learning things, but I didn't say so. "I'm glad you're going to stay," I said instead.

"You are?" Suz said skeptically. He peered up at me. "Why, you really are! How amazing."

I didn't know what to say to that, but fortunately I didn't have time to think about it. Father and Mother and Kazul all stood up just then and everyone else got very quiet. Father looked around for a moment, smiled, and started speaking.

First he thanked everyone for coming to help with the wizards, and then he introduced Mother formally as "my wife, Cimorene." All the dragons and elves and other people shouted and applauded; the din was tremendous. Then he introduced me, and I had to stand up and be clapped at. After that, Kazul said that the dragons were pleased to be of assistance, and everyone sat down and started talking again. The whole thing didn't take very much time, which surprised me. I'd thought speeches at feasts were supposed to be longer.

Even with short speeches, the feast lasted longer than I expected. Shiara left after a while, to go find Nightwitch and talk to the little dragon. I stayed at the table. I didn't have much choice; every time I tried to get up, someone new would pounce on me and start asking questions. I got very tired of it, but I couldn't seem to get away. I was glad when it was finally over.

THE NEXT FEW DAYS were a little hectic, but then the elves and dragons who'd been in the battle went home and things started to settle down. Morwen and Telemain were almost the last to leave, because of Telemain's shoulder. Morwen had to stay to take care of it, and she wouldn't let Telemain go anywhere until he was well.

"It's simply ridiculous," Telemain grumbled at breakfast on the third morning after the battle. "I am quite capable of traveling with my arm in a sling."

"Yes, and the first time you ran across a slowstone or a pool of transformation water you'd take your arm out of the sling and start tinkering with it," Morwen said. "Which would *not* be good for that shoulder."

Telemain glared at her. "I disagree."

"Disagree all you like, but you're not leaving the castle for another two days," Morwen said. She picked up a basket of muffins, took one, and passed the rest to Mother.

"Two days!"

Mother raised an eyebrow. "Is our hospitality unwelcome?"

"No, of course not, but . . . Cimorene, I have a tremendous amount to do if I'm to be ready for the wedding in time."

I hadn't heard about any wedding being planned, but I was carefully not looking at Shiara anyway. Then Father looked up.

"Wedding?" he said.

Morwen smiled. "Telemain and I are getting married."

Shiara and Father and I all said, "What!?" at the same time, but we were nearly drowned out by a chorus of startled meows from Morwen's cats.

"Yes, married," Morwen said to one of them. "And it has nothing to do with you, so you may as well be quiet and accept it."

The cats made unhappy noises for another minute, until Morwen frowned at them. Then they all got up and went over to a corner of the room, where they sat muttering to each other with their tails twitching.

Morwen watched for a moment before she nodded and turned back to the table. "They'll get used to the idea."

"Um, congratulations to both of you," I said.

Father was looking at Mother. "Cimorene, did you know about this?"

"Not exactly," Mother said, and smiled.

"I see." Father shook his head. "Well, congratulations."

"Thank you," Telemain said. He started to reach for a plate of sausages with his bad arm, and Morwen stopped him.

TWO DAYS LATER, Morwen announced that Telemain's arm was well enough for him to travel. She promised to invite all of us to the wedding, even the dragons, and then she and Telemain left the castle, followed by a string of disapproving cats.

Shiara and Kazul were the last to leave. I was a little taken aback when I heard. I knew that Kazul lived in the Mountains of Morning, but it hadn't occurred to me that if Shiara was going to be Kazul's princess, she would have to live there, too. I didn't say anything about it, though. I felt too silly for not having realized it before.

Father and Mother and I went out to see them off. Mother gave Shiara some advice about princessing, and Father told her that if she was going to glare at dragons, she'd have to learn to glare politely. Then they both went to talk to Kazul. Shiara looked at me.

"I'm beginning to wonder whether I really want to do this or not," she said. "Does he really expect me to practice glaring at people?"

"No, just at dragons," I said. "If he wanted you to glare at everyone, he would have said so."

"Well, I think it's—Nightwitch!" Shiara bent to retrieve the kitten, who had been investigating one of Shiara's bundles a little too vigorously.

"Where did you get all of this, anyway?" I asked as she straightened up. There were three bundles in the heap Nightwitch had been climbing, and I knew Shiara hadn't had any of them when we'd arrived at the castle.

"Morwen gave me that one, and Cimorene gave me the others," Shiara said. "She said I would need them if I was going to live with Kazul. I don't even know what's in all of them yet."

I couldn't think of anything to say because just then I realized how much I was going to miss having Shiara around. The Mountains of Morning weren't exactly close to the castle, and I didn't think Kazul would be interested in flying back and forth every day.

Shiara frowned. "What's the matter with you?"

"I was just wishing you were going to be living a little closer to the castle," I said.

"I don't see why. I'm going to have to come here a lot anyway, at least until you get that stupid politeness spell off of me so I can use my fire magic. So what difference does it make? *I'm* the one who has to do all the traveling back and forth." Shiara looked toward Kazul. "I think they're ready to go. Come on, Daystar."

She picked up one of the bundles and started walking. I didn't say anything, but I felt a lot happier than I had a few minutes earlier. Getting rid of that spell didn't sound easy, and until it was gone Shiara would have to spend quite a bit of time at the castle. I was sure that if I had enough time, I could think of some reason for her to keep visiting after the spell was gone, and even if I couldn't, Mother would be able to. Smiling, I picked up the other two bundles and followed happily after.

LOOKING FOR MORE GREAT TALES OF FANTASY AND ADVENTURE?

TURN THE PAGE TO DISCOVER MORE BOOKS THAT TAKE YOU WHERE MAGIC, DRAGONS, AND OTHER MYTHICAL CREATURES COME ALIVE!

FROM THE *NEW YORK TIMES* BEST-SELLING AUTHOR JASPER FFORDE

THE CHRONICLES OF KAZAM!

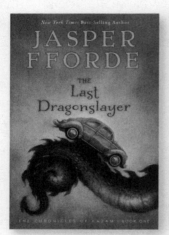

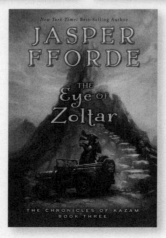

IN THIS DELIGHTFUL TRILOGY BY JEAN FERRIS, HAPPILY-EVER-AFTER GETS TURNED UPSIDE DOWN, INSIDE OUT, AND COMPLETELY OVER THE TOP!

BOGLES ARE AMONG US IN CATHERINE JINKS'S CHARMING AND CHILLING BOGLE TRILOGY!

STEP INSIDE MR. ELIVES'S MAGIC SHOP—
A PLACE WHERE BOYS HATCH DRAGONS, TOADS TALK, RATS DELIVER MESSAGES, AND SKULLS SPOUT SHAKESPEARE!

THE MAGIC SHOP BOOKS
BY BRUCE COVILLE

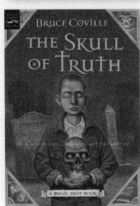

**THE DAY SACHA FOUND OUT HE
COULD SEE WITCHES WAS THE WORST
DAY OF HIS LIFE . . .**

FROM CHRIS MORIARTY

 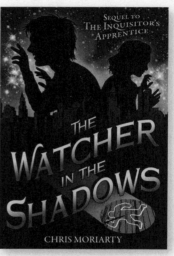

"FANTASTIC . . . A GREAT MAGIC TRICK."
—CORY DOCTOROW

EVEN MORE GREAT FANTASY STORIES
NOT TO BE MISSED!

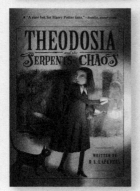